CW01281476

Mike Eicherly was born in Garden Grove California, January 10th, 1969. He currently lives in the Mission District of San Gabriel, California. Together, he and his wife have three children. His passions are horror films, love stories, music, books, cashmere socks, family and Lucky Baldwin Pubs.

This story is dedicated to all who lived in Los Angeles, California. Located on the 700 Block of Los Angeles Street. 1998–2008. This book is yours.

'Your number is 4. You don't look 4. 4, is solid people, practical, uninspired. 4 is unsuccessful. The number 4 is of poverty and defeat.'

– Vincent Price
Night Gallery. Season 1- 1971. The Return of the Sorcerer

Michael Eicherly

4: A Morbid Love Story

Austin Macauley Publishers™
LONDON * CAMBRIDGE * NEW YORK * SHARJAH

Copyright © Michael Eicherly 2023

All rights reserved. No part of this publication may be reproduced, distributed, or transmitted in any form or by any means, including photocopying, recording, or other electronic or mechanical methods, without the prior written permission of the publisher, except in the case of brief quotations embodied in critical reviews and certain other noncommercial uses permitted by copyright law. For permission requests, write to the publisher.

Any person who commits any unauthorized act in relation to this publication may be liable to criminal prosecution and civil claims for damages.

This is a work of fiction. Names, characters, businesses, places, events, locales, and incidents are either the products of the author's imagination or used in a fictitious manner. Any resemblance to actual persons, living or dead, or actual events is purely coincidental.

Ordering Information
Quantity sales: special discounts are available on quantity purchases by corporations, associations, and others. For details, contact the publisher at the address below.

Publisher's Cataloging-in-Publication data
Eicherly, Michael
4: A Morbid Love Story

ISBN 9781645756446 (Paperback)
ISBN 9781645756453 (Hardback)
ISBN 9781645756460 (ePub e-book)

Library of Congress Control Number: 2023911951

www.austinmacauley.com/us

First Published 2023
Austin Macauley Publishers LLC
40 Wall Street, 33rd Floor
New York, NY 10005
USA

mail-usa@austinmacauley.com
+1 (646) 5125767

"The gifts of lucifer are not ordained from the word. They are *chosen* from *his* fallen offspring."

– Anton Levey 1969

"The Rite of God never existed, as our ancestors spoke, from the Nephilim and sons, Capricorn South. The Angel of Light is God. God's sword, the angel of light spewed among the unbegotten faith. The wretched souls that displeased the master were punished. Like John the Baptist. Where is his sword, his faith? He worshiped a God that served his head on a plate. You are all hypocrites. I have delved into the valley of darkness. I have seen the underworld. The new Earth. A world of sweet pain and pleasures beyond *his* creation. I have served the god of light and evil. There is only one. And his name is Satan. May his name be praised for all eternity."

– The last words of **Henry Faustino**
NSA Facility 1999

"The devil attempted destroying God's people by altering their DNA. We will achieve this goal by introducing 'Killer Cocaine & Methamphetamine to the New World Order."

– The last words of **Henry Faustino**
NSA Facility 1999

"People of the world, unite and defeat the U.S. aggressors and their running dogs! People of the world, be courageous, dare to fight, defy difficulties and advance wave upon wave. Then the whole world will belong to the people. Monsters of all kinds shall be destroyed."

– Quote from a famous Eastern Leader.

"Respect God and Ghost. However, keep away from *them*."

– Confucius

"There are demon-haunted worlds. Regions of utter darkness."

– The ISA UPANISHAD: (India, ca 600 B.C.)

"Fear of things invisible is the natural seed that which everyone in himself Call-eth Religion."

– Thomas Hobbes, Leviathan 1651.

Note to Reader

The author is well-aware of the fact some of the content of this book *may be* offensive. I stated this in book two of this trilogy-**Distinctive Tendencies,** this author does not agree with thought process, beliefs, or actions of the *fictional characters* in this story. Like is said before. This story is fake, not real. A few sections of this book are based on a Journal found in a loft. Downtown Los Angeles 2004. Yes, I lived there. I butchered the journal and created a whole new story. (This Story) Troy is based on my travels to Hegang. Keep in mind, I am one of the few Americans that's ever-set foot there. A province only 40 minutes from the Southeast Russian border. When I wrote this last chapter of the trilogy, please be aware that I listened to 'Beethoven, Chopin, Toys in the Attic and Ziggy Stardust and The Spiders from Mars. This helped ease the pain. And finally, Use your own imagination. Stop trying to steal mine…

Chapter 1

Henry Faustino died at NSA facility, August 6th, 1999. After years of rehabilitation, human behavior studies and counseling, Henry Faustino was categorized as a Lost Cause. Henry Faustino died spewing blood, cursing God, Jews and Christians. He said that his concubine of evil, Beatrice Meadows, will bear a son. A son of light. A son that is chosen to sit at the head of all tables. He will help lead a world of fire, destruction and chaos. A son that will sit next the Antichrist.

On his deathbed, he told the NSA that the *New World Order* is at hand. He told the NSA that his computer software will rule the minds of billions worldwide. Youths will commit suicide, woman shall abort all newborns, we shall decide who breeds, lives and dies. School teachers, university teachers, doctors and lawyers work for us. Even police officers and some government officials. He screamed, "All you bastards, sons of Abraham shall pay. The day of torment is at hand."

The NSA turned off the voice recorder and cameras. They disintegrated his body and that is the end of our friend Henry Faustino.

In the 1960's, Beatrice was a RN. She worked in Alhambra, California, at the medical center. Her job with this terror cult was to target young babies. Mostly for demonic rituals. Henry's brethren feed on boiled infant flesh, laced with cayenne pepper, sea salt, and barbeque sauce. The flesh was garnished with red potato, with steamed vegetable, Irish Butter and Sea Salt.

Beatrice would target children mostly born autistic or with other health problems. Henry referred to these infants as 'Children of the Damned. The tarnished ones. Gifted to us from the master; for our works'. Ones went missing, some were switched. It all depended on what the gods instructed her. Beatrice killed, she tortured, she maimed and overdosed children. Hoping to create autism and future targets. Through her actions, Beatrice was ordained at the "Beggar's Banquet." She became a ranked member of the organization and church.

As we all know, Beatrice killed her lover Richard Walbreck, then met Henry In late 1950's. She later gave birth to his son in 1979. Hiding the pregnancy and birth from her man Gerald and his lover Cherise. The child was born under sign of Gemini. Beatrice and the nurses observed the child proclaiming he was perfect in every way. The birthdate was June 6th, 1, at 6:00 am. According to Henry the child was born under the rite of Capricorn South, Henry's ancestors.

Henry showed the math to the church. He placed a decimal and six zeros in a Texas Instrument calculator.

1979 divided by 1999. Then inverted the numbers. Which is the date the antichrist will be revealed in Syria. He inverted the numbers and added his birthdate, which proclaimed the prophecy of his newborn. 666.

His newborn son was named Darius Faustino; and to be worshiped by the brethren worldwide.

To fulfill the prophecy, Darius would be given up by Henry and Beatrice. They placed the young infant in a Catholic Orphanage. The orphanage was overlooked by a decan from Ireland. His job was to report young talent to the organization. The decan was pleased with the good news. That the son of fire was born. The decan would later kill his wife in the name of the church and Darius.

Darius was bigger, stronger, smarter and more athletic than any other child at the orphanage. German Dodgeball was his favorite sport. He played fierce and with vengeance. Children from the opposing teams were sent to the nurse with broken noses, and bruised ribs. The same was for baseball, his third favorite sport, and rugby. Darius not only outperformed, but he also annihilated the competition.

On Darius' 12th birthday, he was adopted by a CIA agent and wife. The CIA agent is head of all covert operations worldwide. A man more powerful than president of the United States. The wife, a college professor at Georgetown University, and social debutante. Their names are Jack and Emily Whitford.

Later, Darius would be baptized at Saint Patrick Catholic Church where he would take on a new name. A Christian name, then continue his private education. His new name will be Brian James Whitford.

Chapter 2

Excerpt found in Brian Whitford's Journal.

I have now reached the rebellious stage of my life. DC is the land of the dead. Land of the lost. The land of mindless bodies intent on destroying others and their families. I have always done the right thing. Things I haven't wanted to do. Things to please my parents; and now, I want out. It's my turn to be pleased. I've seen the DC streets and the loyal political party losers. Intellectual losers that walk the streets, looking for votes so they can later destroy jobs, take innocent people's homes. Create panic and contempt, racial hate in the streets. It makes me sick. Only if the public could see what I've seen. Learn what I have learned. Their sins, their lies, their dirty sex and get-rich-quick schemes. The way they talk in private. The way they are in bed together. Their guilty conscience, as they spill their enemy's bloods in the sewers. This is the fun part for me. Reading these assholes. Reading their minds as I walk the DC streets. Political mayhem and lost causes that suck the life out of American democracy. Worst of all, the innocent and naive taxpayers. If they only knew what I have learned. Heard what I have heard.

At night, the poseur punk rock wannabees. The Curt Cobain worshippers. The high-class black hookers, that work the five-star hotels. Politicians shake their heads, while smirking. Later having sex with them in hotel rooms.
I walk the sick streets of DC. Thank god, for this time, it is my last.

I walk onward toward the upscale restaurant where my parents await. I walk over the homeless bodies, by the bars, monuments. The fuckin' taxis and Arabic drivers with ulterior motives. We must all be politically correct in this town. Everything and everyone in Washington are right? However, not grade schoolteachers. The ones who teach children false motives and meditation techniques. Teach that the new world government will protect them, give them life after college. After the loss of Amber, my true love, I find their theories evil and self-serving. This really pisses me off. And my new girlfriend; my parents set me up with. What a fuckin' disaster. Everything, I mean everything about DC makes me resentful. I'll write a book and get even. I'm moving to Los Angeles, and I can't wait. Moving to where real people are.

I wonder if I'll ever see cool rock bands. Live bands like Black Flag, Shattered Faith, Germs, Adolescents, Circle Jerks, Bad Religion, and X. Maybe the Stains will get back together. God, how I wish. Bands that make Los Angeles what it is today; cool. Bad Brains were kicked out of DC. Kicked out because they are black and wrote the truth. I heard The US Bombs Kick Ass. Can't wait to see them. Again, political hypocrisy is the offspring of this evil in DC.

I have watched *'The Decline of Western Civilization'* at least 100 times. Now that's Rock-n-Roll. Everything I ever dreamed about in Los Angeles. Biorhythmic, high-energy Rock-n-Roll. Some of the women are hot too. Especially the dark styled witchy ones.

DC, why am I here? But first the hippies in LA, societies never-ending disease. Shoot what you want, snort what you want, screw who you want; then blame it on the government. I cannot fuckin' stand liberals, communism and hippies. We learned about those assholes at West Point. Again, if you only knew.

But first, my parents. How do I deal with them? I don't hate them. I don't' like them right now. I want to be independent and alone. Have sex with real woman. I'm just upset. And that is it. I've done everything for them. Now it's my turn. I can't wait. Wait to get laid inside the Roosevelt Hotel. The same room Marilyn Monroe slept in. I've heard many cool stories about Los Angeles and the ghost that swarm the streets at night. Now soon, this city will mine forever. I heard the Mexican chicks are hot and sexy also. I cannot wait for Los Angeles.

End of Excerpt.

Jack is 60 years old and a good man. He's worked hard his whole life and has a plan. It's called Anglo Saxon Theory. And now Brian's last Washington meal will be at a pretentious, political restaurant, called 'successful.'

Jack is 60 years old. He grew up in Indiana as a cornhusker, paid his way through college, and was a star running back at Penn State. Jack is a rock, the strength of his family. Through the eyes of many, he can do no wrong. No evil hand can touch him. Jack is an "upright man, who shuns evil and fears God." This is what the church says about him.

Job is his Jack's favorite book in the Bible. He said it reminds him of politics in Washington. When it comes to politics, Brian sees his father as Jesus Christ. An old soul. One of the last *true* American's, willing to be sacrificed for societies' own good. Jack works in the CIA. What he does nobody knows. No-one will ever know. Not even his beloved wife and adopted family Jack is the type of man you don't mess with. Not even the Bushes or Kennedys will attack him. It has been rumored Jack started the war in Panama and Nicaragua, then ended it. This is what rumors circulate at West Point. This is Jack's best trait for the Agencies. He ends everything he starts. Unlike our fuckin military today. Jack's record is unmatched. The only thing he ever said about his work is "our enemies will all die from political heresy." Other than this, the man never speaks… (ever)

Jack waits impatiently with his wife Emily. Emily is 45 years of age and is "ultra-beautiful." Many say she looks like a mid-forties Jaclyn Smith and is good with business. Emily, when not teaching, manages her time investing. Building a family fortune. Monitoring their enemies and planning her son's political future. She is obsessed with wealth, reputation, social gatherings, and pledge drives for the homeless. She is well liked, while investing money into poverty struck communities. She proclaims that *Eminent Domain is the future of Washington. As well as most major cities in America.* Emily is fond of ribbon-cutting ceremonies and *meetings* at the Ritz Carlton. Emily has dark hair with highlights. Light brown eyes and white pitched skin. She wears a navy-blue dress with diamond earrings. She is proud of her figure and not afraid sporting her cleavage. Her knowledge is worldly and vocabulary superior. Especially when she addresses politicians. The ones she dislikes. The thieves, liars, and hypocrites. The ones her family has put away years before. In Jack's eyes, this is a good thing. His wife can do no wrong. The perfect political adversary. She is the perfect feminist. She is also Brians' favorite family member.

Brian walks into the restaurant. As he walks, he notices *all* eyes fixated on him. Success is not your typical yuppie restaurant with white tablecloths, an open kitchen, bar, and *servants* draped in black. It's le crème de' le crème of political bullshit. White candles light his way. Everything is dark; so, politicians can hide their sins. As Brian walks toward his table his hands start to tremble. He feels nausea. His stomach starts cramping. He can vomit any second now.

Jack watches Brian mannerisms closely. Emily grabs Jack's hand, reminding him to relax. Brian sits down at the table like a diffused James Dean character. Jack already knows what his son is going to say. What he plans. His deliberate acts of emotional anarchy and contempt against the family; even his country.

"Son, I'm opposed to your Los Angeles move."

"But how did you...?" Asks Brian.

Brian has a confounded look about his face.

"Don't interrupt me, Son. I know *everything,* do you. Everything you think belongs to me. As I was saying, before you rudely interrupted me. You're making a horrible decision son. One for you, and this family."

Brian nervously shuffles his position in the chair.

Emily doesn't say a word, she seldom does during a family quarrel or argument. Her hand trembles as she drinks her red wine. The sound of silverware is heard clanking throughout the restaurant. Patrons pretend not to notice the family; or listen. Brian knows they are. They always are.

"Dad, I'm capable of making my own decisions."

"You've never made one decision your whole life, Son. Everything's been decided by me. And now you're wanting to ruin your destiny? Brian, you're ungrateful, spoiled, and wet behind the ears." Jack's tone is stern and direct. As he speaks, he nods at a man sitting across the room.

"Dad, please let's not go there again. It's always been about you and Mom."

"Don't drag your mother into this. Shut up and listen."

"I'm not. Listen for once please." Says Brian.

There is a pause for a moment. The restaurant goes dead quiet. Spooky.

"Let me finish," says Brian. "For once, up until now, I've done everything you've requested. I have gotten good grades. Never got into trouble and never been arrested. You should be proud of me. They offered me $75,000 plus commission for starters."

Jack looks and Emil, while smirking. Brian does his best trying not to raise his voice. He takes a deep breath then continues.

"Dad, all I get from you are these sores about being a loser, not aggressive in life, lacking direction. Up until now, I feel like some type of sick project of you and mother."

Brian picks up a glass of red wine, looks it over, then drinks.

"I took the offer. After tonight, I'm gone. And I will succeed, with or without your support, Dad. You are both going to have to deal with it, or…"

"Or what?" says Jack sternly.

"Nothing," says Brian.

"Yeah, that's what I thought you said. Seventy-five thousand? that's chump change. Where's your pride, son? You're a very capable young man. Your mother and I spent years, raising you at the highest level. Your too dumb and too young realizing the *sacrifices* we have implemented. Your mother and I have given you the best schools, and the best private tutors. You can be president of this great country someday. Have you ever thought of that?"

Jack makes a fist, then slams it down on the table. The whole restaurant goes silent, while looking. Jack looks at his son with disgust, then clears his throat. Brian has been through this before. There is no winning. A debate or argument with his father is like taking on the NSA. You will lose and be destroyed. Once Jack slapped Brian back of the head, for not opening a shopping mall door for a woman. Jack is strict, believes his way is the only way. He believes in discipline, again- 'Anglo Saxon Theory.'

"Look now, honey, the cocky son of a gun knows everything. He's an expert in disguise. A mental giant. A real man of the people. A real, Ahhhh, screw it, talking to him is like talking to a doorknob."

"Dad, I don't—"

"Don't interrupt, gosh darn it. I am not going to watch my son ending up a turkey. And you know what happens to turkeys. You learned that at West point. Didn't you."

"Yes, sir I did. They get caged, plucked, stuffed, and baked."

"Honey, I don't think this is the time of the place," says Emily.

"No, he needs to hear this. Do you know what kind of people reside in Los Angeles? Do you? They are not our kind of people. It is a class system of poverty out there. The crap I know that goes on would make your head spin. Murder, thievery, political hypocrisy, the police shootings, segregation, the opium epidemic. Socialist infrastructure in the Downtown city Government. It's a political disaster zone. Everyone owns a gun in that damned city. And there all criminals. The place is useless, over fifty percent of the population is on welfare. Do you know, if there is a terrorist attack, they are under-funded and ill prepared? Makes me sick to think about it. No wonder so many assholes move there. The mold, fungus in the air. Are you out of your mind son? And It's the perfect haven for enemies of the United States. Especially Central Asia, China and North Korea. I say, destroy the fuckin' place, before it's too late. start all over again. Teach people some manners. Eminent Domain is the future son. So, get used to it."

Jack slams his fist on the table again. Brian has no retort. He sits with his face downward. He knows his father speaks the truth. Brian knows Los Angeles can be a cruel place to live. However, he must find out for himself. Branch out as a man. Create his own destiny.

"Jack, stop this," Emily says softly toned.

"I will tell you this and tell you this once. You get on that plane tomorrow, your cut off. Not one cent. Do you get it? Your mother and I are not going to let 150 years of family tradition and some pipe dream of yours get in the way of our goals for you."

Brian picks up his wine glass, finishing in one drink. A waitress, 20 years old, with blond hair, timidly walks to the table.

"Sir, are you ready to order?" Jack's table goes quiet. He looks at the waitress, then orders cheerfully.

"Yeah, Three rib-eye steaks. Cooked medium. And make it the premium cut. Not the crap you normally serve everyone else around here." The waiter nods in agreement and walks away. Not another word will be spoken the rest of the evening…

Chapter 3

Brian's alarm sounds at 4:00 AM. He didn't sleep last night. He stayed up, writing in his journal, trying to remember the good times in Washington. Brian knows not all were bad. He knows his mother and Father love him. He knows he's smart. He knows he'll survive. It's Jenna. A young woman, chosen by his father for him to marry. She reminds Brian of his mother, and for *most* young men, this isn't cool. Brian's Father works with Jenna's Father. Her Mother is friends with Brian's Mother. It makes Brian want to vomit. Every time they meet, it's the same old story, same conversation. "When are you both getting married? Think of your children. How smart, privileged, beautiful they'll all be. You both will look so good in the Whitehouse one day. Especially Jenna. Jackie O would be so jealous." What a loud of crap that is…

Brian sits on the side of his bed and watches the alarm clock click with those familiar sounds. Sounds of his Fathers disapproving voice, stresses of West Point, and Jenna reminding him of the fuckin' picnic this Sunday. Brian smiles to himself then chuckles. He remembers standing her up on purpose. Meeting with one of his best friends, going to the pub; watching the Redskins and Bears play. Getting drunk on Fish, Chips and Stout. Funny thing is about the picnic, in the end, Jenna invited one of her friends. It didn't turn out as bad as Brian thought. She always does this to Brian. Sabotage a meeting with mischievous acts of pleasure. Brian's friend tells him, "She's trying to seal the deal. Hook you in. Later, after marriage, the fun will end. She'll throw in your face, that you slept with her best friend. You'll never hear the end of it. When she's overweight, she'll always talk about her friend screwing you. Run for your life Brian." In lieu of the Guinness and fried food, again, Brian, places his hand over his mouth; ready to vomit.

Brian grabs his alarm clock, throwing it across his apartment. It's a Felix the Cat Alarm Clock. Too him, one of the most irritating things ever built. Jenna bought it for him. Half the time, the fuckin thing doesn't work. Or sets off too early or too late. Anyway, today is the greatest day of his life. Better than the day he trained with the Seals in Lebanon. Shot a four-barrel Kilroy and blew up a warehouse. Not then, but today, is the greatest day of his life. His day of freedom. The grand departure. Delicious Los Angeles. And all the hot sexy woman that he'll have sex with. He was researching the Golden Gopher. The add said 'A laid back lounge with a killer jukebox and perfect drinks. Join us for movie nights.' Yes, today, is the day, Brian will become a man. This is where he will go first. The Golden Gopher is it. The day of freedom. The day I finally become a man. Brian looks at the dating ads for the LA Weekly. 'Hi, my name is Tim. I believe in a well-balanced diet and exercise. Will you work out with me? Lol…. get it' Brian takes a sip of beer then chuckles. What a douche bag, Brian thinks.

Brian looks over his apartment for the last time. He admires the boxes his mother so neatly packed. One of the boxes reads, "Valuable objects, be careful!" He looks at his study desk that faces the window overlooking the courtyard, he will miss. And all the friends he knows in the building. He wonders if Jenna known about the Hungarian Delegate up the hall. Man, her pancakes were good, thinks Brain. Yummy pancakes, German Lager. Brian thinks about the good times, then grins.

Brian looks over the clothes his mother left for him. Dark blue jeans, a black leather jacket, a three-pack of Calvin Klein under ware, a three-pack of Calvin Klein T-shirts, black socks, Prada shoes, a distressed belt. Brian looks over the assemble and smiles. He knows his mother has good taste. Especially clothes, and automobiles. She did teach Brian how to look good. Brian looks at the Tumi bag she left him with a well-stocked German grooming kit. Brian looks inside the bag and finds an Ebel black leather band watch and envelop. Brian looks in the envelope. He finds $10,000 in fresh mint $100,00 bills. The note says, "Remember this, Son. Love spends better than money. Do not be a stranger. I will miss you." Love spends better than money. I'll remember this when I read the 'LA X-Press.' Thinks Brian.

Brian feels an uncomfortable sentiment as he looks over the money. He looks out the window, then walks toward the shower. As he walks, he notices a picture of him and Jenna on the kitchen countertop. It is wrapped in a British Sterling frame. Mother obviously put it there. Brian looks at the picture and runs his finger over Jenna. He grins and looks at his study desk. He re-gathers his thoughts and heads toward the bathroom. There's no turning back now. He knows what he must do. Go live…

Jenna, in her black C-class Mercedes, waits for Brian. Jenna is 24 years old, red hair, green eyes, 5'5", and 125 pounds, natural double B breasts, and attractive.

Brian sits in the passenger seat. On the radio plays 'Roxy Music; More than This.' Brian listens to the song knowing she selected. It's another one her lame attempt keeping him in Washington. *That song,* he thinks, *that is the song we first listened to when we made love in the back seat of this car.* I swear to heaven thinks Brian. Jenna is like one of those daytime soap operas. It never ends.

"Remember, you're not leaving me if you do, I swear—"

Brian quickly interrupts, "Swear what?"

"I'll kill you." Jenna laughs nervously as she ashes her cigarette out the window.

"I'm not leaving you. I just want to get things together before you move out. You know, the job, the apartment, new set of wheels. The apartment also, I know how you like that Berlin-style loft look. Anyway, if the job doesn't work out, I'll be home like that." Brian snaps his fingers avoiding eye contact with Jenna, if he doesn't, he might get a bit sentimental. He's to hungover for any in-depth conversation.

"I may not even like Los Angeles."

"Well, you know what we say about Los Angeles in DC," says Jenna.

"Yeah, and what's that?"

"Los Angeles is the city of lost angels. The land of over-ratted pleasures." Brian laughs as he grabs one of Jenna's cigarettes.

"You sound like my father." Brian chuckles.

"Promise me one thing?" Asks Jenna.

"What?" Brian said sarcastically.

"Before you buy furniture, take a picture and send it to me."

"Yeah, Yeah, I know. We discussed this a million times before."

Jenna reaches into a bag and takes out a sandwich.

"Better eat your egg sandwich. You can't go hungry." Jenna quickly unwraps the sizeable breakfast sandwich and tries feeding it to Brian.

"Here." Brian turns his head away in disgust.

"Smells like an old woman's wet foot," says Brian.

Brian is a bit hungover from last night. He and a few old West Point buddies had a few drinks. He thinks of his friend from Israel. He left to study "psychotic computer behavior." It is a theory he and buddies discussed at school. Keeps his mind off Jenna's meaningless bullshit.

"Not now, I'll save it for later. I already ate."

"Ate what?"

"Jenna, stop playing mom. I'm not hungry now. I'll eat it on the plane. Thanks anyway, it is sweet of you." Brian leans over and kisses Jenna on the cheek.

"When am I moving in with you?" asks Jenna.

"Not this again. We've been at this a thousand times. I am not in the mood right now. Especially after the meeting with my parents last night. And you're not helping much."

Brian takes a deep breathe, gags from the smell of the sandwich, then cracks the window open. Wait a second, that not the sandwich that smells like rotten snake eggs. Holy shit, Jenna just passed gas…

"Sorry, I'm still a bit confused. Brian, so tell me, what's so bad about DC? Your friends and family are here. I am here, your father offered you a kick-ass position at the State Department. Is it me, for once be honest with yourself? Tell me—" Brian quickly interrupts.

"Jenna, cut it. Enough about my family. And can you please, roll down my window. The switch is locked."

Jenna regains her composure and throws the cigarette but out the window.

"OK, then. Brian, you are right. The decision is yours. I must respect it. Besides, I heard many of the women out there are plastic. Superficial. Dumb and fake blond. I'm not worried. I know you love me."

Brian sighs, then rolls his eyes.

"I'll remember that; Jenna."

"You want to hear the truth?" Asks Jenna,

"Dazzle me," says Brian.

"Very funny," Jenna Says.

"Truth is, I don't ever want to leave Washington. I am doing this for you. Just remember that" says Jenna.

Brian cheerfully tries to change the subject. He takes her hand, giving her a sign of false sign of reassurance.

"Can you roll up the window please?" asks Jenna.

Brian shakes his head, sighs and sets the window upward a few inches.

"There, that should be better. Holy crap. Smells like rotten eggs," says Brian.

Jenna interrupts quickly.

"You better not cheat on me. Remember this, everything you do wrong; I'll know about it."

Brian looks her over curiously.

Jenna lets of an evil grin.

"You're stuck with me for life, Brian."

Brian looks at Jenna and nervously laughs.

"That's a cheerful thought." Jenna laughs, then nudges Brian in the arm.

"So, you'll be watching too. Everyone is always watching."

Brian looks out the window admiring the trees and green lush landscape as Jenna babbles on about their everlasting love. What if *they are watching? Who gives a fuck thinks Brian, maybe they'll learn how to have sex. Make love to a real woman.* He sticks his hand out the window feeling the cool breeze float throughout the car cabin. This will be the only thing he misses about Washington.

Jenna's black Mercedes pulls up to the drop off the curb. She places the car in the park then sighs deeply.

"Well, I guess this is it," says Brian.

Brian gets out of the passenger door as Jenna opens the rear trunk. Jenna meets Brian at the rear of the vehicle. Brian reaches in the trunk and takes two bags out.

"This is a new beginning for us, Brian."

Jenna remains positive in lieu of her sadness. Brian doesn't speak. He adjusts one of the rolling cases and smiles.

"The move is for both of us, right? Brian, right?" Brian says nothing. He places his sunglasses over his eyes as he looks in all directions.

"Want me to wait with you?" asks Jenna. "I don't mind."

"No, you don't have too. This is difficult enough already. Why don't I call you when I'm boarding? We'll talk about our plans then."

"Promise," says Jenna.

"Promise."

Brian jesters a hand, pinky swear.

Jenna's eyes begin tearing. She places her right hand over her mouth then looks away, she quickly moves in closer hugging Brian. She begins sobbing.

"Hey, look at me," says Brian. "Don't do this. I'm only a few hours away." Brian takes a white handkerchief and hands it to her. "I do love you. You know this."

Jenna gasp for air. She senses Brian is lying.

"I don't want you to leave without me. Don't you understand how much you're hurting me? I can't breathe without you."

Uncontrollable feelings of sentiment overpower Brian. He starts to cry. Brian pulls Jenna into him closer. He hugs her closely and kisses her, then brushes her tears with his hand.

"You'll be with me soon, promise," says Brian.

Jenna places both arms around his waist, then buries her face in his chest.

"This feels like death to me." Says Jenna.

Jenna places both hands around Brian's face, kissing him. A voice over the intercom wails. The voice announces that flight 414 to Los Angeles is now boarding.

Jenna pulls away as Brian reaches in his coat and takes his ticket. Brian solemnly looks over the paper.

"That's me, better get going."

Brian takes his luggage and slowly walks away toward the glass doors. Jenna stands at the side of the car looking at him with teary eyes. Brian looks back as Jenna blows her a kiss. Jenna smiles at Brian.

"I love you!" says Jenna.

Brian pretends not to hear. vanishes through the glass doors. He's quickly consumed by the passengers walking to their destinations.

Brian looks out the glass doors for the last time then waves. Jenna waves goodbye then gives Brian her best smile. An overwhelming feeling of dread and fear overcome Jenna. A brisk of cold air runs through her body. She turns around and sees an old woman. Draped in black, pilgrim style shoes, black cape, and black sunglasses. Her skin is dead grey and her eyes white. She points to the East, then evilly smiles. Jenna turns her head in the direction, then looks back at the old woman. She's gone. The demon is gone. The same demon that's been haunting Brian's family's bloodline for centuries has spoken again. This demon will no doubt, follow Brian to Los Angeles. Tempt him, teach him, make love to him, nestle him. then in the end, destroy him. Jenna feels horribly uncomfortable. She fears this may be last time she'll see Brian. Her true love and soul mate.

A nun walks by Jenna and gives her a pamphlet. She smiles ever so lovingly, then walks away. The pamphlet reads "Evil people do not believe in Love. They believe in Self-Serving Damnation."

Chapter 4

Brian enters the plane. He's the last person. The flight attendants' smirk at him, as he feels all eyes upon him. The plane is silent. So silent, Brian can hear the passengers breathing.

"We've been waiting for you," says the flight attendant. Brian walks to his seat. The seat number is 14.

Thank God for an aisle seat thinks Brian. He tries placing his carry-on in the above cabinet. His right leg touches one of the passengers. The passenger looks at him and frowns. There is no room in the compartment. The other passengers glare at him, as they shake their heads in disapproval.

"Shit, sorry, Ma'am," says Brian.

"Ouch. Watch it, young man!" Yells an elderly woman. Brian's embarrassed. He begins to sweat from his forehead. All Brian can think of is settling in and having a few drinks. It will help calm his nerves. It always does.

"What the hell is your problem man? Let's get on with it!" A passenger from the back of the plane yells. Brian continues to place his carry-on bag in the above compartment with no success. An agitated flight attendant hurries toward Brian. She has been on route from Canada, Alaska now Washington. She obviously isn't in the mood for any shenanigans. Brian is already late. He will have no friends on the flight, until up in the air, and drinks are served. Oxygen helps ease the worries of meeting strangers too. The plight of a man who enters the plane late, will not be heard. There is no room for negotiations. Especially is coach class.

"What's this guy's problem!" Another passenger yells next to him. Brian tries slamming the above cabinet again.

"Shit, what the—?" says Brian. The flight attendant tells Brian he can place the bag at his feet.

"Touché, sound's good," says Brian. He sits down and sighs. The plane is already moving and ready for takeoff. The flight attendant hurries him and tells him to fasten the seat belt.

A passenger in her 70s, with dark red lipstick, yellow scarf around the neck, and green blouse, a large nose, gold sunglasses with black lenses looks over Brian. The elderly woman smiles as the plane accelerates down the runway. The elderly woman doesn't say a word. She looks at his crotch area and smiles, then licks her lips.

For heaven's sake. She looks like one of those deranged old women from a Seinfeld Episode, Brian thinks. The odd-looking elderly woman slips off her Prada loafers, then continues smiling at Brian. Her feet are dead white with blue veins that consume all angles. She sports bright orange toenail polish. The toenails are longcut and pointy. Brian wonders if his future wife will have such ugly feet. I mean these tires look like you can hunt and stab boars. Brian won't allow it. He was taught by his mother to look at a woman's feet, hands and neck before you do *anything* else. Gross dirty ugly feet are disgusting too. Reminds Brain of an old legend his grandmother wrote him. He received the letter at the orphanage on Halloween. It's Called 'Legend of Old and Smelly.' The woman does not say one word. All she does is smile mischievously, while touching and rubbing his inner thigh. Her hand is old and decrypted with plastic artificial green nails. She wears an oversized black opal gold ring on her left index finger with an eye in the middle of it. Her married finger shows a gold ring, black faced with pentagram. Brian looks down at the ring and sees the eye wink at him. Brian shakes off the illusion. The woman finally speaks.

"This style of transportation is a bit trite and meaningless; don't you think young sexy man? In my days we traveled by trains and automobiles. The sex, especially oral was invigorating. Simply wonderful. And I mean on both ends of the stick."

She looks at Brian's crotch again, licking her lips. Breathe smells of garlic pasta sauce, lipstick on her dentures. "Delicious." Proclaims the deranged old woman, "Delicious."

Brian smiles and laughs aloud. He has not slept in the past 4 nights.

It is just another illusion, thinks Brian. The after-effects of Carlsberg Lager and the toxins of Jack in the Box, really did him in last night. Especially the Polish Delegate he met in the hallway before leaving.

Brian has seen a few illusions in the past four days. He heard voices in his apartment. Voices telling him not to move to Los Angeles. Voices telling him Jenna is his soulmate. Voices telling him that his *destiny* is Washington. His true love is home. He woke last night drenched in sweat, then drank 4 glasses of whisky. Took a 10mg sleeping pill and went back to bed.

At 4:00 AM, Brian saw an elderly woman draped in a white robe, the apparition floated in a backwards and forward, motion until he felt a tingling sensations all over his legs and arms. Brian felt his body muscles ache, and his temperature rise. The aspiration appeared was cursing him, pointing at him. Trying to tell him something. He woke himself out of the trance, cursed the apparition and prayed. The apparition vanished.

Brian knows it was just sleep deprivation, another illusion. He knows he will feel better when he arrives in Los Angeles, rest and starts his new routine.

Brian looks at the elderly woman smiles, then politely removes her hand from his crotch.

The captain is heard over the speaker discussing the travel route, and points of interest. The captain says they will reach Los Angeles in about 4 hours. I man back of the plane yells. "Right on Dude!"

Brian closes his eyes and smiles. The word Los Angeles brings great comfort to his ears. He adjusts his back seat, then adjust his body in the chair. He wanted to fly business class. He always flies business. It was Jenna that booked his ticket. He knows it's her way of punishing Brian; for not taking her with him. She's already sending texts, showing Brian what furniture to buy, what colors. What lofts to look at downtown. She likes Pacific Avenue and Southern Pacific lofts. The sales individual stated they intend to attract more serious professional types. More married couples. Brian looks at the phone smirks, then turns it off. He saw a loft on Los Angeles Street on the 700 block. One renter called it "Cheap and Dirty." This is what Brian wants for now. Who cares what she thinks, right? Brian closes his eyes knowing soon, he will have a new life. This relaxes him. Now, he can sleep.

Brian wakes from his slumber. His dreams were violent. He dreamed that the plane was crashing. The best part of the dream was, he didn't care. In his dream, Brian stood in the middle of the aisle cursing the other passengers, warning them of their demise and the sins they have committed. Warning them to the trials of judgment and hell and repentance. He watched passengers get their heads cut off in judgement and laughed. He laughed so hard he ended up vomiting blood. The blood turned into a large demon, then devoured the flesh of the passengers. Then Brian dreamed he was at a little league game. His father staring at him from the stands. The bases were loaded with two outs. Brian strikes out, the other team cheered as Brian walked away. His father did not wait for him. Brian walked home in the rain, feelings defeated and useless. Then he saw *them* again. Men and woman draped in black, following him, then as he ran, chasing him home. Floating in the air behind him yelling 'you are the chosen one.' At first Brian was ahead of the stalkers, then he began to slow down. His heart felt heavy, he could no longer breathe. Just as he was about to drop, he woke up.

In the seat in front of him, a young Caucasian girl peeks over her seat starring at him. Lost expression on her face. She is about ten years old. Extremely pale, dark circles below the eyes and pigtails. She wears a red turtleneck, with jean overalls. The young girl stares at Brian, as she places her dead white hands, with black nail polish below her chin. At first glance, Brian thought she was an undersized woman, washed out from drugs. Or a young girl who is extremely malnourished. As he stares back, he sees the silence of a desperate young girl suffering. One that may be suffering from leukemia, or ankylosing spondylitis. The young girl looks dead and frightened. At first, Brian pushes out his ears, sticks out his tongue, making a monkey face. The girl does not respond. He tries a few other expressions that make his nieces laugh, no luck. The young girl's expression doesn't change.

"Hello there," says Brian. "Where is your mom?"

The young girl doesn't answer. She continues to stare at Brian, eyes dilated. They almost look snake-like. Demonic, Nosferatu. Eyes of a cloaked demon. One Brian has seen, many times as a child. A demon with bat ears and big black eyes, a mouth with fangs looking as if he's screaming at you.

"How are you? My name is Brian. Can't you talk?"

The young girl finally speaks. "I already know who you are," the young girl says. Brian's eyes widen, now he is curious.

"Who are you asks Brian?"

"Your unborn daughter," says the young girl. "We will be waiting for you." She raises her eyebrows and grins.

A white envelope falls from the girl's hands. It hits the floor, next to Brian's shoe. Brian looks to the floor and sees the envelope has a symbol written in black ink. Brian leans over, picking up the envelope sits up. He looks it over. Brian clarifies that the symbol is written in Chinese script. Below the script, in English, the envelope reads, "Do not open. Ever." As Brian looks over the envelope, he feels a sizeable round hard object inside. Curiosity strikes Brian. He thinks it may be a valuable coin or a historical relic dated back to Imperial China. It may be worth hundreds and thousands of dollars.

"This must belong to you," says Brian.

The young girl shakes her head then speaks, "No, it's yours, Daddy. It is from *them*. I wouldn't open it if I were you." The young girl shakes her head left to right, eyes gleaming like a demon.

As Brian looks over the envelope, he remembers his studies of sociology and Eastern Culture Euphemisms. Brian stands up quickly and looks around the plane. All passengers are gone. He looks back at the girl. She has vanished.

Brian's is now awake. He lets out a scream, then quickly remembers where he is. He stands up and looks around the plane. He sees passengers glaring at him. A few in the back are laughing out loud calling him a white freak. "Yeah, he like one of those white punks on dope," says the passenger.

Brian looks over the front seat in front of him. He sees the young girl is gone. He looks to his right seeing the old-deranged woman is gone. *Here I go again,* Brian thinks. *Another fucked up bad dream.* I need a drink. I should have had a drink before the ride. I'll never learn.

Brian looks toward the floor and finds a white envelope. It is the same envelope as in his dream. He picks it up and looks it over. He notices the same Chinese symbol, the round object inside, and instruction is written the same. Brian stands up and calls out to the passengers.

"Does this belong to anyone? I have a white envelope here, with a Chinese letter." All the customers stare at Brian, shaking their heads no. A few passengers yell out. One calls him a dumb ass; another complains that his sleep is now disturbed. A woman tells him to shut the hell up and have a drink or take a pill. Her children are sleeping.

A different flight attendant stands in the aisle next to Brian. One that is sexier. Black hair, white skin, big brown eyes. *Shit, she looks like the young girl's mother,* he thinks. She looks him over and pats him on the shoulder.

"Sir, would you like a drink?" Her voice echoes the sounds of a bad dream.

"Excuse me?" replies Brian.

"Would you like something to drink, Sir?" Brian looks around the plane, then looks over the envelope.

"Sir, you are disturbing the passengers. You need help?" Her tone is stern and direct. This is not a question.

"No, I'm OK. It's just that…that."

"What is the problem?" asks the flight attendant.

"Was I asleep? Wasn't there a small girl sitting in front of me?"

"Sir, I don't understand."

"In front of me. A small girl. She dropped this." Brian shows the envelope to the flight attendant.

"Look, she was sitting in front of me. And what about the older woman next to me. You know, the one with the funky outfit, green nail polish?"

"Sir, the seat in front of you has been vacant since we departed."

"And the woman?"

"What woman?"

What Brian sees is a businessman in a suit glaring at him, as if he wanted to stab Brian for waking him.

"But I saw her sitting there. She was sitting in front of me, starring and, and well, the old woman was—"

Brian's head begins to feel faint.

"Well, what, Sir?"

"She gave me this." The flight attendant looks at the envelope.

"What does it mean?" asks Brian.

"Do I look Asian to you?"

She does, thinks Brian. The flight attendant takes the envelope holding it over her head.

"Does anybody on this plane own this envelope? Anyone?" Passengers look at the flight attendant comment saying no shaking their heads. She smirks then gives the envelope back to Brian. Another man tells Brian to shut up. This time cursing him.

"Sir, according to the flight roster. There is no one in this place under the age of 18. Also, before each flight, each aisle is cleaned. I'm sure someone would have claimed it claimed since Canada."

"But what if—"

"Sir, again, the aisles are inspected before each departure."

"You never noticed me sleeping or anything?" Asks Brian.

"Sir, you have been awake the whole flight?"

"What?" replies Brian, agitated tone.

The flight-attendant shakes her head, then singles a potential problem to another attendant.

"Sir, you already ate your lunch. Look at the trash basket in front of you." Brian looks and sees wrappers and empty coke can. Brian regains his composure. He looks toward the back of the plane and notices a large male in hill-billie, blue overalls, starring at him. He looks like the football player in the movie 'Sixteen Candles.' Brian's pulse begins racing. His heart skips a few beats.

"Sir, are you OK?" Brian nods yes. He takes a napkin and wipes his forehead.

"So, Sir, how about that drink?" The flight attendant smiles gleefully.

"OK, a Jack Daniels will be nice."

"No problem, I'll bring two of them."

The flight attendant walks away. Brian stares at her buttock. *Nice,* Brian thinks. *Hope the women in LA all look this good.* Brian sits back takes a deep breath. He looks to his right and sees the elderly woman again. She smiles and pats Brian's inner thigh; then gives him her cell phone number.

The message says, "Old and Willing. Be careful what you wish for. It may come to you." 213-666-1801. Brian looks at the elderly woman and smiles. She raises her wine cup, then cheers Brian.

"I must be losing it," Brian says to himself.

"Don't worry, honey, wait until you reach Los Angeles." "They're all losing it," the elderly woman says.

Brian looks at his Ebel wristwatch. The time says 4:00 PM. Brian takes a deep drink of Jack Daniels, then speaks to himself. 'This is what I get for flying coach.'

Chapter 5

Brian's been in Los Angeles for two weeks now. Every rental he has looked at, Jenna has supplied the information. Mostly hotel style, overpriced, undersized lofts occupied by married couples. Some with kids running around, running around, screaming all day. Not Brian's style. He want's something artistic, sexy and real. So far, he bought a brand-new Volkswagen. A 2005 Black GTI. It has a 2.0-liter 20 valve motor and is well balanced. He plans on a Black Mercedes AMG soon. Brian bought 4 suits from a supplier on Los Angeles Street. The proprietor's name is Roger Stewart. Brian bought two button Hugo Boss-black, navy, dark grey and brown. When spring hits, hell buy a Khaki one. He's impressed by the quality and the tailor-cut, so perfect, Dean Martin would smile. Brian also bought cashmere crewnecks, turtlenecks, and V-neck vest. A wide array of black t-shirts, some dress shirts, ties, shoes, belts and 4 four of jeans.

Brian will start work in two months. For now, it's party time. His time to roam the streets of Los Angeles. Get laid, meet dirty woman who work in pornography, drink and eat hamburgers, tacos and burritos every day. After all, Los Angeles is a Burger Town, right??

Brian grabbed LA Weekly and looked for a Motel. Something dark, steamy, sexy. Something that represents a young man freedom, *chaotic fate*. Brian found a Motel West of Downtown by about two miles. Something. rumored to be gouged with forgotten children and young adults looking for a new life. 'The Bahama Inn.' is perfect; and Jenna is furious. 'They are bungalows offering overrated pleasures and self-defeat!' Jenna screamed over the phone. She threatened, him, cursed him, said she is sending someone to watch. Brian doesn't care. This is what Brian wants. At least for now. The Motel is known for transient drug dealers, loser wannabe 'Slash' guitar players, singers, song writers, screenwriters, and prostitutes. It was fuckin' paradise to Brian. Everything he ever imagined since he left Washington. The people he met, were 'fantastic.' And what a vacation for Brian it is. He thought of his Father the whole time and grinned. 'If Mr. Perfect could only see me now.'

Brian ate Mexican food, went to a hostess bar on 4th street, drank tequila, shoot pool; mumble to himself and he paced his hotel room, drinking, getting high on weed, as he recited lyrics to 'Grand Funk Railroad,' and 'The Faces.' He wrote song lyrics for a punk rock guitar player from Indiana. Stayed up all night and ate at Tommy's Chili Burgers for breakfast. Brian watched cool movies like '2 Days in The Valley, Manhunter, Slam Dance, To Live and Die in LA, Breathless, Blade, The Big Lebowski, Big Wednesday and the Mechanic. He was in paradise. 'Los Angeles, Nostalgic Cinema, all the way.'

A few nights Brian stayed in. He was a bit hungover, and tired of chemical induced foods. One night, Brian sat and stared out the window. He was surprised of the night life on 3rd street. It appeared more interesting than any movie he has ever seen.

It was a sticky summer night. Brian watched a dark, sexy, sadistic looking woman as he drank beer. She would slowly walk up and down the sidewalk. Neon signs lighting her way, flicking cigarettes at vehicles, as they passed by. This is where he met Simone. A white witch prostitute from Romania. Brian watched her walk back and forth on the sidewalk, smoking, drinking Red Bulls while displaying her assets. Brian felt excited, lustful, overwhelmed with curiosity and sinful desire. He was lost in her body movement and ghostly figure, that laid out the night's destiny. Brian became so excited, he relived himself in the bathroom, then rushed back to gaze at her. Brian could swear that he saw her stop at look at his window several times, while grinning. He wondered if they could read each other. Either way, it was sexy, period.

One night, Brian heard her yelling inside one of the rooms. Then sounds of a lamp hitting the floor. Pounding on the wall; then cursing. A door slammed. Simone exits screaming atop her lungs. "You owe me $100.00 you white trash American pile of dogshit. I'm connected, I will murder you."

Brian intrigued, opened his door, and spoke to her. She smiled, introduced herself, then asked Brian if he had any smokes. Brian replied no, but he does have plenty of booze and food. He introduced himself, as she aggressively shook his hand. A catastrophic handshake. Not like any other handshake; a civilized woman would bring. Her handshake was as if she is.

torturing a penis. I mean, she hated the fuckin' thing. Brian asked her if she understood the theory of 'Penis Envy.' She laughed, then took to Brian immediately.

Brian escorted her to his room then offered her Vodka. She was most appreciative. Vodka and microwave hotdogs. Farmer John Hotdogs. Dodger Dogs "Perfect!" the borderline looking woman hailed, as Simone engulfed six hot dogs plain, with buns. She drank eight shots of vodka straight, burped, then goose-stepped to the bathroom. Simone partook in defecation. I mean, this woman's shit stunk horrible. So bad, Brian almost vomit, right in the middle of his room. He opened the door, trying not to laugh, then looked for another cool movie on 'Showtime' or 'Movie Channel.' Understanding as Brian may be. Some things are to be kept sacred. One is the smell of a street woman's crap, laced with synthetics.

Brian masked the smell, by lighting two of her cigarettes. Brian never smoked, however; tonight, his most triumphant, he just may start.

You see, Simone was unlike any other woman Brian has ever met. Not because she appeared to be a drugged-out street girl. She seemed smart. An expert at the art of hustling. She also looked good. She stood 5 feet 6 inches, weighed about 120 pounds, and has real breasts. This is a rarity in Los Angeles. Her hair is jet black, eyes blue, and skin white as snow. Fuckin' sexy thinks Brian. Maybe I should talk to her. Really talk to her, get inside her maybe even save her. The last two weeks Brian watched her. Yet to the best of his knowledge, she never had sex. It appeared that customers would drive up, shed look around, then take a small box out of her purse. Then hand it to man driving the vehicle. Brian noticed zero money being exchanged. The arrangements always ended up in a fight. A few times, the police showed. They sided with she, then warned the guy about being a turkey in their town. Brian wondered if she's spreading illegal surveillance software. Basic coding to hack the 5G-Digtital Networks, throughout Los Angeles County. You see, Brian knows that if an Army is built, using free energy as weapon. Human existence can and will be destroyed. We might as all live in a HUGE MICROWAVE OVEN. Brian learned this West Point. The more people extracting Free Energy, the more Dominate, the wavelength. It destroys human flesh, causing bone and brain disease.

After the smoke cleared and smell dissipated, Simone asked Brian if she could stay in his room for a few hours. She mentioned that she owned a gangster from Albania five-hundred dollars for rent. He will be looking for her soon.

Brian, out of curiosity replied yes. They both sat on the bed eating at Tommy's' Chili Burgers and Fries, drinking booze, and surprisingly; Brian had a good time. They watched 'Family Guy, Married with Children, Malcom in the Middle, and the Benny Hill Show.'

At 3:00AM, Simone wanted to play a game. They both sat down Indian Style on the bed, touching hands. Simone asked Brian to close his eyes and concentrate. She asked him to figure out why she came to America? Why she does what she does? Why she hates men so much?

Brian closed his eyes. They start to flicker, and his body became tense. Electricity ran through his body, as he felt goosebumps all around his arms. Brian did see things he thought he would never see. He saw her as a child being sold for bottles of Vodka, he saw Russia threatening Yugoslavia, then her family in Crimea. Then he saw Ukraine. He saw peoples' throats being cut. Houses lost, jobs lost, total despair. He saw her Father being shot by gangsters then her sister being raped.

Brian awoke screaming in pain hollering. He told Simone everything he saw. Simone started to cry, telling Brian, he spoke the truth. Then Simone asked if she could spend the night.

She took a shower as Brian brushed his teeth, then shot down his last whisky. As they both lay on the bed, with one lamp lighting their way; Simone told him things. She told him of many things. Why he resented his parents, his home his girlfriend. Why he came to Los Angeles. She told him about his new job. She even knew it was in commodities and investments. She also informed him that people were watching him. Brian quickly sat up, stood from the bed then look her over. All he noticed was a crooked smile about her face. The smile of poker thief, or someone who lied to get someone in trouble. To him, it was a smile he has never seen before. The smile of pure evil.

The things Simone told him about. His secrets, his sexual desires. The type of woman he wants to marry. How he doesn't want Jenna. And most of all, his life's goals. Simone also informed him that he will be a great leader someday. The people watching him are powerful. They have been in existence for thousands of years. You will be led by an ancient light. A light that was ordained through God himself. An angel born from the light created by God.

She told him his destiny was written many moons ago. By the high priest. Ordained from the master.

Brian laughed. He told her. "I studied people like you at West Point. If people are watching me, it is probably my father or his goons. They probably paid you to fuck with me. Screw with my head. Listen and listen well. Lucifer is a god of light. I know this. He is powerful. His power is ordained through God, his Father. If he is so great, and God, why has he not sacrificed himself for his people. Jesus who is the one and only God; did this for all humanity? God is love. Our love for each other, is proof God exits. The god you speak of is a god of hate, lies, and deceit. He hates his Father and all his creation. In the end, he begs the true God, his Father for mercy. He is then locked away for one-thousand years. You know God ordained these acts. Because he agrees to have his own son killed, the antichrist. In the end, the devil loses. This has been written for thousands of years."

Simone glares at Brian, then turns to her side. She cannot speak, she only cries. After a few minutes she falls asleep. Brian tries waking her. She will not wake.

Brian sits up another two hours in the chair beside the bed. He thinks he can stay up and watch her but retires the night... He lays down on the floor beside the bed, then falls into a deep sleep.

Brain wakes at 8:00AM. Mouth dry, head pounding, felling as if his stomach is full of battery acid. He stands up, checking his pockets. He finds his wallets, then opens it up. All his credit cards are gone with $300.00 dollars. Brian laughs, gathers his Tumi Bag, runs to the bathroom, vomits, then decides; better find another Motel. Something a little higher class. Maybe I will try the rooms above 'King Louie.' Thinks Brian. But first, a breakfast burrito. One at that cool Mexican place with the Jukebox and hot looking waitress. The Jukebox with 'Freedy Fender' and 'Carlos Santana.'

Brian checks his coat pocket. His Banana Republic denim jacket. He finds a letter in the side pocket. It has the heading of Holiday Inn, downtown. Must have been the location of one her last victims.

The note reads.

"Dear Brian, you a good man, and I am blessed meeting you. However, be warned. There is an Evil Presence on you. I read it in your dreams. It has been stalking this earth for over 100,000 years. Dating back to ancient Emerald Isle.

He is one of your ancestors. Please be careful. who you meet." She leaves a phone number for he to contact her in case of emergency. The phone number is 213-666-1801.

Your New Friend, forever.
Simone.

Note to Reader:

It should acknowledge. Simone is indeed Cindy Walbreck. She is now out of Prison. Her Grandmother inherited her body, before the fire in 1994, through ancient witchcraft rituals. Now she recruits for Henry Faustino Army.

Chapter 6

In front of Pico House, Downtown Los Angeles, stands Realtor Jane Marshall. She's in her early 60s, 5'5", bleach-blond, orange hair in a bun. She smells of Aqua Net and Opium Perfume. She sports an orange and navy-blue Channel dress, with white stockings and green pumps. She also wears an orange scarf around her neck, big gold earrings, and a golden dragon broach with red eyes. Dark red lipstick offsets her assemble. Most of her lipstick is stuck to her yellow dentures. She lost her teeth due to chaotic drug binges in the seventies and eighties. She enjoys her fake teeth. Her boyfriend says they're sexy. She smokes Salem Menthols daily. When with a client, she has a bad habit of smacking on nicotine chewing gum. She drives a 1993 Mercedes E-Class. It's green with a beige interior, in perfect showroom condition. The accents are gold, with 17-inch AMG chrome wheels. It was a good buy she tells everyone. A bargain at La Brea Discount Classics.

Realtor Jane looks up at Pico House rooftop, then taps her walking cane three times on the concrete. A cold breeze goes through her as she gasps for air. She looks nervously at her gold and diamond Rolex. Her truck driver boyfriend bought it for her at Santee Alley on their 20th anniversary. She likes the hot dogs at Santee Alley, as well as the discounts. She also likes to people watch with her abnormal boyfriend, pretend to hear what they are saying and thinking. Realtor Jane also enjoys McCormick & Schmick's. It's also a good place for prospecting young clients. She is known throughout the Basin as *The Death Realtor*. This is due to her lust for death properties throughout Los Angeles. In other words, homes of unnatural deaths, lofts of pain, lost lives, and suffering. Why go on a death tour when you can go see Realtor Jane? She knows everything and anything about LA's haunted past. Brian liked Realtor Jane over the telephone. He thought she was humorous. Like him, out of place and from another time. She reminds Brian of Flow on the 70s television show 'Mel's Dinner.'

Brian pulls up to the curb in a new Volkswagen 2.0 Turbo. He's late for the appointment. He despises being late, however; he's still getting used to the LA traffic. Brian met Jane at the civic center downtown. They were having a realtor convention. Brian knows realtor conventions are known for good-looking woman. At least they are in the Washington area, and Brian has had great success in the past.

"It's me, Brian. Sorry, I'm late. Not used to the traffic yet." The realtor curiously looks him over. She grins. She likes what she sees. Brian is her type of man. A man of destruction and chaos, a real wrath child. A man she has waited to devour, feed on, and possibly become his sex slave.

"Hi, Brian." She offers a handshake. Brian accepts and looks at her "no-fly zone."

"Traffic has always been a hassle in this city," says Jane. "My family moved here from Oklahoma in the early 19th century. Boy let me ya tell ya. Those were the days."

Jane loses herself in the moment. Becomes a bit dazed, then snaps out of it.

"No worries honey. Everyone's always 15 minutes late."

"So, what do we have here?" asks Brian.

"Well, here it is. The old 'Pico House.' Oh, baby doll, you're going to love this place, it has an illustrious past." Brian and the Realtor walk together toward the entrance. Brian opens the door for Jane.

"Oh, how nice, thank you. Finally, a gentleman in this town." She adjusts the bun in her hair, then pulls on her skirt.

"So, what's so special about this building? It doesn't look like much," asks Brian.

"Are you serious?" The realtor looks over Brian. He has a blank expression on his face.

"This great here building represents everything wonderful about this fair city. Hellfire, I can feel the energy standing here. Makes me a bit rambunctious. If you know what I mean."

She nudges Brian on the arm.

"Oh, I forget, you're from Washington, aren't you?" Brian nods yes. The realtor takes a deep breath, then adjusts her bravado.

"Well, this place is very old. It used to be a hotel. Old style locals used to rent here. You know, people of class and community status. Starting off in the business, then making it big. It is one of the first buildings constructed in this city. Lovely place. Hollywood royalty used to live here." Brian strolls through the lobby and looks at the pictures on the wall.

"It feels old, what are the rooms like?"

"Small, but cozy. Enough for two young adults, getting it on."

Realtor Jane laughs aloud. Brian tries to ignore her comments.

"You mentioned over the phone, this place is special? I don't get it?" The realtor shakes her head, rolling her eyes.

"Well, it is. Especially if you are a horror fanatic. You like horror stories, horror movies, Brian?"

"Sometimes, it depends."

Realtor Jane clears her throat, then adjust her jacket.

"Well, the story goes, in the late 1700s, early 1800s; there was a group of Chinese railroad workers settled here. One night, after a lot of drinking and hollering, crazed Mexican and IRISH cowboy gangsters ran amuck. They went through the courthouse and building. They executed 23 Chinese men. Real blood baths wonderful it was. Knives, machete's, guns, hand axes, sledgehammers, you name it. It was a real blessing. Absolutely marvelous. Anyway, it was told this land; the boys of Santa Ana and Los Angeles would have no part of anyone taking it over. They wanted things their way. It was their town. And this here town is what they established. Isn't that something Brian?"

Brian looks over Jane, white face, eyes widened, checks red.

Realtor Jane looks the place over like a long, lost lover. She shakes a chill from her body.

"I tell ya boy, this place turns me on." Realtor Jane laughs aloud.

"Like I said, wonderful place. It's one of *our* favorites you know…" She pauses for a moment as her cell phone rings. She doesn't answer. She too busy fixated on Brian's good looks. His crotch, his buttocks, all she can think about is oral sex. She wants Brian now. She wants to role play. She, the dirty older, hooker. Brian is her customer. Getting it on in the upstairs bedroom. Bending over the sink. Talking dirty telling him to call her his 'Old Slutty Slave.' She gets turned on by these types of men.

Realtor Jane catches herself, then shakes off the moment. She shakes her head, then continues.

"Security staff hears mysterious footsteps throughout. Also, some have seen ghost leaning over that balcony there. Isn't that swell?" The realtor smiles as she desperately smacks on her nicotine gum. She craves Brian, as she would a six-foot-tall cigarette.

I could just roll him up and smoke him, she thinks.

"Sure, I guess. However, I do not think I would be comfortable here. It feels claustrophobic, like somethings' on my shoulders." Brian has a look of shock about his face. He thinks this woman is clearly deranged. The realtor looks over Brian with that crazed grin again. Like she already knows him.

"Do you have any other rentals in this area?"

"Oh, honey, take your pick. Let us see, I have a list right here? Wait a sec—"

The realtor shuffles papers through her fake Prada bag. She sighs, places her cheetah glasses on, then opens the listing book. "Let's have a look here."

"Off of La Brea Blvd. Marvelous area. I have a one-bedroom. No, wait, even better, a two-bedroom, on Ardmore Blvd. It's rumored that Charles Manson son lived there. Isn't that something?" Brian is now in definite shock. He shows no emotion.

"I need a moment to think that one over," says Brian. The realtor's phone rings loud. It stuns Brian as Jane answers.

"Yes, Oh, hello. Uh, Uh, yes. I have a beautiful place up on Silverlake Mountain. It is rumored that the original owner butchered his family with a chainsaw. He then dumped the bodies in the lake…" The realtor pauses the conversation, while she listens to the customer.

"Fantastic, marvelous place." As the crazed realtor carries on about the history of these Silverlake murders; Brian walks outside and takes a deep breath. He cannot believe what he has heard. Yet he is confounded by this woman's personality. He decides he must move on with her until he finds the perfect home.

Brian and the Realtor Jane are now on Los Angeles Street, at the 700th block. They both stand in a modest loft around 620 square feet. It is located on the fourth level. It is comprised of a modern kitchen, dining area, walk-in closet, and private bathroom. The walls are brick and plaster, painted white, and ready for move in.

Jane and Brian are both exhausted. They have looked at four different apartments. All exceptional. All haunted, all laced with sex, drugs, murder and black magic.

"Hey, Hun, this is the last place I'm going to show you. It is late and I'm hungry. Besides, it's date night. You know what that means baby doll?"

Brian pays no attention.

She looks at Brian with a disgruntled expression. "It means, Bobs' Big Boy, beers and sex after." The realtor walks into the bathroom and looks herself over in the mirror. She takes out her lipstick and freshens up her yellow dentures, then sports her oversized D breast. 'Damn, I am one sexy bitch.' She says to herself.

"You are a picky one, I must say. A bit pellicular also. Uhhhh, Uhhhh." She watches Brian from the mirror, as he walks around the loft.

"You got a girlfriend, Brian?"

"Yeah, back home."

"Is she pretty?"

"Yeah, why do you ask?" Brian walks into the closet and looks it over. The realtor re-adjusts her fake Channel suit.

"Well, if she's not what you want, there are many fine-looking women in this here building. In other words, I can hook you up. If you know what I mean? Remember this Brian, you need to be careful who you date out here. You know, don't rush into something you'll later regret. I assume you are the straight type. If you are, you'll do simply fine." Realtor Jane continues to stare at Brian through the mirror. As she looks, she sees an aspiration of man in a white hat and white suit standing in the corner starring at Brian. Jane doesn't say anything. She smiles, then exits the bathroom. Brian laughs, back turned, he looks out the window at the courtyard.

"Brian, you may want to check out the tub. It's big enough for three people if you know what I'm saying." The realtor grins evilly. Brian brushes off the statement, pretending he didn't hear. He quickly changes the subject.

"How are the couples in the building?" asks Brian. The realtor walks out of the bathroom, heads over to the kitchen, and looks over her paperwork.

"Good people, most of them. Mostly your age. There are always a few bad apples that fall of the tree. The young man next door to the right is in advertising. The couple upstairs, oh, you're going to love."

Brian feels comfortable in this loft. His nerves are easy, and the muscles in his back are relaxed. The hairs on his arms are not standing. And no goosebumps. Not like the other apartments he saw today. Most of them made him feel uneasy, dizzy like someone is watching him.

"What's the building's history?" asks Brian.

"Well, this building used to be a hat factory in the 1940s. After that, a shooting gallery."

"Shooting gallery?" asks Brian.

"Drug's Brian. You know, shooting gallery. Morphine, Opium, Heroin, China White, Mexican Black Tar."

Brian looks at the realtor with a confused look about his face. She shakes her head then jesters a syringe in her arm.

"Brian, like this, you know, vein soup." Brian walks to the window and looks out again.

'Darn boy must be braindead. Or a retard.' She mumbles to herself.

"Is there anything in Los Angeles that someone hasn't died in?" asks Brian. The realtor laughs aloud.

"Honey, I like your sense of humor. Don't worry bout that. You'll do fine. They also do."

"Brian, everything, and everyone has a past. There isn't any way of escaping that. What's important is you like this building. You like the amenities, you like the street, you like the shops. Obviously, you have a new job. I say go for its Hun. At $1,100 per month, you won't find a better deal." The realtor's phone rings again.

"Look it over for a few, Brian. I got one more appointment tonight."

Brian walks to the refrigerator. He checks the cupboards and oven. Brian walks back to the oversized window again. He is fixated on what he sees down in the courtyard. For some reason, it reminds him of home. He witnesses a tender side of Los Angeles. Downstairs he sees 'Henry's Market.' Everyone is walking out of the store is happy, smiling. He sees many women and men of his age. Couples, walking, talking, holding hands, holding each other, walking dogs. One gentleman is playing a lame attempt of 'Johnny Cash' on the guitar. Couples are drinking beer and wine beneath the yellow umbrellas. Some are reading books. He sees a fitness room and waterfall to his right. This makes Brian smile. This reminds him of his loft apartment at home. Brian looks at a couple sitting, laughing, drinking coffee. The young man leans into her and kisses her passionately.

"I like it." Brian proudly turns around and smiles. "And I'll take it."

"Excellent, how do want it, honey?" asks Jane. "Oops, I meant, when do want it honey?"

"How about now?"

"Now?" Jane acts surprised, knowing it was already his.

"OK, I have the lease papers right here." The Realtor shuffles through her bag, as her phone rings. Again, the volume of the phone rattles Brian's nerves.

"Oh, hello Vic, how's it hanging? Oh, yes, Wilshire Blvd. Yes, it's still available. Magnificent opportunity for you and the wife. Yeah, that's right. Three people were killed with an ax." As Realtor Jane carries on about how lovely the murders were, Brian walks back to the oversized loft window. He looks down at the couples, then notices a woman unlike any he has ever seen. The most existing, sexual, sensual, seductive women, ever… Brian listens to the Realtor blab on about killings' as he looks the woman over. Brian is finally home. And the city his. All his…

Chapter 7
14 Days Later

Brian's moving truck arrives in front of building, 700 block of Los Angeles Street. Brian had to wait two days before there was enough space in front of the building. The front is the best for moving. It has an elevator and makes things much easier. Without the elevator, Brian is out of luck. He will have to walk four flights of concrete stairs in 90-degree weather, with the taste of fallout in his mouth. Jeans and T-shirt wet, money soaked in his pocket. Under ware crawling up his anus. Moving is hell. Even for a strong young man, who is debaucherously ambitious.

The side building entrance offers distractions. The first is dust and smells. Smells of human waste, and drug-sweat. Graffiti and absurd messages. "Why buy a paper or look on the internet? I live here. You can call me anytime." His favorite is, "Beware of the underground railroads. Children of the damned live there. Or Punk Rock Rules Los Angeles, and Always will." Brian looks at another message written on the wall. He finds this one quite amusing. It reads. "Warning, Evil Spirits Have Been Summoned. Get Out While You Can." Another message is written on the stairway walls. It's a telephone number 213-666-1801.

Fantastic building, Brian thinks. *No, wait. It is cool, and it is historically relevant. Everyone in LA says "fantastic." Things are "cool." The place has a hipster crowd. An independent mindset. I like it…*

Brian's brain is running wild. He is looking forward to the Golden Gopher, the X room, Blue Room, fourth street, seventh, ninth, Spring Street DJ club, with the Converse symbol on the outside wall. Figueroa Street. The Bars that offer kettle-cooked potato chips with steak. The awesome whisky and vodka bars that pour $30.00 drinks. The best part is the four finger pour. Not the watered down two-finger crap in other cities. He cannot wait.

And the women, Brian thinks. *The women in Los Angeles are the most beautiful women on Earth.* Therefore now, Brian is here. The woman, the eccentrics, the eclectic and interesting people. And of course, the food, booze and a job where he can make millions of dollars. A job where success and power will begin.

Brian is in the lobby of his new home. A same-sex orientated couple walks by. Brian says hello. They say hello also. Brian wonders who did this to them. He would like to beat their boyfriends senseless. They are too good looking to be same ex-orientated.

The two women offer goodwill, and information about the roof-top parties. They discuss the parties and DJs who reside in the building. The music producers, porn studios, art walks, clothing designers, the best stores, and all the other crap that happens downtown. Brian thinks these girls are cool and hot. So, he gave them his phone number. They may be same sex orientated now, after I'm done with them, they'll be bi-sexual. Brian thinks.

Brian holds a box with a Mexican helper. Brian found him outside Home Depot around fourth street. Or was it third street? He does not remember. What he remembers, was the Mexican restaurant playing 'Freddy Fender, Crazy Baby.' The night after Simone robbed him. Brian put that song in the juke. Mexican patrons with cowboy hats nodded in approval. After Freddy, Brian played 'Chuck Berry.' He left the small restaurant with five phone numbers. All men saying that they are connected. They own sections of the town.

The waitress brought him four tacos, a bean and cheese burrito, chicken enchilada, with Bohemia for under $15.00 Best of all she told Brian that she liked this music, then winked at him. Her seductive hips waving back and forth to the music. Brian brought his new Mexican friend to the restaurant also. Since then, Brian's has had a hard time getting rid of him. Now he helps Brian moving. The Mexican helper was also way grateful for the lunch. He is from Monterey and has six children. He's very, proud of his 501's and sports a Mexican football national team Jersey. Brian never knew his name or asks. The man never offered his name. Only said his family is connected to Mexico City. Guess this is one of the reasons Brian liked him. Some things are best never said. He only gave Brian a cell phone number with the letter G.

After lunch, Brian tries to enter the elevator again. Brian's wearing a lampshade over his head. After six Bohemia's, it does not bother him much.

Next tenant that enters the building is a drugged-out white girl, 25, 5'3", bleach blond hair, cowboy boots, green handbag, an oversized T-shirt with tank-top under. She also sports big earrings, an overabundance of jewelry, with aviator frames. She is good looking. Very, good looking. She has the bravado and energy of a woman that is new in town. Excitement and wonder written all over her face. For some men, the bad ones the face reads naive. Brian thinks she looks like Hope Sandoval.

A male accompanies her. He is around 30 years old with a big beard. Brian cannot tell what nationally he is. He looks almost Middle Eastern. He wears ridiculous-looking jeans. They are flared at the bottom with flip flops. His toenails are yellow and rotten, proof he's unemployed; and doesn't respect women. He has tattoos all over his arms. The ink represents meaningless bullshit. The kind of crap that a poseur would order of a wall in some parlor off Melrose Avenue. There is no history or meaning behind the art. He's your typical asshole. Just another "Passenger," with dreams and aspirations of being a Hollywood, blood-sucking asshole. The type that would bend over for any useless opportunity. He's not from LA but tells all the woman he is. He tells women, he's a music producer, screenwriter with *many* connections. The only things he's connected to, is the lies he tells. Also, the drug dealer he buys from…

Brian looks at his underwear sticking out, and his oversized belt and wants to *correct* him. Correct him by beating the loser senseless. He also sports a beanie hat, chain wallet, and backpack. A beanie hat in 90-degree weather. What do you think about that??

What's in the backpack? I'll tell you, Some underwear, stolen towels from the Bahama Motel. Stolen hotel soap, stolen hotel shampoo. Stolen toothpaste, and of course weed. Not good weed. But weed manufactured by a 13-year-old training in South Figueroa. Oh, and stolen white underwear and T-shirt. 1 pair each.

This guy tries acting black when he buys from this kid. He also tells the blacks he is a professional hip-hop producer. A professional grower, with many white connections. This drug addict, white trash fucker will travel to Long Beach on a train. All the way there, just to buy $20.00 of China White.; because there isn't any speed left to control his victim-girlfriend.

Brian looks the guy over. He knows, *He wouldn't last a day in his town.* His father would *destroy* him. Brian snaps out of his instincts. He finds himself in the elevator, with this god-forsaken creature.

"Hey, man let me get that." The drugged male says. His hands shake nervously. He pushes the elevator door.

"Thanks," says Brian.

The drug out guys' girlfriend, looks over Brian, then smiles. She likes what she sees. Her boyfriend notices her starring and is upset. The drugged-out male smiles mischievously. He finally introduces himself as Troy and moved from Hegang. The elevator goes quiet. The Mexican worker wears a lampshade over her head, looking over the enemy Troy. The Mexican clenches his fist. The couple looks at Brian and the Mexican. They stare at each other, and both laugh aloud. The Mexican clutches his fist harder, hold it up, then remembers not to be deported. Troy looks at the control panel and pushes every floor on the panel.

He thinks, *it's funny—Everything is funny.* Especially in his deranged mind.

"Can you push the fourth floor please?" asks Brian.

"Fuck you," says Troy. "Hey, man, I'm just joking. It's cool. Hey, wait, I am not joking. No, I'm not. What the fuck, I'll push it. All push all of them. Screw it, I'll fuck everyone and everything. Ohhhhhhhh, fuck, I love this shit." The deranged asshole looks over Brian.

"Hey, man, where the fuck you from?" the assholes right leg shakes as he speaks.

"Washington," says Brian.

"What part, man?"

Troy looks toward the ceiling and yells out, "Fuck!!"

"DC," Brian says. Brian looks over the deranged drug attic. Troy lowers his glasses, looking over Brian.

"Mmmm," says Troy. "So, man, you like to party?" Brian is a bit agitated. He doesn't answer. He sees this guy Troy is a pole puncher. A reach around Sally. A lipstick warrior. He wants to snap this asshole's neck, then send the girlfriend home to her parents.

"Well, welcome the fuck to LA, baby. Owwwwwwwww!" Troy slams his hands, on the elevator walls, like a drummer.

"I'm a drummer, man. Did you know that? A fuckin' drummer. The best in fuckin' LA. Hurry up, hurry up, hurry up. I am bored. Let's get on with it." The Mexican looks over Troy. He mumbles in broken English. "We should throw him off the roof."

Brian nods in solemn approval.

The elevator finally makes it to the fourth floor. The deranged couple exits first. Brian and the Mexican exit afterward. Troy knocks a small box out of Brian's arms. It falls to the floor making a clanking noise.

"Shit, please, be careful. My mother packed that for me." Troy stops and laughs. His female partner lowers her aviators, then smiles at Brian.

"Hey, baby, look at this guy in all. He loves his Mommie. How sweet. What a fag." Says Troy. "The fuckin' glasses. All smart and sexy. Shit, I love this guy. Look at him. So, what's your story, man. You a fag or something?" Brian tries ignoring the asshole. He thinks of his training back home. He knows he will undoubtingly end up in jail if he beats Troy.

"I say we invite him over, baby. You can suck his dick. He looks like he can use a good dick sucking."

"Whadda, you say, Mr. Washington?" His girlfriend slugs her boyfriend in the arm hard.

"Hey, lay off, bitch. Whatcha self. Or else." Troy finishes his 40-ounce bottle of Natural Light. He places the empty bottle atop Brian's moving box.

"Hey, a present for you. Welcome to Los Angeles, shit head." Troy grabs his girlfriend's hand and forcefully leads her to their loft entrance. He opens the door, then pushes her in. the door slams shut. You can hear the man howl inside and down the hall.

"Yeah, bitch, get naked!"

The door to the couples' loft opens again. Troy sticks his head out.

"Hey, fag, we're in Room 443. Come by later. Let's get high." Troy shows his middle finger at Brian. Then lets out a cynical laugh. He slams the loft door.

"Hello, fuckers!" The dope fiend yells behind the loft door.

Brian and the Mexican listen to the drugged idiot boyfriend, behind the door, for a few seconds.

The Mexican man speaks out, *"Basura blanca, pedazo de mierda."* Brian laughs. He's fluent in Spanish and three other languages. The Mexican worker shakes his head as Brian continues to laugh. Brian just found a friend for life.

"Don't worry, amigo. Any problems, with that *pendaio*, give me a call. I got connections in this city." The Mexicans' English is more proficient this time. Brian admires his sense of humor.

"Don't worry about that guy." Says Brian. "I can take care of myself. He would not last a day where I'm from. In Washington, we call turkeys like that, dead people."

It is now 4:00 AM on Sunday morning. The television in the background shows a porn movie, while ambient music plays in the background. Troy quickly walks toward the couch. He grabs a small wooden pipe, then sits down. He takes a drag only to be disappointed.

"Shit, baby, we are almost out of drugs. Soon it will time, get some more."

The loft is dark with blinds closed. Rays of blue-grey light shed through the blinds as candles light the rest. His girlfriend looks tired and much older than yesterday. She is still attractive, but borderline. Almost at the point of no return. Her complexion shows that of Johnny Thunders, before his end. Her skin is yellowish, with dark circles under her eyes. She has not slept for 9 days. She spent most of the night staring in the walk-in closet. She saw many things. Things, spirits, demons, or is it the drugs? She will not say a word to anyone.

She thinks about the time he met her. Fresh off the train from the North. He told her about his connections. That she had stage presence. Features like 'Charlize Theron.' She must dye her hair blond and lose some weight. He will help her. He will show her *everything.* She didn't have a place to stay then. He promised she can stay with him until she finds work. Until she finds her dream position in Hollywood. He told her many things. Most of all, he said he loved her. Where she is from, the way she was raised, these words, mean something. A promise, that will should never be broken.

The days, weeks, and months are now gone. Now her innocence. She looks in the mirror and sees a ghost. The ghost of her dead mother. A ghost of a father that told her, "Hollywood will take you in, then spit you out. Your just their type." Her father said this with tears in his eyes…

She stands in the bathroom looking at her decaying body. Bra with no underwear. She puts on a pair of jeans. They used to be snug. Now she wears a large belt holding them up. She looks at the tattoos on her arms, and lower back. She was high when she got them done. Now she resents them. Even if Troy's gone, she'll always be reminded. She thinks about what people would say if she returned home. The slurs, the humiliation. "We told you not to go there. Now looks at you. Are you proud of yourself? You slut." She feels hopeless. Every day, she thinks about escape. How she can be released from this dream, this dream called hell?

She looks at her bare feet and sees dirt on them. It is from the interior's concrete floor. She used to clean. Now she doesn't have the time or energy. Days float into night. Nights float into mornings. The time of a drug addict is fast and furious. In time, you forget to bathe, use the toilet. It's easier to piss in a motel bed, or your own. Why ruin my high by moving? Cigarette butts lay about the floor, along with fast-food wrappers. The walls are sprayed with paint. The so-called "art" that was applied during a seven-day binge. The walls now make her sick. There is a stripper pole that sits in the middle of the loft, where is she forced to practice. He makes her practice every day. Even when she is sick. If she disobeys, she is punished. Punished like Patty Hearst.

She puts on a black tank top, picks up her white Persian, then walks to the middle of the room. She looks her boyfriend over. He is desperately trying to scrape meth resin from a pipe, mirror, and particles found on the loft floor. The drugs are purely synthetic. Keep in mind, if he's being dragged down, this asshole with drag her with him. In the end, it will be her fault. She didn't strip enough. She lost too much weight; she lost her looks. He will leave her, then find another victim at the Downtown Train Station. No man will ever be better than him. Have his knowledge or taste, connections. Connections she's never met. Just a room full of junkies humping dreams of delusion, damnation and death. She stands in front of her boyfriend staring. Stares if she is admiring a relative, she never knew. One she was forced to attend at funeral service.

"What the hell you are staring at, woman. Get me a beer." She walks over to the kitchen and opens the refrigerator. Inside, there is little food. A bucket of KFC, some Oscar Mayer Hotdogs, bread, cheese, butter, ketchup, mustard, and half-eaten chocolate cake. Some of the cake has green dots of mold.

I'll feed it to the asshole later, she thinks. Take off the green dots first. She will rejoice when he is praying over the toilet and diarrhea squirts from his ass. He'll blame it on the bad drugs. Then she can blame it on the drugs. Says she's sick too. Force herself to vomit. This way, he cannot abuse her.

The cat cries of hunger. She places the cat on the ground feeding her what's left of the chicken.

"Baby, we're out of cat food," she says. He takes another hit of the wood pipe, then quickly lights a cigarette.

"That cats expensive. I say, get rid of the fucker." The young woman looks at him with disgust. She opens a beer, then timidly walks over to him. She knows he can strike at any moment.

"We should get rid of you," the girlfriend says.

"What did you say to me?"

"Why are you so mean all the time?" Girlfriend asks. "You used to be so sweet."

"I'm not mean. I'm trying to—"

She interrupts him. She picks up the cat and holds it close to her chest.

"Get a job," she says.

"What?" Troy escalates his voice trying to intimate her. She changes the subject quickly.

"Don't you dare touch her. I swear god."

"Swear what?" he asks. "What? What, are you going to kill me again? In your dreams bitch."

"I'll kill you," she says. "I'll do it when you least expect it."

"That's what I love about you, sweetie. You're always talking out of your ass," Troy says. "You need an army to kill me, baby girl. And for the cat, that fucker is useless. All she does is eat and shit. Shit and eat. Then whine all the time. I mean look at the cat box. It shits the size of fuckin' burritos. The whole fuckin' house stinks shit."

"Why don't you clean it," she asks.

"No, you clean it, girl. Look at yourself, you are useless. All you do in peace the floor and mumble all day."

"You're the one that stinks. I say she and I move to Las Vegas. She dances around the room like a ballerina, holding the cat. I'll be a dancer, become famous, leave you behind. Stupid."

"What did you say?" The boyfriend stands up from the couch. "Girl, you are fucked up. Look at yourself, skinny bitch. You can't dance worth a shit. All robotic, no rhythm, no sex appeal."

"I am not useless. Or a robot. You are the stupid robot. You're the one that cannot make any money. All you do is talk. Talk, talk, talk. And treat me like one of your whores. What's wrong with you all the time?"

The young woman kisses the cat, then places her down on the floor. She walks toward her boyfriend cautiously and takes a cigarette from his pack. She sees he's still upset about her comments. Work and money. She knows she can dig at him about *everything*. Even the fact he cannot perform in bed if he's not high. She sips the beer, then places it down lightly. She looks at him smiling.

"What the fuck are you staring at!" He grabs a controller from the coffee table and turns on the stereo. Some crap, corporate, washed out, dance tune plays over the radio. Now it is time for his revenge. What for? The fact he can control her. This is all he's wanted since the beginning. To have a woman, he can control. To break down and make him money.

"Dance for me?" Troy asks.

"No."

"It's dancing time, baby girl," he speaks avoiding eye contact. He stares at the dark walk-in closet, then grins. He turns up the stereo volume just a bit.

Nobody will hear her scream, he thinks.

"I said dance. Dance!" His tone is stern and direct.

"No." She places her hands over her face.

"Dance, dance, dance!" His girlfriend turns her head in anticipation of being hit.

"Look at yourself. Did I say I'm going to hit you?"

He has done worse, she thinks. The worst part is, he has convinced the neighbors that she is a sadist.

"No, it's just that I'm so tired. I need to sleep." Her voice shivers.

"I said fuckin' dance woman." She places her hands over her face and starts to cry.

"No, No, I don't want to."

"You're going to dance. If you don't, you get the other." He looks her over then grins. His grin is unnatural, inhuman, that of a demon. As he speaks the young woman looks at the closet. She sees the darkness move slowly toward her. It consumes her every memory. She closes her eyes as *it* speaks. She tries to ignore but cannot. All she can hear is an evil voice asking her to dance repeatedly; inches away from an echo in her head while she screams bloody murder. No one ever hears. Or nobody wants to. He always turns up the music as loud as it will go. Sometimes for hours.

The pounding of her fist echo in her mind as she holds her head. She hears herself scream, "Let me out, please, honey, let me out. Let me out. I will do anything you want. Please, please let me out." He will not answer. All this demon does is sit in the light, mocking, terrorizing, killing her dreams. Finally, after hours, the light shines through the door. It is the demon smiling. He hands her the dope pipe.

"Are you ready to behave?" Troy says. "Behave, and I will love you. Maybe for all eternity." He grins...

The boyfriend continues chanting in her face, "Dance, dance, dance, dance, dance, dance, dance, dance, fucking dance!!" She finally breaks. Ahhhhh, just what he wanted.

"Shut up!! She sees visions of her future. Visions of a hell hole. Visions of cries for help. The vision of a dark angel, negotiating her death. OK, OK she says. I will do it. stop doing this and I'll do it. Please, stop hurting me." His girlfriend continues to cry. Troy stands up, then hold her closely.

"Baby, look into my eyes." She turns away. "No baby, right here. I'm here sweet girl. It's just me and you. Look into my eyes."

She feels another presence in the room. They're not alone. They never are. The presence sits on her shoulders, while choking her throat. Laughing in her ear.

"Right here, look, baby, look." She tries turning away. He grabs her head and holds it still.

"I said look into my eye's woman. Look at me." She gives him direct eye contact. There is no use in fighting him. It will end with pain and screaming. It always does.

"Baby, I love you. You know that. Since the first time. The very first time I saw your face, I fell in love with you. I knew we would be together, forever. Baby, you own me, all of me. There is no other for me. Do you understand? She covers her eyes and face with her hands. Together, we are destiny. I'm not hurting you. I'm teaching you. I don't want to hurt you. I'm teaching you to be a stronger woman. Please, don't make me hurt you. Just make me happy, this is all I ask. Make me happy, and our *priest* will be happy. Everything will be OK. And it will be over soon. **Look into the camera baby. Look here, look into my eyes.** Don't you love me?"

"What kind of stupid question is that?" she asks. "I just don't like you right now." The boyfriend smiles then falls on the couch.

He laughs aloud and yells, "Fuck you all, mother fuckers!' Now dance baby. Dance!"

To avoid the closet, the doorway to hell. She complies with his request. She always does and always will...

Chapter 8
14 Days Later

Brian is asleep. He dreams of a time he was playing Highschool Baseball. His team was down by one run in the final inning. He was up to bat, with bases loaded. His Father sat quietly in the crowd looking him over expressionless. Cheerleaders gawking at him, licking their lips with desire. He struck out; his team lost. Thereafter, the sky turned black, then it started to rain. Nobody said a word to Brian. He hurried, placing his gear in bag, then looked for his Father. He was gone. The crowd mysteriously vanished, his couch, his team. Brian walked home alone in the rain. All by himself, in the dark for five miles. Some of the cars driving by mocked him, laughed showed the middle finger. Their heads moved violently in circles, swayed side to side as they cursed. Faces look distorted, almost inhuman.

Brian wakes violently. Heart racing, puddle of sweat on his chest. He hears a couple yelling in the distance. He's never sweated before while sleeping. Not that he remembers. His lower back is tight, feet and hands are numb. So, numb they hurt. He can barely move them. He shakes of the nerve pain, then sits aside his bed.

Brian notices different shadow areas throughout the loft. They appear to be crawling over the walls and ceiling. His senses are aroused, his manhood erect. He hears things never heard before. Things that speak of erotic behavior and masturbation. They say there's a woman in the building. She waits for him. They even tell him the apartment number. That she wants him. Wants to give Brian oral sex.

Brian pays special attention to the cursing. They tell him that God hates him, and he's all alone in the city. He has no support. His father hates him, he's watching him.

Brian shakes his head, and the voices vanish. Brian thinks it's the booze and bad diet lately, he decides to pay no attention for now. Small amounts of white-blue mist are seen in the air. He feels an eerie presence, as a shadow in his closet begins to grow.

Moving boxes sit across the lofts concrete floor. Mostly furniture boxes and bath fixtures lay about. He ordered everything from West Elm, The Loft Store, Restoration Hardware, and IKEA. Yes, he did it without Jenna approving of his orders. This upset her terribly too. She called his phone over one-hundred times, telling him he's disrespectful and will be sorry. She'll be vengeful. Sorry she'll have to throw out everything that's not to her standards.

Brian looks at the clock above the entry door. A dark shadow moves across the clock. Brian stares at his front door. rays of light stream through the cracks.

Then he sees the shadow of shoes under the door. Again, Brian pays no attention. He thinks it is probably the security guard.

Brian snorts, clears his throat, wipes his eyes, then cough up a big dose of phlegm, spits in the sink. He observes a Coors bottle siting by the bed, below his feet. He picks up the bottle, then finishes it in one drink.

Brian lays back down, taking a deep breathe. He thinks about his new career, his newfound freedom and the Romanian woman. He can't stop thinking about her dirty sex appeal, her black hair, red-blossomed lips. She reminds him of that hot looking prostitute from that 'Firefly' television program. She makes him chuckle every time he thinks of her. Tonight, she makes him erect. He pours a glass of Makes Mark, sits on the bed, and thinks of her living up the hall. Sometime at while sleeping, he feels he can hear her. Her voice so faint but direct. 'Brian cone to me she says. Come to me. Brian swears he heard her recite address from Downtown. How awesome that would be. Dirty Porn sex with no connection, no responsibilities or love. He takes a drink of Bourbon than grins. Problem is, Brian knows these feeling of lust and desire, create children. Brian stands up from the bed, walks to the bathroom, then opens his medicine cabinet. He grabs an over the counter sleeping pill, 25mg, then shoots it with his Bourbon.

Brian remembers the in-depth discussion with her regarding God's people and the 144,000 thousand. How she is god's child. He is angel of light. She his child of light. How her god wants to create an alliance with God. She told him that the 144,000 will be tempted by the angel of light. They will join him, and a new Earth will be born. He opens his wallet, taking out the letter she wrote.

It smells of Opium Perfume and tabaco. The heading reads Bahama Inn. That wonderful place will haunt him forever. This he will keep forever. He finds it quite amusing how a group of people or organization would rebel against Gods will. He thanks God he didn't have sex with her. At least that what he knows. He thinks it's what he knows. He rubbed his gentiles in the morning and crotch hair. There was no smell, at least now overbearing. However, he swears he did smell a bit of orange peel or rose perfume. Maybe it's just his mind, maybe it's the smell of erection, the smell of desire; endless lust. It's been an odd month for Brian. Not bad. He's slept with eight woman. All safe sex.

Brian chuckles to himself then begins to relax again. The Hydrochloride and booze are slowly kicking in. The Romanian woman reminds him of West point and the training he undergone. The weekend parties at the local strip clubs. There was one woman wide eyed, like a snake. She sat on Brian's lap talking about the Devil and Jesus. Lashing her tongue on his closed mouth, neck and earlobes. She informed Brian that she was a messenger, and that Jesus hated him. He was born unto the angel of darkness. There are people that want him dead. His father was cursed by God. Later, Brian found out; she was from Southern Mexico. Way downward South by the equator. She also insisted that Brian giver her his phone number. He must be her love slave. This way, she will protect him.

Brian thinks of the old woman on the plane. He knows she moved somewhere else. Probably first glass. She did wear on overabundance of expensive jewelry. The darn phone number. Perfect, a 70-year-old Hooker. I am in LA, thinks Brian. What a fucked-up place I live, as Brian laughs to himself. He suddenly feels comfortable. This is his new home, and nothing will bother him. Nothing will get in his way. Brian hopes the sexy Korean girl that lives four doors down, knocks his door this morning. She Offered him pancakes, sausage and beer again. The one he met in the laundry room. The one wearing a tank top, jean shorts, barefoot, black toenail polish; asking him to come over to her apartment, for a quick drink. He thinks of her sweat smell, her taste, her fluids, tasted so good Brian couldn't resist, her small frame. How easy it was to maneuver her. She referred to herself as "fun size." The screams when she climaxed. Those wonderful, pleasurable screams of extasy.

The next morning, the wine bottles and dried semen between her legs. She begged him for more. Then the pancakes, with orange juice and tequila. So far so good thinks Brian. Los Angeles is already paying off. However, I have a long way to go.

Brian thinks of Jenna; his stomach turns. He tastes bile and nicotine. In his throat. He never smoked before. Not until he moved from Washington. The cigarettes seem to mellow him out. They also go good with the booze and sleeping pill. The Vicodin that is being passed in the bars and clubs. Better stay away from them, thinks Brian.

Brian sets his mind back on the hot looking Korean gal. The one he bent her over the dryer as he guided her hips unto him. Fucking incredible, Jenna would shit her pants. It happened late at night when they were both drunk at around 3:30 AM. Guess they both needed clean clothes.

Brian looks back at the clock. It reads 3:00 AM. *Why I am so friggin' horny?* thinks Brian. He doesn't want a serious relationship. All he wants is sex. Sex and alcohol. The things he was denied in Washington. Things only acceptable through marriage, with no marriage. A yoked marriage. After that, according to his friends, it's all downhill.

Brian wonders if he'll get punished for abandoning Jenna. He should have settled himself in the past two weeks. Settled in and find a new church. There is a church in Pasadena. He has been looking at on the internet. The pastor teaches the Bible, and the music is awesome. He thinks about his family. He wonders if they will show up at his door. even worse, Jenna.

Brian reaches into his nightstand and takes the white envelope he found on the plane. He looks over the Symbol, then turns on the internet. He looks at what the symbol stands for. It means, "to throw oneself into a well; suicide." Ancient Chinese writings also categorize it as a warning. He wonders if the person who left it really knew what was written. *"Do not ever open this envelope."*

Brian rubs his index finger over the object. "Maybe the person who wrote it didn't want to lose the gold coin inside. Again, he thinks about how much it may be worth. Maybe, one of the emperors owned it. Maybe, it dates back over five-thousand years."

The temptations are astonishing. Thinks Brian. He remembers of the girl on the plane. At least what he thought was a girl. He had not slept for over four days then. He was probably hallucinating. The plane was like the show, twilight zone. It reminded him of Mental Diminution. Forced through abnormal RF-Frequencies. A type of brain attack during the Cold War. Forced offerings, false realities, realized without knowledge. The human spirit does not accept; however, the brain overtakes you. A diminution his family discussed after the assignation attempt of Ronald Regan and James Brady. Brian regains his thoughts as he looks over the envelope. A chill runs through his body.

Screw it, I'll open the envelope when my life is settled. I'll open it in front of my hot new girlfriend after a night of drinks and sex. I'm young. I must experience darkness before I succeed, thinks Brian. *What is the point of working for Dad if I have no life experience?* Brian's brain will not stop thinking. It is all over the place. He knows he must get it together. Lay off the booze for a few weeks.

Brian stands up from his bed and heads toward the bathroom. He's naked, course. Best way to look when the door knocks. Especially in Downtown Los Angeles, 2005. He grabs his shaft, checks it out, then burps. Overall, it looks OK. No damage yet. No scratches, no dents, or bumper damage.

Brian notices the whiskers on his face. He wonders if Jim Morrison lived this way. Brian's been on a bender, and he's enjoyed every minute of it.

Brian burps then sit on the toilet. As he sits, he looks at his bed. A pillow from the bed is suddenly tossed on the floor. It must be the booze, thinks Brian. More hallucinations. He looks at the box in the middle of the loft. It is the one his mother gave him. She bought him a designer lamp from Belgium.

Only Mom would pay $2,000 for a lamp. It proudly sits atop the original box. Brian smiles as he looks at it.

Brian finishes in the bathroom. He turns on the water and washes his hands. Just as he turns off the water. The lamp is pushed by an unseen presence forcefully from the box. It falls making a shattering noise. The noise startles Brian. He quickly throws down his face towel. 'What the hell?' He says to himself aloud.

Brian walks quickly toward the main room. He looks over the broken lamp. A look of disappointment fills his face. Brian picks up his pillow and looks it over. He looks at the bed, then his bathroom. The bathroom floor closes by itself.

The laughing noise of a young girl is heard in the loft above. The laugh is followed by running across the floor. Then sounds of cue ball, from a pool table; being rolled across the floor. Brian follows the noise, as it rolls from one end of the floor to the other.

Brian looks over the ceiling and inspects the fire sprinklers. The sound of JAX's is being thrown upstairs and spread across the floor.

The sounds of a young girl laughing is heard again. Next the sounds of a rubber bouncing ball, or basketball bouncing on the floor. The young voice upstairs begins singing the *'London Bridges'* nursery rhyme.

Brian continues listening as he hears large footsteps running across the floor. The force of the footsteps, rattles Brian's nerves. A man's voice is present. It sounds husky and muffled.

"I thought I'd told you to shut up," says the man.

"No," says the voice of the young girl.

"I said stop it. They'll hear us," says the man.

"Stop it, ouch. You're hurting me."

Light footsteps are heard running across the floor upstairs. They sound of the young girl.

"Come here," says the man upstairs.

"Try stopping me." The sounds of lighter footsteps are heard running across the floor again. Then heavy footsteps.

The loft upstairs goes eerily quiet. Brian hears sound of a siren, beeping down the seventh street. It fades away when it reaches Skid Row, East.

Brian walks to his bed then lays down. He looks upstairs, then readjusts his pillow. He hears the upstairs front door open, then shut forcefully.

The sound of a female is heard. This time Brian cannot decipher what is said. She sounds as if a hand is over her mouth. The voice is muffled yet strained. The woman sounds as if she is struggling to breathe. Brian looks at the lamp, then at the ceiling again. Upstairs, the sound of a cue ball slowly rolls from the front door upstairs all the way to the loft window.

Brian will not sleep again. This is the fourth night in a row he has been woken at 3:00 AM.

2

It's now sunrise. Brian is a bit dizzy. It's been an interesting weekend, to say the least. He met three women. He dominated a jukebox, played pool. Ate IN-AND-OUT-BURGER for the first time. He really like the three by three, cooked well done with grilled and raw onion. He eats two of them with two French fried potatoes and two oil cans of Foster's Lager. Burgers, booze, punk rock, and hot woman. So far, he's impressed. Brian observes his standing mirror, then exits his loft door. He opens the door, then looks back inside. The women will love it, he thinks. Not Jenna, but the women of Los Angeles.

Brian stayed up late cleaning, arranging, drinking beer, and dialing in his new home Best to all, he got it done with no rest. He is confident where he's going with his life. It his first day at his new Job. Merrill Lynch. He's happy about it, even if he must fake it for a few days. Get acclimated, meet the co-workers and the women.

Brian wears brown polished designer shoes, a cashmere V-neck sweater with a tie, and a stylish sport coat. Brian walks toward the elevator. He hears 'Soundgarden' playing from one of the lofts, and it makes him wanna puke. Brian was listening to '*X-Wild Gift*' this morning. Now that's rock-n-roll. The other, crap music, fucked it all up. Now thoughts of his hometown will haunt him all day. He wonders if his neighbor next door played that shit on purpose.

Brian walks inside the elevator. He hears a woman yell for him to wait. The woman is in the mid-20s. New York, artist type with tattoos, and long coat.

The guy is in his early 20s. He is Japanese holding a skateboard. He wears a Ramones T-shirt, Bennie cap, dark Levi's, with black high-top converse. He is also laced in tattoos. The skateboard is a Z-PIG which is rare. Large independent trucks, with black Scott Powell wheels. Rail guards, and skid plate. Brian likes his style and says hello. The Japanese skateboarder doesn't say a word. Maybe, he doesn't speak English. Anyways, he is in a world all his own.

The elevator stops on the second floor.

The manager from the leasing office enters. She is around 35 and from Orange County. She moved to Los Angeles because of a bad relationship. She is attractive of course. Most women from Orange County are. She's 5'6", wearing a navy suit with a white spread collar. Blue pumps. Brian looks her over. She is sexy, in a professional sort of way.

"Hey, Brian, how's the moving going?" she asks.

"I'm just about settled. A few boxes need to go through. Still a bit un-organized."

"How I hate that feeling," she replies while looking at her smartphone.

"I know, tell me about it." Says Brian.

"So, how do you like everything else?"

The elevator makes it to the second floor. They let the others exit so they can talk. Brian, being a gentleman; holds the door open.

"How nice. Finally, a gentleman in this city," says the leasing agent.

"The building is nice," says Brian. "Haven't had time to really meet anyone yet."

The leasing agent looks Brian over and smiles. She asked him out for drinks when he signed the final lease. They went out of course. She's a lot of fun. Brian's keeping her phone number well at hand. Brian can't help to notice the broach under her collar. Oddly enough, the exact same dragon broach Realtor Jane wears.

"I know, tell me about it," says the leasing agent. "It takes a few weeks. Los Angeles is different than other cities. The people that move here seem to pack an attitude with them."

Brian laughs aloud.

"So, how do you like everything else?" Asks the agent.

The elevator makes it to the first floor. They let a few other tenants out first.

"Everything is fine." Brian says.

"It's a fun building," says the leasing agent. "Many professionals and artists. Some writers, musicians, and directors also. Wait until the summer rooftop parties begin. One of our production companies is throwing a barbeque party, with a DJ, the end of this month."

What is with the DJ thing in Los Angeles thinks Brian. I mean, these fuckin' fake musicians are playing at health clubs in West Los Angeles. What next, Motel lobbies? Car dealerships. Clothing stores. What a fucking joke. It's so irritating. I mean, you're trying to work out, relax. You know what I mean? The next thing you know some lame ass DJ, plays Barbara-Ann by the Beach Boys. Those assholes have one good song, and it's Don't Worry Baby. Brian now clears his thoughts.

"Sound good," says Brian. He clears his throat, *trying not to laugh.*

"You better go, Brian. I'll be there."

The leasing agent walks down the sidewalk next to Brian.

"I have a question, actually," says Brian.

"Excuse me." Her phone rings.

"Yeah, I know wait. I said hold on a second. What's up?" The agent says.

The leasing agent nervously looks at her watch. Brian cautiously walks toward Los Angeles Street. He watches the cars passing, people hurrying by. Just about everyone is starring into a smartphone. They appear detached from the world around them.

The leasing agent finishes the phone call. Brian timidly approaches her.

"I have a question. That is if you're not too busy?"

"I always have time for you, Brian."

"Upstairs, the last few nights. Maybe I'm not used to the place. I know this sounds stupid."

She looks him over curiously while thumbing through her phone.

"I don't know what to say," says Brian.

"Brian, you can tell me anything. I work here. It's my job."

"Well, at about 3:00 AM, I heard noises upstairs. It was nerve-racking."

"What noise?" The leasing manager asks.

"It sounded like a young girl or woman was playing with a solid type of hardball. Then it sounded like someone else was there. A man, maybe a big, tall, strong type of man. It sounded if she, a young and older woman was being detained, or something. I think she may know him though. It was creepy."

The leasing manager looks at Brian with no expressionless. She looks almost angry. She has the look of someone who drove over her dog on purpose. Her eyes are piercing through Brian.

"Brian, that apartment upstairs has been vacant for two weeks. The previous couple, both moved back to Japan."

Her response sounds a bit scripted. She avoids the subject by answering her phone again.

"I'll be there in two minutes. Mmm, Mmm, OK. OK," I said!

"Brian, you said it was late, right? You were drinking, you probably were hearing things. Tired, new loft, new sounds, stress. Feeling unorganized. Like you said."

"Yeah, you're probably right," replies Brian. How the hell does she know I was drinking, thinks Brian.

"I said, be there in a minute! She yells into her smartphone. Look, I must go. Anything else, Brian?"

"No, that's it. I feel stupid. It's probably nothing."

"Probably so. Look, if you need anything else. Anything. Call me. Here's my card."

Brian accepts the card, knowing he already has it. She smiles back and walks away quickly. He admires her silhouette for a few moments, then walks to Henry's market. He grabs a cold Starbucks coffee bottle, then exits the store, through the side gate and out to Joes Parking Lot.

Chapter 9

Brian drives to work in his new black Volkswagen GTI Turbo. He drives West down 7 Street admiring the architecture restaurants, and storefronts.

He looks at Braazo Pizza, then smiles. Reminds him of his first date. The date was quite simple. Brian was at the Metropolitan having sliders and beer. There were two woman watching poker on television. Why? Who knows? Anyway, after Brian read cards over the television, one of the girls was so impressed she joined him for Pizza. She quietly left in the morning as Brian pretended asleep. She left her panties, her perfume scent. That was nice. 'Oscar De La Renta' the pink box. Incredible smell. Also, a letter with phone number. Guess she had something to do that morning. Anyway, I should call her, thinks Brian.

Brian snaps out of his daze and notices a wide array of characters walking the streets. The streets are busy, and everyone is in a hurry. Face expressions are different in Los Angeles compared to Washington. In Los Angeles, everyone has a look of desperation and agony, even transparent sin. In Washington, the people; they have arrived. They either accept their way of life or move. Los Angeles resembles a big washing machine. You go in wet, then exit dirty. Not many people you meet are *clean in spirit.* Sometimes you may end up dead. After a few years, after the monies gone; *visitors* usually end up crying over the phone. Begging Mom and Dad for more money, or to come home. Talking about the glory days of the red states. LA is full of Red-Staters in 2005. Negotiating a deal, for their return home. What I learned about LA so far, it's not a forgiving city, you should see the Korean Gal in my building. She hooked up with the wrong man. I warned her, she didn't listen. Now she's strung out. Imagine that? A USC graduate smoking synthetic speed. No job, no direction. I wonder if her father belongs to the Lions Club. Wonder if he's secretly watching her? As for the loser she supposedly loves. If daddy's watching, I would not be surprised if he dusts the guy. In Los Angeles, worse things have happened every day. Especially when it comes to Politics...

You see, California I learned, is a Police State. People who visit don't know this fact. Think about it, next time, before you visit Los Angeles. Brian takes a cd out of his leather car carry case. He places it into the dashboard stereo, then searches for track seven. The song is 'In the Morning.' Big Head Todd and the Monsters.

Brian stops at the corner of 7th and Figueroa, trying turn right. He screws it all up **again**. It is impossible to turn, and the cars keep speeding up, they laugh; not letting you enter the enter section. He hears a voice yelling in echo as he passes the intersection. "Hey man, Fuck You!"

Brian wonders if his work will be this chaotic. As the light turns green, the crosswalk people begin. Brian directs traffic and edges slowly into the pedestrian walk. People walking by shake their heads, some uttering insulting slurs. Some giving the middle finger.

Brian is almost at the corner, ready turn right. The traffic light turns green, then quickly red. An LA 3 second green light. Holy crap, now the cars speed up through the intersection. Other pedestrians curse Brian for blocking the walkway. "Hey fucker. Watch your white ass. You're in LA now. Stupid out of towner, don't know shit."

Brian floors the accelerator pedal as the 2.0 Turbo spins its front tires. The Volkswagens' power is deceitful. He almost swerves into three other pedestrians. The cursing vulgar and ghetto. Brian laughs aloud. He wonders if an angry mob will attack his car like the South-Central Riots.

Brian finally makes it to the financial district. Things are much different driving. He also notices *most* people are white now. What a shock Brian shocks. Next time he may walk to work, listening to 'The Velvet Underground, Beginning to See the Light.' Brian finally on Figueroa, kissing the 110. He finally finds the parking structure for his work.

Brian notices an odd-looking woman. Her hair is mangled. She wears a fluorescent pink hair pick, a white tank top, with nipples piercing through, pajama pants, and flip-flops. They are fluorescent green.

"Sir, can I have some money?" asks the woman.

"How much?" asks Brian.

An erroneous question for such a medieval morning, thinks Brian.

"Enough to get some food. I haven't eaten for days," says the woman.

Brian takes out a ten-dollar bill and hands it to the woman.

"Sir, yo, Honkey, I'll suck your dick for another ten?"

"No, thank you. I'm in a hurry. Maybe next time." Says Brian. However, thanks for the offer, I'm flattered.

"Shit, baby, I'll look you up, in the white pages. Get it?" The woman laughs hysterically. "I can't believe this shit. Look at this white boy, he can't afford a 20? Shit, I must be in the wrong country. Whole damn world is ending. Shit." The deranged woman walks away mumbling and crying out about end of the world.

The odd-looking older, Caucasian woman walks by Brian's car. She asks for money. Brian gives her a ten. Then she begins singing 'Sunday Kind of Love.'

Brian looks over the woman and thinks, *Its Monday, what the hell is Fridays' like?* I wonder if Friday is more mellow. If people miss work hung over? Brian chuckles to himself and enters the garage. His red lights vanish as he pays the attendant and turns to the left.

Brian attended the Monday meeting, introducing himself to everyone. It wasn't too painstaking. Especially even though, he stayed up drinking whisky and decorating his loft. After the introductions, the new recruits watched a movie about the history of Merrill Lynch.

Brian liked Lisa immediately. She reminds him of Gwyneth Paltrow in 'Great Expectations.' Rob is an asshole and talks loudly. He is one of those Hollywood Douchebags that pretends he is connected in the industry. Too Brian, he looks like Gary Buseys poop...

Brian's boss Richard is having an affair and wasting too much company money on his mistress. Brian in the zone. He's reading everyone. Like looking at a magazine. He tries to maintain and not get to deep inside. If he does, he'll zone out, starring look like a lost dog. Brian's always had this gift. Your years it frightened him. His father told him it's a family gift. For Brian, it's easy. For now, it's this Rob character that intrigues him. That and Lisa's hips, and breast.

Brian's office isn't that bad. I have a corner unit, overlooking a view of downtown. The architecture is beautiful in Los Angles. Much better than I ever expected. I enjoy looking over the city, starring at my newfound freedom. If my father could see me know. He will, but first; its' time to kick some ass.

The organic tea isn't not bad either. Plenty of fresh fruit, bakery goods, and the coffee is gourmet. If I play my cards right, close the right customers, I'll have Richard's position in about ten years. Wow, think of that? Mid-thirties and an Operating Manager. Fat salary, big house in 'Pacific Palisades 6 car garage, ocean view, and a powerful wife. One that will walk through the earth with me. Profits up, customer retentions at over 90 percent. This is Brian's goal.

Brian has only two hours to review three investment models. He sips green tea, then check his watch. It is 10;00 AM. His phone rings, and his heart begins to beat fast. Alright calm down, take a deep breathe, quick meditation, and its' showtime. Thinks Brian.

He takes a deep breath, then wheels the leather chair behind his desk. He looks at the phone. This is the one. He knows the boss will listen in; on all three calls today. The boss will assess his knowledge, and retention skills. Analyze his knowledge about Securities. Buying and selling money. The index of the United States Dollar. This is what Brian will do. It is all very, simple. Buy and sell money. Here her goes…

Brian picks up the phone as an angry voice is on the other end. He has been waiting for a returned call about investing in Mexico. That's a tough sell in the year 2005. Brian listens to the customer and comments.

"Mexico's not a good investment for you right now, you try Ireland or Australia. There are many reasons why," says Brian.

Brian listens to the customer tells him about what every *other investor* says. "The old true and tried tales of Mexico, no oil, no military, no pharmaceutical presence, means no money. Most of their GDP is agriculture. Because of now, Socialist Rule, their government has regulated most of it. I have reviewed your file. You need a fast return. I am looking at Finland right now. They got a good thing going over there. Why don't I call you later at 2:00 pm? Discuss the details." The customer agrees. Brian hangs up the phone. Then smiles.

Not bad, he thinks. *I'm a bit rusty. By 2:30 pm today, I'll own this guy.*

Brian's phone rings again. This time, more quickly.

"This is Brian. There is a pauses for a moment. Hey, Tom, how are you? Yes. I understand. Well, this will make you feel better. You're not in the red yet. The LIBOR is fueling the Euro right now." I've been on the phone with Barclays. With the China Real Estate market on the move, being tied to the US dollar, you 're more than strong. We need more money from you to create an index that's profitable.

Brian listens to the customer as he agrees. "I'll call you back at 4:00 pm. Discuss the index."

Brian hangs up the phone. He feels confident talking to the customers. Like he's done this before. Maybe in another life. This is a good customer, and according to his model, solvent.

Brian knows his boss is grinning ear to ear. If he can retain the next customer, He will keep his position and the sweet desk. If not, he will be out in the bull pin.

Brian takes a drink of his green tea, while checking his emails. He notices there are 1,500 welcome emails. Most of them women, with their pictures. Holy crap. One of them looks like Jenna. Brian thinks it is. 'Remember Brian, I'll watching you.' What a screwed-up woman. Thinks Brian.

Brian's phone rings again. This time the desk portfolio sends it over. Woman over the speakerphone talks.

"Brian, be careful with this one. He is ready to walk. Good luck."

"Good luck" is the equivalent of the kiss of death in the business.

Brian stands up for a second, then looks out his window. He moves his neck is a circle and takes another deep breath. "Hello, this is Brian." He looks at the customer model. The investor is Frank Petersen. He sees he has been investing with Deutsche Bank for over 20 years. He wants in on the Euro. He believes it will surpass the US dollar, long enough to colonize Belgium's banking and finance. and the German economy will soon control most of Europe. He also wants to invest in Greece, Italy and Spain economic, Real Estate infrastructure. He sees Mr. Petersen has a net worth of over 600 million US Dollars.

Typical German thinks Brian. *He is smart. They always are.*

"Hello, Mr. Petersen. Good day to you, Sir. He did? Well, that is nice of him, Sir. I do my best. If you don't make money, we do not make money. There is a long pause from Brian as he listens intently. I see you are with Deutsche Bank for 20 years. I must say, Sir; your numbers are beyond impressive. 600 million. You know the old sane about German investing. If they don't join you, buy them." Brian hears the customer laugh aloud over the phone.

"This is good. Germans never laugh when it comes to money, and worldwide dominance. Your investments with us in the Western Baltics have done well. We'll discuss the advancement figures later, however; I must tell you about the arrangement Sweden and Norway made with Finland."

The customer replies as Brian sips his tea, "Wait a few days until the deal is signed. You will be satisfied, and our customer for many years. Yes, in four days to be exact. Very, good then, thank you, Sir. Good day to you. I'll call you with the details. What I need sir, is 100 percent commitment. Good day to you too sir."

Brian hangs up the phone and sighs. He takes a deep breath. He feels sweat under his armpits. He thinks of his father and all he taught him. He wonders if he's listening. He has the power to do so. In fact, he has the power to do many things. Brian feels sentiment toward his family. Brian will call him tonight. He will tell him what happened today. His father will be proud. What Brian's doing will build wealth. Not only for our family but for the rest of this great country. Brian's father will tell him, what he always says. "Son, you will be a great leader amongst men."

Brian's door knocks four times. Brian snaps from his day-dream A head peaks through. It is friggin' Rob. Rob is not from Los Angeles. Where he is from Brian doesn't have any interest. He looks like the irritating guy in that fuckin' movie. You know, the one with the giant insects slaughtering and eating humans? *Great movie,* Brian thinks. Rob has over-tanned skin skinned, big oversized white teeth, spikey blond hair. A fuckin' disaster. Brian curiously looks this douche bag over. He can't resist, getting to know this fool.

Brian already knows he'll discuss and tell lies about the woman of the office. How he's slept with most of them. How he knows all the best spots in downtown. Especially the ones with hot women. Rob's not a bad person. He's just a misogamist. It is not his fault. He has never had a steady girlfriend. Not for over six months. He was never really a good athlete. He has tried skateboarding, surfing, playing guitar. Even sailing. That ended in a disaster. Everything he's tried failed. His father never respected him. At the age of 18, Robert was kicked out of home. He used to toilet paper and egg houses until he was 16. Stay home when he was 18 listening to RUSH and playing Dungeon and Dragons.

After his true love left him for his best friend, he binged on booze and dope. He bought her a ring. Not the six-month salary type, but the two-year salary type. Now he wants revenge. Most of all, on women. On women until God finds gifts him the right one. Now Rob's in Los Angeles. The land of stolen hearts and lost dreams. The land of overrated pleasures. Worst of all, lost love.

Robert represents all these things. This is Robert. Therefore, he is here. Everyone better gets used to him. Again, this what Brian reads in Robert.

Rob walks into Brian's office then slowly closes the door. He sits down in the chair, playing self-catch the corporate super ball. Brian watches with amazement. Rob is one of those guys that throws the damn at you. Yes, while on the phone in your cubicle. And yes, Rob has pictures of Kobe Bryant, and the Kings all over his cubicle. He's not fans of either team though. You see Rob is connected to the operating manager. He'll never leave. The only reason he has a cubicle, is so the other employees can't stand hearing him talk…

"How's it going DC?"

Brian rolls his eyes.

"I got a few things going. Nothing special." Says Brian.

"Welcome to the boomtown, baby. Time for us to Rock-N-Roll." Robert continuously throws the ball in the air, then catching.

"Our clients. Is it always like this?" asks Brian. If so, we'll make a fortune.

"I don't know, Boss, why does it matter anyway. Fuck the client, it's all about pussy." Brian is fascinated. Robert is unlike any other young man. He is rude, obnoxious and foul mouthed. Brian tries to lighten things up a bit.

"So, Robert."

"My name is Rob."

"Is there a difference?" asks Brian.

"What?"

"Oh, nothing. Tell me about yourself, Robert."

"There's nothing to know. I moved here from Connecticut five years ago." Rob continues playing catch with the corporate ball. Brian intercepts the ball and throws it in the trash.

"So, what's up why are you here?" Asks Brian.

"How can I say this," says Robert. "Think of me as your official host in this city. I'm going to pop your cheery, man. Introduce you to all the babes. I promise you, if we hang out, you will meet woman."

"What if I already have a woman? One back home," says Brian.

"There's no way you have a woman," says Robert.

"How do you know? I've been here for over a month. I've been out already."

"No way, bro, your way to wound up, and stuffy."

"Stuffy?" Brian refrains from insulting him.

"Yeah, stuffy. You got to relax man. Play the game. Like I do. That's why I'm your new bro. You're going to learn what I know about LA home slice. Dude, think of it this way. I'm saving your sorry, boring ass. You're too wired up, man. Relax, DC."

"Relax?" says Brian inquisitively.

"Yeah, relax. You take this shit way too seriously. It's just work. You got to be like me man. All I do is sit around, drink coffee, eat, and bang all the ladies. I mean, look at me man. Smell my success. And I look good. Check out the suit bro. First class all the way."

All Brian smells is Allure Cologne and cheap vodka from last night. Rob leans in and whispers to Brian.

"Dude, have you heard?"

"I'm on pins and needles," says Brian.

"Dude, you haven't heard what the chicks here are saying about you?"

"No. I haven't. I usually converse with Rick most of the day."

"Rick's a FAG. Don't listen to him. He's a fuckin' useless. As a boss, the worst in the industry." Rob looks over his right shoulder toward the door, then lowers his voice.

"His job is closing a customer, right? He hasn't closed shit. Then the asshole yells at you all day about closing. He can't close, but he conducts meetings about closing. Wait until you attend. What a joke. Funny as hell. I mean, this year at the party; he should be nominated for this year's dumb ass award."

"You know I get through the day bro?"

Brian's eyes are widened, he cannot wait to hear what nonsense he speaks next.

"I drink, man." Robert Says.

"Drink?" asks Brian. Now Brian understands the meaning of corporate mayhem.

"Yeah, man, drink. You know get toasted at lunch. Meet the slags out on the street. Shit man, I take two-hour lunches when the boss is out of town."

Brian knows why his father disowns him.

"Yeah, drink at lunch and meet chicks. That's how we'll deal with the bullshit here."

Brian quickly tries to change the subject. He's new of course. What if someone is listening? Brian tries to make things somewhat amusing. He asks Rob about a subject; he knows nothing about it.

"Tell me about the women," asks Brian.

"OK. You know that one hot red-haired chick. You know, the one with the big tits?"

"No, I don't know," says Brian.

I heard her talking about you to Donna.

"Who is Donna?" asks Brian.

"It's not important, man. What's important is her huge tits, and she's hot." Brian shakes his head in disbelief.

"Screw the personality, it's about the tits bro. Chicks with big tits, get it on. You'll learn this in time Dude."

"So, this works for you, out there? Robert."

"My name is Rob."

"You know I can't get involve with anyone. It's against company policy," says Brian.

"Stop being such a pussy. She wants you. Take her out. Get her loaded, then screw her. By the time you're done with her; you'll be up the company ladder. I mean, what's she going to do bro, sue the company?"

Rob is delusional. A legend in his own mind. A real prince of peace. A real Macho Camacho. Rob continues lying about all the woman he's screwed. It is enough to make Brian puke or punch him in the nose.

My father would throw him off Washington Bridge, he thinks. *My father would call him a turkey. Then send it to him to the Island.*

Brian is waiting for this deranged lunatic to shut up. Rob will not. He continues going on about women he will never date. Maybe never talk to. Rob is animated. He shakes his legs, arms wave, uncontrolled hand motions. Some of them sexually offensive. Rob jesters a high five to Brian. Brian looks at Robert, then jesters the front door. rob rants on about nothing.

"Dude, fuck it, let's get out of here. Get some coffee," says Robert. Brian clears his throat then nods toward his office door.

Standing with the door wide open is Richard. He stands in his Hugo Boss suit, black slicked-back hair, pale white skin, and beading dark eyes. Brian finally points to his door.

"Hey, it's the big man. What up, Boss?" says Robert.

Rob has the nerve to jester a high five towards Richard. Richard grins at Robert, then denies the gesture. Richard doesn't say a word to him. He walks by Robert, pats him on the shoulder, then sets a manila folder in front of Brian.

"Good job with those models so far. Brian, I need you to close these Norwegian's. They're coming in on Monday. We're looking at around a 15mil upfront on this guy."

"OK, thank you, Sir. I'll do my best," says Brian.

Richard exits the office quickly. As the door shuts. Rob begins talking again. The door suddenly opens. Very quickly.

"Hey, Robert, what the hell are you doing in here bothering Brian? It's not social hour. Get your ass on the phone."

Robert is a telemarketer for the company.

Richard shuts the door again quickly.

"What a dick," Rob speaks in a whisper. Robert quickly opens the door again.

"Oh, and by the way, Robert, I was outside the door listening this whole time. Your production has been down the past three months. It's showtime, get on the darn phone."

"Ahhh, Boss, it's nothing, just guy talk. Also talking about biz—"

Richard interrupts.

"Yeah, well keep it out of this office, and get back to work." Rob starts talking to Brian again Richard interrupts.

"Your still here?"

"Later, bro," Rob says to Brian.

Rob leaves the office, as Richard glared at him.

"Keep up the work, Brian," says Richard.

"Thank you, Sir. I will,"

Richard nods at Brian and leaves his office. Brian now sits alone at his desk. He turns his head and stares out the window. *Soon it will be all mine,* he thinks. Brian's phone rings again...

Chapter 10

Brian arrives home from work. He's had a successful day. He feels good about the company and its future goals. It's a beautiful fall night. Just a bit of orange fills the sky. The early evening wind is still blowing from the Pacific Ocean. The serene sky reminds him of Washington by the Northwest shore.

Brian holds four bags of Ralphs's groceries. Tonight, Brian will cook for the first time. He will cook one of his father's favorites. Spaghetti. A recipe by an Italian. A real Italian. One of his father's best friends. Brian will cook the sauce and share it with his new neighbors. A sauce so delicious, so succulent, so tasty; the whole building will smell of love and Italian tradition. Good Spaghetti sauce should smell like sweet sweat from your lady lover.

Brian walks through the metal gate through the courtyard. Different people from the building are talking. Some are in tears; others whisper to each other. Another woman holds her boyfriend crying.

Brian walks into John's market. He needs three bottles of red wine. One merlot, while cooking. A Zinfandel to taste, a Cabaret with dinner. Two bottles of cabaret if he's with a date. This is what he is hoping for.

Brian looks out the window. Tenants of the building are pointing toward the Northwest building. There are five buildings in this development. One of the buildings have units for sale. They start at $250,000. If things work out, Brian may buy five of them. Brian will check it out this weekend. He may buy two, to start if the capitalization rates are in check.

Tenants are still chattering about. Looks like a Highschool gossip session. He sees expressions of disbelief, shock, confusion, remorse, regret. He has always known how to *read* people. A gift he sometimes regrets. Especially when he is on a date. His mother says it is a gift. It will come in handy one day.

"What's going on?" Brian asks the merchant.

"You didn't hear?" says the merchant.

"I was at work." The merchant looks over Brian and grins. He shakes his head and points toward the Northwest building.

"Many bad memories," says the merchant.

Brian doesn't say anything. The bill is $75.11. Brian takes four twenties from his wallet.

"Keep the change," says Brian.

"Thank you. Next time look at my beer selection. It's the best in the city." Brian walks out of the door.

"Don't forget the frozen food section. It's new," says the merchant.

Brian walks through the courthouse avoiding everyone he sees. He does not tolerate gossip. About anyone or anything. A feeling of uneasiness enters him.

He knows they're not only gossiping but enjoying their self, while doing it. Evil people take great delight in the misfortune of others. Brian knows he'll find out who the evil people are soon. There everywhere these days. Again, a gift he regrets. A gift he never asks for. A gift that others perceive as deranged, morbid, depressive. Sometimes "stuck up."

Brian walks onward toward Los Angeles Street. Two younger men in skinny jeans, hanging from their ass, with beanie hats; walk abreast. They laugh aloud. One of them comment about something being "nasty." They think it's funny. Assholes always think tragedy is funny. They always will.

This must be why my father works in agency, thinks Brian. Assholes everywhere.

Brian walks South on Los Angeles Street. He opens the glass door and sees *her*. The perfect one. A woman he never thought would exists. A body like 'Selma Hayek,' in that awesome movie 'From Dusk Til Dawn.' The one he saw light around. The one and only. The one he looked over from the loft window, while ignoring the deranged death realtor. Now there she is…

Brian drops his bags at the sight of her beauty. He saved the wine. Thank god for that. It is her. 5'5", late 20s, black hair. French cut hair. Brian's always liked that style. She wears a Dolce style black dress, with black flat loafers. Her fingernails are painted black and skin so olive and smooth; Helen of Troy would kill her out of jealousy. Brian likes her dark and vampy eyeliner and peach rose lipstick. She doesn't need makeup though. In fact, this woman needs nothing but Brian's bed. Watching American movie classic until dawn. Listening to jazz, classical, and *'Songbird by Fleetwood Mac.'* After that,

'NADA ONE' by Heart. Candles throughout the room. He will give her anything she wants. This is the woman he wants, and he hasn't even met her yet. Funny how that works sometimes. The one that will walk through the Earth with him. Destroy all their enemies and rule the United States. She is incredible, thinks Brian. And I must have her...

"Oh shit, I'm sorry," Brian purposely bumps into her, spilling some groceries. Brian makes direct eye contact with her. He's immediately stunned by her beauty.

She kneels and starts helping Brian pick up the groceries. Oranges and apples are rolling across the floor. She's on her smart phone talking. She's going on and on, a million miles per minute about her day. How business was. She places the fruit in the bag, then opens her mailbox. She looks at Brian then smiles. She tells her mother in Spanish how overbearing she is. But she loves her. Brian understands her. Her Spanish is beautiful. It is no doubt, she's an educated woman. Maybe from a wealthy, political family.

Sondra tells her mother she doesn't want to be set up with a man. She'll find her own man. One that respects her, not owns her. She tells her mother she doesn't want to end up barefoot and pregnant for the rest of her life. Living on an old wood floor.

Brian thinks, *her tongue is sexy,* as he looks at her perfectly formed feet, hands, arms, hips and legs. She wants to retire to Spain she tells her mother. Brian can't help to laugh. His father owns a 4-bedroom condo in the Mediterranean. Brian laughs again, and she looks at him curiously. She fixates on Brian, as her mother continues yelling through the phone. Brian laughs aloud gain. He must play Spanish guitar and write poetry; she tells her mother. This is what I want mother. The beautiful woman says she'll call later. She quickly disconnects.

"You're a spaghetti lover, I see," she says.

"It's OK. One of the only things I know how to make. That, and baked chicken. And of course; steaks," says Brian.

"Really now," she says inquisitively. The woman walks around the entrance area helping Brian with the groceries. She rushes, not letting him pick up the rest. He kneels quickly, as they bump heads together.

"Ouch, what a way to meet," she says.

"I'm sorry. Let me look. You OK," Brian says.

"Fine," she says.

"Let me look at it." Brian looks at her forehead. Their eyes meet.

"My name is Brian."

"Sondra."

"Nice meeting you."

"Nice meeting you, Mr. Brian."

"Are you OK? Serious. It is my fault. I should have paid attention to."

Brian finishes placing the groceries in the bags. Sondra looks him over again. She likes what she sees. Brian is different from all the others.

"You're not from here. Are you?" asks Sondra.

"How do you know?"

"I just do. It's your mannerism."

"You're right. I just moved from Washington."

"You're a State Department brat?" Brian laughs.

"Got me on that one. How did you know, I'm not from here?"

"There's something about you. I don't know what it is yes. A certain type of gentleness. You're a good man."

"Or—" Brian interrupts. Sondra takes the last grocery bag.

"Or what?" asks Brian.

"It's nothing. Never mind. I don't make sense. I'm Sondra by the way."

"You already told me your name. Must be the bump on your head." Sondra looks embarrassed for the moment. She likes Brian already.

"I'm Brian." He offers a gentleman handshake. One of his fathers. One only a woman of class and elegance would recognize. She accepts his handshake, makes eye contact, then smiles. Sondra's hands are silk. The softness of her skin melts in his hands. Brian looks at her hand and black nail polish, then smiles.

"You already told me your name." They both laugh.

"You have beautiful hands," says Brian.

"Really, now. No men never told me this."

Yeah, bullshit, thinks Brian.

"Well, I guess, there aren't many real men in this city." Sondra admirably looks at Brian. He reminds her of a man. A man she read about in Don Quixote.

"What's going on around here? Everyone in the courtyard kept pointing at the building, acting weird, and rude. I just got home. I was going to cook some spaghetti—"

Sondra interrupts.

"Spaghetti. That's sexy." Brian cannot believe what he just heard. She may the perfect one. He regains his composure. He hopes she doesn't see him sweating.

"People is this development are rude. Stay away from the rooftop parties. They always end in disaster, with vomit all over the place."

That's it. Brian found his woman.

"Everyone's standing by the store is acting if someone had just died.

"Some people were laughing some pointing. I don't understand the people here." Sondra does not answer. She diverts the subject.

"Can I help you bring this up? I live on the fourth floor," says Sondra.

"Sure, I live on the fourth floor also. Cool, we're neighbors." Sondra smiles. She will not say another word until she reaches her destination. She likes Brian and his smell. This is good enough for now.

The fourth floor is the large floor. There are over 20 units. Premium unit. The average loft size is one thousand feet. Sondra leads Brian on a route he has never seen before. As they walk, Brian notices a courtyard down below. There is a hammock and vegetation. It would be nice if they lay together. Watch the sun rise, and it filters upon their bodies.

Brian' hears music from some of the lofts. 'Bob Marley' 'Moby' and electronic music. Cliché as always. They walk through another hallway he has never seen before.

In front of a loft stands a Los Angeles police officer. He looks at Brian and Sondra as they pass. He has a cold look about him. One of a marine, who has seen battle. A marine that has seen too much death. He has a look of revenge. Revenge on all the assholes that kill innocent people. Good people. People that are lured into a world of *slavery*. Both physical and economically. Not just sex, but *any* slavery. Anything that makes these monsters money.

A chill rushes through Brian's nervous system as he passes. His arms light up, he feels energy flow throw his head. His legs feel weak. Brian, Sondra, and the police officer never say a word.

Sondra finally speaks,

"I can't even look at that loft, it creeps me out. I have lived next door for over three years. At first, they used to party. Everyone does here. After some time, I heard them yelling at each other all the time. The yelling was abnormal. Not like most couples. It made me feel sick. I don't want to think about it." Sondra shakes off a chill. She feels as if a presence is behind her. She refuses the bad energy. Then sports a nervous smile at Brian. The memories of a woman screaming in agony and pain. A woman suffering from bondage and despair. A woman crying for help. A woman that will never be the same again. Sondra swears she hears her whispering in her ear when sleeping. Maybe a dark sinister presence that enjoys destroying Catholics. That is what voice sometime said at night. Sondra heard the spirits cursing her. Calling her a whore. That Jesus hates her. That we are your friends, your new family. You must join us, or your family will die. Sondra tries not to tear, as they reach Brian's front door.

"Well, I guess this is it." She looks at Brian and steps backward. She avoids eye contact.

"See you later," says Sondra.

"Hey. Why don't you have dinner with me? I bought all this food. I won't eat it all, and I don't want it going bad. Also, we have wine." Brian holds up a few bottles.

She looks at Brian and smiles. She enjoys wine.

"That is if you are not busy. I don't mean to impose," says Sondra shyly.

"Now, that would be nice. Impose, what is there to impose on. I want you to impose, please. There are a few good movies on tonight. '2 Days in The Valley and 'Edward Scissor Hands."

Sondra laughs. She wants to kiss him but will refrain.

"Since you said please, OK."

"So, come one by around 8:00?"

"OK," says Sondra.

"OK, see you." Brian walks away and opens his door. He watches Sondra as her hips lead the way. She sways her hips like a love goddess in a 1940s classic movie. That movie Elizabeth Taylor was in. That Paris movie. Black turtleneck, black skirt, and swaying juicy hips. Or even Sophia Loren. As she walks, he can't believe how beautiful she is. He also thinks about what Jenna told him about LA women. He wonders if Sondra is different. He will soon find out. Forget Jenna for now. Sondra is all he sees; all he wants and desires.

Brian stands over a large pot. He uses two jars of traditional, and two jars of marinara. He has 40 cloves of garlic, Irish butter, olive oil, four green bell peppers, two red bell peppers, four tomatoes, coarse black pepper, sea salt, bay leaves, half a large onion, Italian seasoning, and thick-sliced, white mushrooms, brown sugar, and Italian sausage.

He bought fresh Italian sausage. He will not use it. A woman of her beauty may be a vegetarian.

Brian's loft is beginning to smell like love. It is just what he wanted. He will accent the meal with Mama Bella Garlic Bread and Italian salad.

If she stays later, they will use the excess bread for dipping sauce. He thinks of lying in bed with her, listening to 'Chopin and Tchaikovsky' maybe 'Mendelssohn'. Later end the night with 'Miles Davis, Kind of Blue.'

Brian images feeding her bread dipped in sauce. Watching her mouth wrapped around the bread. Hearing her moan with pleasure. The pleasure only Italian food will bring. He imagines her sleeping in his arms until noon. Later, they will have steak at Flannigan's.

This is good. Oh, yeah, this will be good, he thinks. *It always is…*

Brian's dining table seats only four. A crystal vase his mother gave him holds yellow tulips. Brian's not that ambitious. Any other color would be improper. Two bottles of red wine sit on the table. One Cabernet, one Merlot.

Sondra sits at the West end of the table. She looks amazing. She wears a red dress, with red heels. This time, she is garnished in jewelry that accents her red nail polish. She is sexy. Not only sexy but beautiful. So beautiful, no makeup can ever enhance her beauty.

Brian would like her to slip off the heels, carry her to the bed, and have sex immediately. Any man would.

This is what Brian wants. Sondra has evolved, in his mind as beautiful to a god. A demi-god he must indulge in. Taste, feel, touch, then consume. This is his prerequisite of bride ship.

Sondra pours her second glass of wine, then slowly stands up. Brian tries to concentrate on his meal. His hand trembles as she walks by touching Brian. Sondra walks around the loft, looking over everything.

"You have a nice loft. Very decadent; Masculine" says Sondra. She finishes her wine and softly walks back to his table. The sounds of her heels make an erotic tapping noise. Brian finds his immensely erotic. Sondra will not pour another glass. Brian will.

Sondra stands up and nervously, walks throughout the loft again. She notices his closet is open with the light on. She peeks in. Everything is exquisitely arranged.

Metal hangers for shirts. Wood for pants. All the color patterns flow. He has a dresser closet to the left with a shoe rack, drawers, and watch display. The display shows four different Swiss Watches. He has five suits. Everything is in perfect order. He has T-shirts, cashmere, and merino sweaters folded neatly. Four pairs of jeans. The suits are made in Turkey, Colombia and England.

Sondra likes this. She sees a white electric guitar with a Mesa Boogie amplifier. It is a 1972 Les Paul custom. In the other corner of the loft sits an acoustic guitar. Sondra pics up the guitar and places the strap over her shoulder. It is heavy. The best part is it feels sexy. She wonders if Brian can play.

"So, you play guitar?" Sondra asks.

"A little bit, nothing special," says Brian.

"What can you play?" Brian looks her over and smiles. He wants her now. But will not tell. He thinks about her naked wearing that guitar, and how the oyster in-lays complement her skin.

"Maybe later, I'll play you 'Luna Negra.'"

Sondra hearts jumps. A man who plays Spanish Guitar she tells her mother.

Sondra walks to Brian's bed. The bed is impressive. She looks at the nightstand and picks up a picture of Brian and his parents. She looks at the picture and smiles. Brian pretends he doesn't notice.

"So, this is your parents?" asks Sondra.

"Excuse me?"

"This picture, your parents?"

"Oh, yes. They live in Washington." Sondra looks over the picture with admiration.

"They look sweet. Your mother is beautiful. I can see by your father's face, he's deeply in love. He is a very, lucky man. I can also see where you got your good looks."

"Who?"

"Your father, silly."

"Well, thank you," Brian cheerfully says.

"No, brothers, sisters, girlfriend?" Brian gathers his thoughts for a moment. He knows he can tell the truth or lie. He does what all men do this age. He says nothing. Sondra waits for an answer as she observes the bed again. She rubs her hand over the bedspread.

"A wife?"

"No, just brothers, sisters. Dinner is ready. Come and get it." Sondra walks quickly to the table. Her breast moves with each step.

Brian takes her chair and offers a seat. Sondra is impressed by Brian's manners. She feels comfortable with Brian, however, a bit guarded. This has happened once before. The result was disastrous. Brian has 'Nina Simone' playing over the stereo.

"I like this music," Sondra says. Brian smiles as he serves pasta and salad.

"It helps me relax. I grew up listening to this music. I like 'Brahms.' Also, you know what they say, 'music will save the world.' Cheers."

"What do we toast to?" asks Sondra.

"New friendship," Brian says.

"Cheers," she says.

Sondra no doubt is impressed. Brian admires her abietite. He thinks, *It's sexy. A woman who doesn't enjoy fine food in the home has no passion.* Brian has been thinking about sharing information with her about the neighbors. You know, the drugged-out male, and tweaked out girl. Female. Not just yet. He will wait. Wait until they open the third bottle of wine.

About 45 minutes pass. They enjoy each other. Most of all, they're comfortable. The food was pretty, good. They dined and talked like two lost others in a 1940's movie. *Sondra thinks she's got him pegged already. She knows him.* She'll meet some half-backed psychic at Venice or Universal City Walk. They'll be on a date. Then she'll find out his passions. A past life lover. A warrior that saved Sondra from War in Spain.

Not an unusual for the IRISH, she thinks. *They are everywhere.* Brian opens the third bottle of wine. They both enjoyed the Claim Jumper chocolate cake with Italian coffee. Now it is time for zinfandel, then the story. Brian offers her another glass of wine. She accepts a quarter glass.

Brian asks the question, "I'm a bit curious. I am new here. There was a lot of action downstairs this evening. What's wrong with the building? Some of the people seem a bit detached, self-serving. Kind of evil."

Sondra takes a drink of wine, then sighs.

"Pour me another."

"You're not a lite weight anymore, are you?"

"First, I want you to know, I'm not friends with many people in this development," says Sondra. "I live alone, divorced, and hard working. I live here because, it's close to my clothing store. What I tell you, is what I know from listening. OK?"

"OK," replies Brian.

Brian looks at Sondra. He wonders if he's scaring her away. If he's being a hypocrite, a gossip freak. Sondra gulps down her drink.

"Give me another." Brian pours the wine. His hand jitters a bit.

"I used to hear them sometimes. It was horrible, evil at its worst. You see, the guy who lived next door to me; a real creep was named Troy. At first, he used to hang out in the courtyard. Every woman that would walk through the gate, he would approach. His approach was sleazy. The same approach all outsiders use when they move here. I am a movie producer, writer, production analyst. Real bullshit. Sondra takes another sip of wine. It's the same crap they all pull here." Sondra notices a pack of cigarettes on the table.

"Can I have one?"

"Sure, that's why they're here." Brian quickly lights the cigarette.

"Thank you. Anyway, he used to hang out on the rooftop parties, fondle some of the women. Offer drugs to people. It was disgusting. We all noticed he looked high all the time. He would stroll the downstairs tables and liquor store. Pants down low, boxers hanging out. He would tell the woman to 'Look at me, I'm bitchin, a DJ, a drummer' I know all the nightclub owner's, we will all get in for free. A real joke." Sondra takes another drink of wine.

"This is the rumor. Troy, he used to hang out at the Union Station, looking for girls. The weak ones. The ones with dreams and aspirations. You know, making it big, actresses, models, you name it. Some of these girls would do just about anything to make it on the screen. You know, get noticed in Hollywood."

Sondra pauses for a moment, takes another drag of the cigarette, then sips her wine. Brian takes a cigarette and joins her.

"Anyway, he found this girl, she was very, beautiful. I think she was from Kentucky, or somewhere close. Weird thing was nobody knew her name. Every morning, she would walk in the courtyard with her little dog. Cutest little thing. She would waddle around, dazed. Most people thought she was stoned. At night, sometimes, I would hear her scream. You will learn in this building, many women scream. It may be a pleasure, it could be bondage, who knows, right?" Brian nods in agreement.

"The police were called a few times. I think mostly because of the loud music. Nothing ever happened. The rumor was, they were just into kinky sex. Then one night, when Troy's girlfriend was asleep. The small, cute dog got out."

"Doesn't make sense," says Brian. "We have stairs, locked doors and elevator."

"Precisely, my thoughts, exactly. That's everyone thoughts. Anyway, the dog was found dead in the morning. The poor little guy was thrown off this 5-story building. Worst part is it was done last Halloween. I guess Troy had a hell of a story to tell. He said he walked downstairs, to get air. He was drinking that night. When sitting below the umbrellas he fell asleep. Someone took the dog, then threw him off the roof. This is what the asshole Tray says. Anyway, rumors circulated. Some of the tenants said the freaky couple are into witchcraft, and the animal was killed for demonic ritual. Troy covered up the kill, buying his girlfriend a baby white Persian Kitten. In Los Angeles, this is not uncommon. This is what the Police said. It's happened before. Dog gets out. Someone kills it. Due to homeless people. Everyone knows this is crap. How would a homeless man get inside the building? Unless he was let inside, given money to kill the dog. This is my theory. The next thing, I know, is what happened today. Troy's dead."

Brian looks her over curiously. She knows she is telling the truth. Yet craves more.

"Why didn't you help her, get to know her?" asks Brian.

"Brian, like I said before, there are a lot of screwed up people around this area. Even the good ones are into some weird stuff. I work all the time. They do not, at least work conventional jobs. Look what happened. What am I supposed to do? I could have ended up like him."

"That's a sad story," says Brian as he drinks his wine, then stomps out the cigarette. "There's more truth that, nobody will ever know. That's between the Los Angeles Police and the victim's families. I think that Troy killed the dog to create a motive. Just in case, the abused girl scrubbed him out. Do you think I'm crazy Brian?"

"No not at all. I was just thinking about that too."

"Really,"

"Yes."

Guess were a good team, Brian.

Brian sees Sondra is uncomfortable now. This is a screwed-up story. Brian tries to lighten the conversation.

"Look at things this way Sondra. The Menace of Santee Court is now Dead."

"This is what I'm afraid of Brian. I know things. I lived next door. I heard many things. Ok Brian, listen, I'll tell you." Sondra takes a long drink of wine.

"Pour me another Brian."

"At night the weird drugged out couple used to taunt me. Speaking through the wall, playing scary music, saying they want sex with me. They used to pound on the wall when I was asleep."

"Did you call the Police?"

"Yes, I did, however, when the Police knocked on their door, there was no answer. The Police said, they will only knock on their door 6 times. I mean 6 calls in one night. By the sixth phone call, the cops looked at me as maybe crazy, or on drugs. They started asking me more questions, than about the harassment. This is why I'm scared. I feel these assholes research the Police and de-classified information."

"Don't worry Sondra, I'm connected to Agency. I will protect you. With me, nobody, I mean no one will touch you."

"Promise?"

"Promise."

"Pinky swears?"

"Yes, for sure baby."

Brian and Sondra wraps pinky fingers.

Brian offers another glass of wine. She does not accept. Sondra informs Brian she must leave early tomorrow. She has a supplier meeting from INDIA. Brian walks her down the hall to her door. Brian will not bother trying kissing Sondra. She does not offer either. Brian fears he may have pushed her away for now…

Chapter 11

Troy and his girlfriend sit in their loft. It is early Sunday morning. They visited the East Melrose District. An area comprised of massage fronts, and dark dive bars. The bars with opportunistic people looking for opportunistic chaos. They went to a nightclub in East Hollywood. Not the good ones. The ones where everyone knows each other sharing the same vices. The vices are drugs, booze, smoke, sex and the never-ending quest finding dope. Happy boy is who Troy was looking for. He promised Troy an eight-ball of 'The Bomb.' Freshly cooked, and cock hard ready. Worst part in East Melrose district is finding a dealer you trust. Is he reliable? Will he let you crash at his house for a few days, spend evil, dark Christmas with you. Where everyone cries about their family back home, discussing getting clean and finding work. Picking scabs in the bathroom, then hiding them with make-up. Asking 'who's coming over tonight? Where are they? Why aren't they here yet?' Let's not forget, the woman who stroll the streets of East Melrose. When desperation sets in. The connection doesn't arrive, they always fulfill your chaotic needs. Finding drugs, using them, and desperate measures that inherit the process, is what makes East Melrose so exciting. At least for Troy.

Speed is most popular, more than heroin and of course, powder and pills. Pills that help you 'crash.' They're cheap and easy to get. Troy and his girlfriend were short on cash. So, he cut the speed he had left, trying to trade weight for substance. Cleaner cut is what Troy wants… They guy behind the bar called it 'The Mass.' He said it shipped from Canada, right through Bakersfield. The Ephedrine was cooked in India, the highest grade, now available., with fears to be eliminated by the CIA. Their friends up North in Oregon are already stock poling. 6,000 drug dealer homes in Oregon. Imagine that is 2005. Total Chaos. Only a few mules picked supplies, then drove to Nevada, Grapevine, Henning, and finally landed in beautiful Hollywood California.

Troy, and his girlfriend, wait at the bar rocking back and forth, hands shaking, and sweat dripping from their foreheads. They try to maintain, the cut he has now, is too weak. More poison than Euphoria. Play it cool. Money is short, so they must watch the alcohol consumption. Pay attention to the USC football game, on the television and maintain from any fighting.

The bar is old, has steel iron entry door, and sheet metal over the windows. It's condemned, underground and illegal. A rock bottom pick-up for the fiends. The ones that can't come down. Once the bar tender sells the dope, everyone is ordered to leave. If they stay behind, they'll eventually be dragged to the alley, then stabbed. This is so the customer could relax, not worry about the outside world around them. The bar does have two pool tables, a juke box, dart board, and small area for live band. The paranoid faithful won't tolerate music after a certain level.

The bar is covered with flyers from the street. Mostly local rock bands, wrestling shows, etc. There are flyers spread all over the hallways leading to the restrooms. It shows pictures of women, who offer services for generous men.

The bathroom and halls smell like vomit and urine. It is obvious that some customers kick their drugs in these areas.

The Rainbow People would vomit if they entered this establishment. Then burn it down.

The kitchen is filthy, dishes piled, fast food remains everywhere. Troy and his girlfriend sit on the floor, corner of bar. Indian Style, chain smoking.

Troy's girlfriend rocks back and forth, discussing the good days. The days when Troy could get an eight ball upfront. Pure China White with Speed. The days when drugs were clean. They felt and tasted better. The music, for now, is slightly above conversation level. This way, no one will hear them. His girlfriend has track marks that Johnny thunders would blush at. She licks them, trying to extract "the final pleasure." She picks at scabs on her body. She rolls them up then skillfully places them in a mirror box. She tells Troy it's for emergency situations. She heard you can chew on the scabs and catch a high. Smoke the scabs if they become desperate. She hasn't tried it yet, however, is prepared-*for anything*...

A scrawny, sickly man smelling like bleach and mothballs, tapes the sides of the metal windows. This way, no light will come in. The patrons used to enjoy the sun and the California ocean. Now sunlight, any light makes them "nervous." The voices they hear surrounding, don't make the situation any more enlightening. They discuss end times prophecy, the CIA and Nostradamus, more importantly, the Sunday Mass about to begin. Troy finally scored. His dealer was stuck in traffic driving from Bakersfield South 5 freeway. A truck ran into a Toyota. 4 people died.

Troy and his girlfriend are home. Candles, black and white ones are lit throughout the loft. In the past, he enjoyed it when she poured hot wax over his shaft. When it dried, it would be nibbled it off with their teeth. All she could do was sit in the corner and watch. Watch and masturbate. This is all Troy would allow.

The police have visited this couple three times, This past month. Troy says he is worried they are on the grid. He hears voices all around him. He thinks, *It's the drugs, but maybe not. Troy hears voices saying the CIA would like to recruit him. That he's talented. Has gifts.*

The voices tell Troy they're from his hometown. They have a job for him when the time is right. 'For now, just listen. Do what we say. Keep making those underground porn movies. The packages will be mailed to your box.'

Troy is enamored by what he hears and excited. He's been talking to his old dope, fiend, friends, over the phone. They swear the network communicated by mental telepathy. Soon no more phones. The cops will never know what they're doing. How they communicate excites Troy also. When he is not having sex, his girlfriend is passed out, the voices turn him on. Troy claims he receives oral sex, from an unseen presence. Tingling and wet tongue all over his penis, then the soft sway of his testicles, as the suction becomes more intense. Then the climax. Soon he will bring her to life and have three-way sex together. The summoned woman is your gift. Git for obeying the master. She was a gift sent to Troy on his 30th birthday. Loft party, after everyone left, she showed. A Romanian woman. She prayed over the loft, then placed her hands on Troy's head. Greatest gift the drug addict loser could ever receive. Now he can have sex. Sex in the spirit world...

Best of all, he and his criminal network; soon they will break *everyone*, and steal money from bank accounts, retirement accounts, and 401k's. '*We are all on an astral plane.*' The voices call him a beast, a god. Troy's work will be noted by high-priest, and he'll be ranked soon. All his girlfriend can do is listen. If she does anything else. She may pay the price. Be sacrificed as he always says. A sacrifice for his unseen lover, that visits at night.

"Soon they will *all* be joined forever."

Electronic music sends messages to his mind. They tell Troy, he'll have a DJ job. This way Troy can recruit young ladies. Ones on drugs. The drugs we manufacture that change the brain. This way *our* whores can be tracked worldwide.

Troy will be a porn producer. Best of all, there will be no cameras. Yet, the videos will be sold world-wide. No health inspectors, and no red tape. Imagine that no production cost. All profit. That is the best business there is.

The woman having sex will never know, they're on film. The cameras will be human eyes. 'Its' fuckin' perfect, says Troy.'

'Our organization will make a fortune, and when she can no longer fuck, we will sell her, auction her worldwide.'

Central Asia, Africa, and the Eastern Europe. Is a good start. Then we'll have alliances in Mexico and South America. All Troy needs to do is meet his new friend at King Edwards tonight at 4:00 AM. His new friend says he has a package with instructions…

Troy's drug supply is just about dry again. It's now Monday night. Football is over. Troy watched as his girlfriend tries resting. Troy doesn't know who won, but he stared. At the television. Troy has enough dope left to last the next two days. That is if they maintain control, not overdo it. In other words, chip at it. If not, Troy will make her dance at one of those underground warehouse clubs, east Skid row.

The voices tell him destruction is the new beginning. You, being destroyed, and resurrected, will judge your faith in us. They tell Troy to never go back home. That she belongs to us. Together you will be a success. First, you must get clean my son. Then *save her.*

Troy tries to lighten things up, as his girlfriend lays down in the bathroom exploring the battle sores throughout her body. He tells his girlfriend she must dance tonight. Tonight, in the loft, **on Webcam.** If they do it, his friends in Nigeria will wire the money. He was told $4,000.00 monthly. All she must do, is perform three times a week. Troy already purchased a secured deposit debit card, from CVS Pharmacy downstairs. Fuck the yellow Mustang, thinks Troy. I'll save and buy a Cadillac cash. That dealer of off La Brea. That or an old Tricked Out, Jaguar.

Troy, and his girlfriend drove back downtown in their yellow, convertible Mustang, with white interior. By the way, the car is in Repo. He's been hiding it a warehouse in Skid Row. Troy wore a Hawaiian shirt last night, with aftermarket Adidas sweats. He thought he looked like 'Brad Pit' in 'Fight Club.' Another reason for Troy to be paranoid. The four-banger Mustang with the loud after-market exhaust, with lowered suspension. The one that could get him pulled over any second. The registration has expired, the brakes squeak, and the tires are bald. A real "Cheese Machine." Troy can never find the time for the DMV. He's hungover, too high for public, in a speed coma. He also claims the Registration bill never arrived through mail.

Troy was able to salvage $20.00 by nights end. He drove one of his friends to the liquor store for smokes. He said he was Horney, asked if he can get head, even a hand-job from the old lady. Troy's not the hand job. No, not at all. So long it's not inner-course, and money is exchanged. "My bitch, is your bitch." That is Troy's motto.

He drives with one eye in the rearview mirror the whole time. He thought he may have been followed. 'Fuck it, he always says. 'I'm always followed. And I don't care. These fools ain't got crap on me, baby The guys I'm in with downtown are connected. They own the Police.'

"What do you say baby girl. My homeboy left us a rock. She stroked off his friend in the bathroom at a gas station in East Hollywood. After tonight, we'll have enough to be on for days. Maybe a week. Find ourselves a new religion. We're gonna score later little girl. But first, let's puck up 3 packs of basics; and 4 forty ounces of King Cobra. I know I guy, He sells me 2 bottles for $3.00. Pretty fucking sweet, hey baby girl?"

The drugged girlfriend chuckles, then spits mucus all over her hand.

"I would rather take a nice long hot bath. Try relaxing for a while. My nerves hurt, so do my bones. My head feels like knives are puncturing the sides. Please make it stop."

"I'll take care of you really good when we get home, baby girl. Just chill, daddy will take care of everything."

2

The drug-out girl stands atop the toilet so she can see herself in the mirror. Harsh reality now sets in. The thinks, then mumbles to herself. 'I used to look like the hot girl in the movie 'Almost Famous,' now I look like 'Night of the living Dead.' My bones are showing in the ribcage, my hair is white, and translucent, and scabs, now atop my feet. I can't believe that I've been sharing my scabs with Troy. My boyfriend likes them now. Especially the ones that are syringed. He said they have good taste and toxicities.'

At first, she screams, then she places her hands over her face. She speaks softly to herself. 'I cannot do this anymore. Please God, deliver me from this sin and evil. I want to be a good girl now. I want to go home. God, take me home.'

She is so dehydrated; she cannot summon tears. The only person she sees in the mirror is a ghost. The ghost of her dead grandmother when she lay in hospital screaming, dying from bladder cancer.

She continues to look herself over, especially the face. She looks and feels like a 70-year-old woman. One with lines on her forehead, lines around her mouth with a few scabs. Lips dry, skin yellow. Her hands won't stop shaking. She wears a black oversized sweatshirt, with white undershirt, jeans that used to fit, and flip flop sandals. Her toenails are painted bright orange with dirt all stuck between the skin. Her hand nails are painted green and purple. Most of them chipping.

One man on the street offered her $100.00 so she can shower at his apartment. He wanted to film her showering for an extra $200. Then cut her hair, then give me her a make-over, feed her, then buy her new clothes off Santee Alley. He also told her about many men from his country would pay her money to visit. She would be a movie star and watched all over the world. She never accepted the offer, however; Troy argued in his favor.

She pulls a scab from her face, then places the scab in her mouth. She thinks there might be a kick inside. She spits the scab out, washes her mouth then walks back into the main loft room. Her boyfriend Troy lays on his back arms in midair. He shows the ceiling his middle finger.

"Fuck you, mother fucker," he says. "Can you see this man. No look, there is a man. He wears a white suit and white hat with black band. Looks like some Hispanic dude."

"Is there anything left?" asks the girlfriend.

"Just enough to tide us until later. Maybe until tomorrow if we chip it. We can't shoot anymore."

"How much later?"

"I made a call. He said he's scoring now. I'll hit Edwards around 2:00 pm."

"I didn't hear you on the phone. Or even dial. Don't bullshit baby. I want to get high and fuck also. Then we'll order pizza. How-bout that? honey girl. Tell him he can visit us. Maybe he'll share."

Troy begins cursing again. He points to the ceiling. Talking to the fucker in the white hat. "Maybe he has the good drugs. Maybe you can suck his ghost dick honey. He'll turn us on to some good heroin."

"Hey stupid fuck ghost. What are you doing here? Give us some drugs or go back to hell. Dirty scumbag."

Troy grabs a mirror then sits on the couch. He tries scraping the resin from a wood pipe. He vigorously scrapes until he sees particles fall on the mirror. Troy doesn't want to share the rest of the dope with his girlfriend. It's already planned. Nobody else will visit the next 4 days. He will make her bet in the end, crawl on her hands, knees crying for more. Make her pole dance, while spreading it on the web. Later, even worse…

"Here baby, snort this." His hands shake, as he hands her a straw. She walks to him grabs the straws, partaking in the madness.

"Check it out, baby. I was able to salvage a few lines. I was praying for this. We can hit our other stuff slowly. Help calm the tide before distribution time." His girlfriend walks to the refrigerator and opens.

"I'm hungry," she says.

"What the fuck you want me to do about it," he replies.

All she sees a gallon of watered-down Hawaiian Punch, molded bread, butter, peanut butter, and kraft cheese. The bread is fresh enough to make toast with melted cheese. However, there is no brown sugar left to take away the aches. There's no more chocolate cake. This upsets her the most. She told him to save some. He never saves her anything. Her boyfriend walks to the bed, takes off his shirt, then lays down. He looks for a television program. He finds a few evangelical programs and listens for a moment.

"Listen to this fag," says Troy. "The preacher talks about revelations and end-time prophecy. The decay of human morals and values? Half of these fuckers on television steal money from the poor, take bonds, take gold, then with the money; fuck whores from El-Salvador. Makes me fuckin' sick baby."

"What about you?" he asks. "What's your take on this religion crap?" She doesn't agree with Troy but won't say anything.

His girlfriend closes the fridge. The cat rubs her body around her calves. She is hungry. No food is left, and she feels hopeless. She feels she isn't good looking enough to walk the Downtown streets anymore. Begging for money, cat in arms.

The girlfriend picks up her cat and sits down in a rocking chair, next to the stereo system. She rocks back and forth slowly, holding the pretty white Persian.

She whispers in the cat's ear, "I'm sorry, angel. Mommy will get you food later." On the ground next to the stereo lays a stack of vinyl records. The girlfriend turns off the CD player.

"What the fuck, did you turn that off for? I was listening to that. It was keeping my head straight."

"I'm so tired of listening to that ambient devil style music. It gives me the creeps. Enough already honey. We can chill other ways."

Troy falls out of the bed, begins crawling throughout the floor.

"Hey, baby, I bet there is enough shit lying about, to last us a week. I bet I can find it. There's gotta be some rock around her somewhere. Mother fucker."

"I'm changing the music," she says.

"Don't fuckin' change it. I'm listening to it."

"Why are you such a control freak? Don't worry, honey, you won't be disappointed," she says. "It's one of my fuck boy albums."

"Yeah, well you better put on something good," he says.

She thumbs through the vinyl records and takes out her favorite, '*Aerosmith, Toys in the Attic.*' She takes out the record as it stumbles from her dehydrated shaking hands, almost hitting the concrete floor. She turns on the turntable. Her hands shake so much, can barely cue the cartridge.

"What the hell you are doing? Fucking things up again."

"Sorry," she says. "Baby, you won't be disappointed." The song begins. She chooses 'Uncle Salty.'.

The song starts as her boyfriend crawls around. He looks like Stiv Bator's'. She tries not to laugh. "Hey momma, I am finding some old rocks. Small ones."

"Ahhh, yeeha, that's it, baby. Here is another one. It's a small clear coated dust rock. Shit. I'll keep looking."

"You know what I want baby?"

"Don't talk about food again, or I'll pound you."

"Get on the bed," says the girlfriend.

"Now you're talking woman. Finally, your being useful."

"Wait a sec." She picks up a cigarette pack on a small round table next to the rocking chair. The cat meows, then runs to the closet. That is where she always stays when they have sex.

Her boyfriend runs over and jumps on the bed. She sees he found a few little rocks. He probably was hiding them. He only shares the emergency supply if I offer him sex. He places a few rocks in his mouth. "Well, sure taste like the shit."

She hopes it's dried up cat piss.

"What the fuck are you doing? Get over here, now fuck!"

She walks over to him slowly then looks him over. She sits down on the side of the bed, methodical and slowly. She doesn't want to upset him. If she shakes the bed wrong. In the closet, she may go…

"I think it's loving time, baby. Let's get on with it," says Troy.

"Don't worry, honey. I'm going to give you the best fuck of your life."

Her boyfriend takes a hit of the wooden pipe. He exhales the hit, then smacks his mouth.

"Yummy." He speaks. "Sees, see what I can do. Told you I can get a few hits out of this."

"I don't want it anymore," she says.

"Fine, suit yourself. More for me loser"

Her boyfriend takes another hit and exhales. "This is good shit, baby. You sure you don't want some? It must have jumped across the room, while I was chopping it."

"Are you happy with this life?" she asks.

"Why do you always ask this shit? Fuck things up all the time, with your stupid questions? You love me? How will we get married, have children? Like it fuckin' matters? You are like some sick psychopathic lunatic. A fucking dog. Love me, love me, love me. What do I always say, uh? Go with the flow. Fuck it, see what each day brings us."

"I didn't ask if you love me. I was just saying."

"Say-what? Say it, woman. Ahhh, fuck it."

"Never mind, baby. I was just thinking." She reaches over and places her left hand over his crotch. He slaps her hand away.

"Did I say you can touch me yet? Don't think, do as I tell you."

"I'm here baby. All for you."

"Don't be a smartass woman."

She sighs deeply, then sits back on the bed. On the right side of the nightstand lays a shotgun. She looks at it quickly, then looks at him. Her boyfriend is content smoking from his pipe.

He turns off the television, putting on a pornographic movie. The sight of it makes her sick. It is the same sequence over and over. Her on her knees, him behind her, then he ejaculates all over her face. Smut, dirty disgusting. This is all he will ever watch.

It's fuckin' disgusting, she thinks. His private collection. She wants the film so bad. She wants to burn it. Thank god, Troy hasn't sold it. He's too high speaking to distributors. She doesn't want sex from him anymore. Especially him. Maybe so, if only I, well if. She looks at the gun again. Why is it that his eyeline is always above me during oral sex? He carries no camera in his hand. Yet, Troy looks down at me the whole time?

She tries to block the sight and sounds of the homemade film. She doesn't dare ask about it. He might punish her.

"Since we're on the subject about love Troy, do you love me? I mean, we have been together now for what? Three years?"

"What's wrong with today? Let's get it on. Fuck, woman. I don't want to hear you talk. Just fuck me now. What does fucking have to do with love anyway?"

She turns away and starts to tear.

"OK, then here it is. I love you, baby. I love you. Is this what you want to hear?"

"Yes," she says.

"Then get over here. Now."

"OK, then," she says. "Only if you promise to love me forever."

"Yeah whatever, you, sick piss head. Just give it to me." Says Troy.

She climbs atop him quickly then kisses him. She knows he's lying. She knows he has been fucking that woman, from the hostess club, on fourth street. *Now, she doesn't care. She wants out. She will leave him today.* She thinks to herself for a moment, then kisses him with her lounge, while rubbing his crotch with her right hand.

"I'm going to love you, then fuck you really good, baby."

His girlfriend stands up on the bed taking off her tank top. Now naked you can see the outlines of her ribs. He unzips his jeans quickly.

"No, no, no. leave them on. Tonight, you will do what I say."

"Take a hit of this first baby, I packed tight for you."

"I don't need it anymore. I want this." She gently rubs her hand over his crotch. Back and forth motion. She notices that he responds by moving his hips. She starts to rub more quickly. He starts to moan. He begins lowering his zipper, as she wraps her hand around his shaft. The aroma from his buttock overtakes the apartment. It smells worse than anything out of the cat box. Troy hasn't showered for days.

"Wait, I have an idea."

Her voice is now at a loveable excitable tone. One he is familiar with. One he can trust. She leans over him while brushing his manhood with her left hand.

"Don't fuckin' tease me, baby. I'm hungry for you. Why can't we just do a 69 and record it?"

She reaches for the nightstand next to the bed and takes out a pair of handcuffs and blindfold. She looks over the slave owner and grins.

"Fuck, girl, what are you waiting for? Let's get it on." His girlfriend cuffs his hands to the bedpost.

This is good, she thinks. *Incredibly good.*

"Aren't you a kinky slut?" Says Troy.

"Remember this? Now it's my turn." She Speaks.

She remembers the times she was cuffed to the bedpost. She thinks of all the times he was binging, dry. How he took out his withdrawals on her. Now it is her turn to withdraw on him.

"Come on, give it to me." She places the blindfold over his eyes, then looks at him. She leans over and kisses him on the lips ever so gently. The last kiss. His last right. This is her sacrament. The years she loved him, and only him. Now her innocence and health destroyed.

Troy says, "Things will get better, I promise."

To her better has a new name. It is called revenge.

"Hold on," she says.

She walks toward the kitchen. Her dirty, blistered feet can barely hold her 75-pound frame. She used to weigh 110. She grabs a cutlery knife from the door.

This is a good one, she thinks. A ray of light shines through the blinds.

The ray of light strikes her face, it almost blinds her. She opens her eyes and sees an angel draped in white smiling at her. She recognizes the light. The light is her guardian that visited her many times in dreams. Her Dead Grandmother.

The Grandmother tells her, "Come to us. Angie."

She wipes the tears from her eyes and walks quickly to the bed. She lay down next to him.

"I'm back, baby." She kisses him again. Uncle Salty is now at its climax. All Angie hears is a song about a woman. A woman just like her. A cry for help. A cry no one would answer. A cry for redemption. Cries of woman who was a sex slave and tortured for three years. Cries of a woman burnt with a lighter. Cries of woman who was locked in the closet.

Not released until she answered, "I promise, I'll be a good girl."

"So, aren't you gonna suck it bitch?"

"So, you want me to suck it," she says.

"Yeah," he says excitedly.

"I'll suck it, baby. You've been a bad man and deserve a real good dirty sucking."

"I sure am. A very, bad man. Punish me, you dirty slut."

She rubs his crotch with her right hand, French kisses him then stops. She stands up on the bed and looks over him for the last time. What a pathetic soul. What an evil man. I must save him. Save him for all women like me. She begins the Lord's prayer. As she prays, he sees a vision. A vision of things yet to come. Visions of fire and torture.

"Great weeping and gnashing of teeth. Things of the Ancients."

"What the fuck are you saying? You fucked up, bitch," he says.

She grabs the loaded shotgun from the bedside. She crams both barrels in his mouth. The chattering sounds of teeth are heard.

"You'll now and forever carry both barrels of my emotions. Asshole!"

He muffles the words, "What the fuck."

The woman pulls the trigger spreading his brains all over the bed and wall. Large portions are left sticking on the white wall, wailing stench. Some parts of the brain lay on the bedsheet, still pulsing with blood.

The cat jumps on the bed for the first time. The white Persian begins licking, savoring, then eating parts of the brain. Angie won't let the cat eat too much. The drugs she thinks, will kill her.

Angie picks up the cat, giggles then speak to her.

"Don't you dare, eat those dirty evil brains. You will end up stupid and smelly, just like him."

Angie dances around with the loft, then looks at Troy's remains. The left-side eyeball is still open, erratically moving. She looks at the eyeball, then coughs up mucus in the eye. She walks over to the kitchen, grabbing a knife. The knife she many times thought using. She jabs the knife in the eye, then spits at him again.

Angie hopes he feels pain. A taste of her pain, the last three years all at once. This is her 'Antonin Dvorak.' This is her New World Order Revenge. She hopes he sees her triumph, her glory. Most of all; she hopes he is hell, Finally, a dark black closet, that he will never escape.

She picks up the cat and walks into the middle of the room. She tears the masking tape from the blinds, then opens the windows. The light shines through her body. It is good. She feels wind from the ocean for the first time. It is good. For once in her life, she knows everything will be good.

She snuggles the Persian cat and speaks aloud, "We are free. At last, we are finally free."

The new woman places away the Aerosmith album. She places on the turntable 'Tchaikovsky' Concerto in D Major, OP.35, For Violin and Orchestra.' Finally, *everyone* on Los Angeles Street, will hear her Voice. Finally…the people will say. She is free…

It's Tuesday morning; Sondra is on her way to work. Police detective and officers surround the building facing Los Angeles Street. She was the First Responder as sunrise. She made the first phone call.

A group of residence stand and observe the last remains of Troy. Not as a human, but a demon in disguise. This is not one woman in the building that speaks kindly of him.

The victim Angie walks out of the building shaking, with a blanket wrapped around her. She holds her cat and looks toward the ground.

Sondra stands there watching her. A woman who was once young, beautiful, a future. Now she has the appears of a 70-year-old widow; one foot in the grave.

Sondra thinks of all the nights she prayed for her. Sondra feels it is partially her fault. What if she could have helped her sooner? What if she put a hit on

Troy? Sondra tried talking to her before. Angie laughed, she said "it's the sex talking and crying. Don't worry about it, it's not me."

Angie looks at Sondra then smiles.

"Thank you." She says to Sondra, then smiles warmly, then places her head downward and cries. Angie is helped in the ambulance. Her prayers have finally been answered. She is now on her way home.

DETECTIVE SANTOS

The woman who shot her boyfriend, is named Angie Ann Kelson. She also went by the name of Angel. Marsha Ann Kelson. She was born in North Carolina, February 20th, 1980.

Her Father is an Electrical Engineer. Her Mother works as a clerk, for a Bankruptcy lawyer. She has one other sibling. A sister that is a sophomore at North Carolina University.

Detective Santos derived Troy's Journal in the loft occupied by Troy and Angie. After the incident, a cleaning woman, who worked for the building, and lived in the same building gave it to Detective Santos.

She looked at him, tears in her eyes. She said "God told me to give this to you. Not the other officers, but you. So, hear it is. Please, I beg you please, do not let this happen to another child."

Detective Santos casually looked around the hallway. Even though it was taped off, it was the same activity as always in Los Angeles. Especially after a murder-suicide. Loud talk, and a lot of chest pounding. In other words, guilty consciences. Some residence, the unemployed, the late-night coffee and pizza eaters; said she *volunteered* for this lifestyle. This is what they heard in the courtyard. This perked the ears of Detective Santos. He calmly listened to the insults, from people who didn't even know her. Late night dope fiends, and computer freaks. What a **MESS** this building is, thinks Santos.

"She was a freak, a drug addict. She lived an impure life and must have enjoyed the bondage. She was just another white girl looking for fame and fortune in Los Angeles." Others proclaimed, "she asked for it, she's an alcoholic, and drug addict. It's such a shame. Bless her little heart."

Detective Santos knows the history of Los Angeles and hate. What some young people are taught from Capricorn South. Now all over the internet. Date sites, porn sites, political and chat sites opening every day. Detective Santos was told by the LAPD that Troy had a habit of watching a website called *Orgish*. It's a fishing site, proclaiming the IRAQ side of the war. Troy distributed the website information to people and residence throughout Los Angeles. He did this by internet marketing corporations. The people of IRAQ. Not the case. It's a *Terrorist* web site, showing murder, be-headings and propaganda. *This site is the biggest in Major Cities across America in 2005.*

One residence told Santos, "Los Angeles was created as a slave labor camp, for minorities. The peoples South the border. Desperate and hungry. They came to this country bare foot and bleeding They would do anything for money. That is why the border is never sealed. So rich people can make money from us. In the year 2005, much has not changed. The people of Capricorn South will have their revenge."

These nutcases are not any different that the cults that run around South Orange County. Thinks Santos. Especially is Dana Point. Santos takes his notes as the deranged hater speaks on.

"The cartel was eradicated so that local and state governments, can manipulate organized crime. When our people get arrested it is your fault, not us. You hired us."

Detective Santos notes a new problem. He gathers his thoughts then writes in his Italian moleskin. It's not like 1994. Drugs came through, women get kidnapped, arrest are made, Prisons are filled. In 2005, enemies of California are utilizing high grade weapons from Southeast Russia, North Korea and South America. In short, we have become docile. The war on crime is failing, the war against terrorism is failing. Santos knows Southeast Russia is the main threats, connected to Hegang. Our government must get involved. Just like in Oregon 1994. What happened? I'll tell you what happened. President Clinton, like Ronald kicked Holy Ass. They destroy these organizations before growing out of control. It is the lives of our children, women and future families at stake. The goals of our enemies are clear. Disable Americans, through drone and satellite technologies. Make sure they can't work. Make sure no one joins the military. Fear tactics are being utilized throughout downtown Los Angeles. People are recruited for a salary, car and other luxuries.

These next writings are from Troy. Some of the highlights brought attention to Santos. According to the writings. America will fall to the Army of Darkness. He mentioned Henry Faustino and the alliances he created in North Korea. Troy wrote that North Korea has access to all mainframe military intelligence. Cuba has agreed to stockpile nuclear missiles, and South America will soon be stockpiled from China. An army is being built, to target members and family of military and law enforcement. Troy writes, China will destroy Peru and their vegetation. Then show technology to replenish their soil. Gaining favor from the people. A Red-Army will erupt in Peru. Missiles pointed at the US. This will spawn the New World Order, and Rise of the Anti-Christ. Henry's goal, my father was to poison the American Farmlands. "Keeping America Sick is our goal. Plain and simple." Target Jews & Christians on the streets of major cities throughout America. Take over rental apartments in Urban Communities. Hack computers wallets, creating financial hardship. Create abnormal levels of stresses through military technology. Causing alcohol, or drug use. This will be done by fear tactics, such as gang stalking, propogandist, internet theory, turning out perverts, alcoholics and drug addicts to law enforcement. According to Henry, private security will rule and destroy American Culture.

Troy also wrote that slavery is the main goal of the organization. Communism is our god.

He claimed, if our people can make slaves of women in the United States, this will proclaim the end of the Western world. He wrote. "What kind of civilization would let their woman, daughters and mothers become slaves? Being kidnapped or raped. We have proven this through abnormal computer technology and brainwashing. Physical slavery will prove America no longer exits. That Satan is the one and only true god."

There is more, much more to this Demonic Diary. Santos will no doubt, read it, write his report, then call his connection at Federal Bureau of Investigation.

Detective Santos sits next to the bed of the victim, Angie He is reading his Bible. He reads a passage from the book of Romans. He reads it soft toned.

"And do this understanding the present time. The hour has come for you to wake up from your slumber, because our salvation is nearer now than we first believed. The night is nearly over; the day is almost here. So, let us put aside the deeds of darkness and put on our armor of light."

Angie wakes, yaws, then stretches her upper torso area. At first, her eyesight is blurry, mouth dry. She speaks slurred.

"Who are you?"

"I am Detective Santos. Member of the Tustin Police Department."

"I didn't kill him. I was defending myself. I should not be here. I did nothing wrong."

"Then who killed him, Angie."

She looks at the Detective, then smirks.

"I don't' know. But I know, it wasn't me. I saw things in that loft. Many thing."

Detective Santos, calmly and quietly, moves a breakfast tray in front of Marsha. He adjusts the bed, tucking her head neatly.

Marsha cannot help to notice the Detective handsome looks. His Hugo Boss Suit, polished shoes, groomed hair, clean skin, and perfect large hands. She is his type of man.

"I took the liberty of ordering everything on the menu. The food came from 'The Pantry.'"

"Thank you, it's my favorite."

"We know." Says Santos.

In front of Angie lies 4 plates of food. They are comprised of French Toast, Spanish Omelet, Home Fries, Two Chocolate Chip Pancakes, and sliced fruit.

Angie immediately shoves the pancakes in her mouth. No butter so jam or syrup. Saliva drips on her hand. She looks frail and weak. As Santos watches her devour the buffet, he can't help to think about the long-term psychological damage.

"Mind If I help?"

"No, thank you sir. You are truly kind."

Detective Santos cuts a piece of cased sausage then warps it around a piece of buttered French Toast. He dips the bite into maple syrup, then feeds Angie. She does not say no. She likes him. Her eyes tear with peace and joy.

"That is so good. Fantastic, I'm in paradise." says Angie. I should of shot Troy two years ago.

This is exactly what Detective Santos wanted to hear. What Angie doesn't know, there is a camera in the room, a witness detective behind the curtain, and tape recorder.

"I haven't tasted anything this good. I have not tasted *anything* for a long time." She continues the buffet, slurps down apple juice, then burps.

"Oh gosh, excuse me." Angie says blushing.

"Slow down, eat slow and enjoy. Your body, your nerves, your digestive system, has been shocked. You have poison running through your body."

"Where are my parents?" asks Angie. She starts to get agitated. Detective Santos knows she and her family history. After all, they are the reason she moved to Los Angeles. He also knows her medical history. She suffers from spinal trauma from a car wreck is North Carolina. It was after her prom. Boyfriend drunk, driving home from the dance.

"Your parents haven't been contacted. Your 25 years old, an adult. You have a right to make your own decisions. Aren't you Angie?"

Angie's face turns bright red.

Detective Santos feeds her a Chocolate Chip Pancake wrapped in sausage, laced with Spanish Eggs.

"I made some bad decisions. Didn't I?" Says Angie

"Yes, you did. We all make mistakes. Your mistakes are not the problem. The problem is your affiliations. Your mistakes were planned."

Angie almost coughs up your food.

"The past three years, you've been associated with bad people. People on a State and Federal watch list. Due to these facts, the District Attorney has an *interest* in you."

Angie gulps, then asks for the apple juice.

"It's not my fault." Angie exclaims. "Mmmm, can I have some of that peach pie?"

"Sure." Santos hands her the pie.

"Angie, we know you're not a bad person. However, some mistakes require accountability under California Law. Likes acts of Malice and Grievous Bodily Harm. Credit card fraud? I have a few questions about Troy. Can you help me fill in the blanks? Explain, how you got to this point in your life?" Angie looks as if she may vomit.

For the next two hours Angie is more than helpful. She tells Santos how they met, what he promised her. The names of people he introduced her too. She told him about a group of people that hate the United State Military, the Police, Sheriffs, and how they proclaim revenge on Gods' church.

She told him about a guy in the building named Brian. Some guy used to talk about him. A big man. He was older and from South America. But he didn't speak Spanish. At least not in front of her. Spanish or any other language. He spoke English just like us. He also had no accent, which was odd.

He talked about his Father and relatives. How they were innocently murdered from the CIA. It was during operations in El Salvador and Nicaragua. He said that this Brian guy was sent to Los Angeles to fuck things up for them. How, he's an undercover informant, and his whole family must be Punished. That Brian's father killed his father.

Detective Santos showed Angie a picture of Brian. She did recognize him. She did say that he is attractive. They meet in the elevator. She said, for some reason, these people attack others who look like Brian. She would walk the streets of Downtown with this individual, and he would point at American people. Men and woman who were attractive. He would call them mother fuckers, making fun of them. Film them with his smartphone. Then later, send their pictures to what he called his police-detective network. She also told Santos he was a leader of Police Agency, that contracts with the United State Government. He carried a CIA walled at detective badge. The man was so scary she said. If you didn't agree with him, on anything, he would strong hold you, get in your face, scream at you. Even hurt you physically. The man said this Brian guy, is under investigations, and screws hookers. Also is a coke head and alcoholic. He said he wants to feed on him, destroy him, then resurrect him a new man. Have him work for his agency.

Detective Santos asked her to remember the man's name. She trembles, as she takes another sip of the apple juice. Detective Santos feeds her another piece of French Toast, she quickly eats, then gasp for air.

"The only name I can think of, is Henry. That is all I can remember. Henry, yes that's it. Henry Faustino. is all I know. Troy told me is a leader of a new movement. A new church. Yes, Henry was his name. That's it."

Detective Santos face turns white. He turns off his recorder, then wipes Angie's face with a cool towel.

He smiles, then thanks her. He told her that he would relay the information to the District Attorney and inform him of all the torture and atrocities that she undergone. He also informed her that she will be safe, no one will hurt her.

Angie asked if she could help with any other matter. He said he has a plan, and she'll be involved later. Now he wants her to rest for a few days. He informed her to drink a lot of water and eat hearty. He said she'll go to detox, then psychiatric care. One from the State of California.

Angie asked who these people are, and why are they in the city?

Detective Santos replied, "They've always been here. They are everywhere, and we will destroy them. Just like we've done many times before. This year 2005, over 500,000 people have moved Downtown District. A percentage of these people are hellbent on chaos, mayhem, propaganda, and financial destruction. They are not human in their soul, their thoughts. These people worship the beast. When you slept, I watched you. I saw your suffering. I also saw your demon standing next you. I am leaving this Bible for you. There is highlighted scripture, from different chapters."

Angie begins to cry.

"Try to rest and dream well. We will get them Angie. This is my word. It is also God's word…"

Chapter 12

Brian sits at his work desk. So far, he's done well. The boss likes him, his customers like him, and his employees like him. Brian has already been assigned a team. He will review his teams' financial models and recommend financial planning.

He takes a sip of his tea, then wipes the lens of his glasses. His designer Dutch Cell Phone. It was a gift from Jenna. Brian admits the phone is awesome. She wrote him a letter explain it encumbers military technology. It looks awesome too. Brian has never seen anything like it. His cell phone rings.

"This is Brian. Who is this?" On the other line is Jenna. Panic strikes Brian.

"Oh, sorry, I didn't recognize your voice." Brian drops his pen to the floor. His hand begins shaking.

Jenna sits at home in Washington. It's raining outside. She wears flannel pajamas, holding a stuffed animal. Her hair is up, and she just got out of long bath. The stuff animal was won by Brian at the Spring Fair.

The stuffed animal reads, "I love you."

"Brian, why the hell haven't you called?"

"Call, I did call. You weren't—"

Jenna interrupts, "Bullshit. You are using the new smartphone I got you?"

"Yes," says Brian. "And thank you by the way."

"By the way? By the way? Brian, what is wrong with you? Is it drugs?"

"Oh god, here we go again—" Jenna interrupts.

"I swear, if it is, I'll tell your father."

"Jenna, I'm at work now. Can't we talk about this later? I'll call you at home. It's been remarkably busy, and I received a promotion also. I have my own team now. Pretty impressive, isn't it?" There is silence on the other end for a moment.

"Yes, it is Brian. Your father and mother have been asking also. How does that make me look?"

"Please, not now, Jenna. I'll call you later."

"You're cheating on me. I know it," says Jenna.

"Jenna?"

"What!" She exclaims.

"Nothing."

"Nothing! This is all you can say too me. I love you Brian, and Nothing!" Brian thinks, yes, it happens….

Brian hands begin to shake. He wants to yell but can't. He feels like telling her about the hot, sexy, sticky woman he's been with. The ones that go to Trance and House Clubs. Take Ecstasy Pills then wanting him for sex.

Brian thoughts go rabid for a moment. He thinks about the women, then chuckles softly.

"Brian are you there? Brian? Brian? Fuckin' Hello!!"

"Honey, I'm sorry. I am busy working. I'll call you later."

"You better call me later, OK?" Brian doesn't answer.

"OK?"

"I knew this whole Los Angeles move was a mistake. You better move back to Washington."

"You're overreacting Jenna. You know I love you. Things are just, crazy right now."

"Crazy enough for you not to call. Brian, I know you. something is wrong. Definitely."

"Nothing is wrong. I will call you later. Promise," says Brian.

"No, something is wrong. Then call your darn parents. And you will tell me now. I had a dream about you last night, Brian. A horrible dream. I called you. You didn't answer."

"Who were you with?" Jenna's voice now trebles over the phone.

"I'm with nobody; did you ever think, I'm tired?"

"Tired of me?"

"Nope."

"You sure about that? You sound different."

"You didn't call my mother on her birthday."

There is a reason for that, dumbass. Thinks Brian.

Brian pauses. He is sweating, feeling nervous. The booze from the last night ready to exit him.

"Shit."

"Shit. That is all you can say? Brian. Shit? What's wrong with you?"

Brian's work phone rings. *Thank God,* he thinks to himself. *It's the front desk.*

"Brian, call, line four," says receptionist over the phone.

"I must go, Jenna. I promise. I will call you later… now bye."

"Promise? I love you, Brian. Call me when your home. I want to see all the—"

Brian quickly hangs up the phone.

"Bye." He says proudly as he turns his chair, starring over the city.

He hangs up the phone. Brian is upset. Not from Jenna, but himself. *Why should he punish himself? If he doesn't want her, be a man about the situation. Tell her the truth. What would Jack think, of his number one son?*

Brian worries if he lost a deal. A deal worth a large sum of money. Brian says to himself, '*All I wanted was a few months of solitude. Is this so bad? All she ever does is yap, yap, yap. Drives me up the friggin' wall.*'

Brian's phone rings again. He hopes it is not Jenna. If it his, he might break the phone, or even worse.

It is one of his customer from Scotland. He called asking if he received the case of Highlander Scotch. Thank God for the Scotland…

Jenna sits starring at the phone. She clenches the stuffed animal rocking her body forward and back. She fears the worst. She claims she can read Brian's soul. It was confirmed by a woman at a flea market in Brazil. Jenna doesn't understand the theories behind White-Witchcraft. Brazil was their first vacation. That was when Jenna proposed to Brian.

Other women are in his presence. The wrong type of women. Women that don't share her same values. Women who are opportunistic. Women who do not believe in God. She knew Brian moving was a bad idea. Jenna will fight for Brian. Maybe even kill if necessary. She learned from her mother how to get a man. Not only marry but keep. No woman will stand in the way of *them*. Or her dreams. Dreams of a family with political connections. Dreams of a family with power and influence. Most of all, the dreams of a family with money. She knows their children will be beautiful. She knows her children will grow to be political leaders. In no way, will she let some cheap slut destroy her dreams. Jenna takes the picture of her and Brian in Brazil. She lays on her bed and holds it against her chest. She begins praying for Brian.

Brian turns his chair and looks over the skyline. He has a large stack of manila folders in his lap. The more work he does, the more comes in. It is a never-ending battle. However, it is a battle worth winning. The more money he makes, the more freedom he will have. Move to Spain, buy a 48-foot yacht. Kick back for a while. Then maybe get married. The stress starts to settle in when he thinks about Jenna and his parents.

It is probably the lack of sleep, and the sounds that keep him awake at night. Especially the sounds that hail from the upstairs loft. Neighbors he has never meet. He has knocked on the door, however; they never answer.

Brian has dark circles below the eyes, and his forehead shows crinkles that were not there before.

He is considering taking Robert up for that lunchtime Martini. Maybe that will relax him during the day. Help him sleep when he arrives home. Tonight, Martinis and Lasagna sound good. Brian thinks about Sondra, dipping her black painted toes in the sauce, then he licks it off, tasting her vagina with the scent of red wine on his tongue.

Robert tells him it's good for business. Not Sondra, the Martini at lunch. It's also a good way to catch a few investors. Ones that are high. "Those are the best customers Robert says." They are easier to convince and more likely to sign at the bar. Robert has closed a few this way. Maybe Robert is right, in some ways. After all, I am still new in Los Angeles. Hollywood signed deals at drug parties and restaurants. Why not swindle a few dollars at the local watering hole. *I must say focused,* Brian thinks. Money is his rite of protection. The money will create lies while negotiating reasons for staying away from Jenna. Most of all, money will give me freedom…

Brian's co-worker enters his office. She doesn't knock. She doesn't have to knock. It is Lisa. *Holy crapshoot* thinks Brian. *Lisa, oh, man, it is Lisa. Robert told me about this one. Man, she is hot. What a fox. She looks like Jane Seymour with highlighted hair today. The way she looked during the fried chicken scene. The movie 'Somewhere in Time.' Outstanding woman.*

Lisa is 5'9", 130 pounds, natural C breasts, epic thighs, piercing brown-green eyes; with the perfect Los Angeles natural suntan. Her skin is godly. Women in New York would spit with jealously. She is stunningly gorgeous. Every guilt about Jenna, now lost, forever…

She was wearing sports Hugo Boss suit, with a red-wine Jil Sander blouse. Brian's impressed by her immediately. She is smooth with her body language, seductive, and confident. The tone of her voice is hypnotic and sexy. Her tone like a French erotic film. Brian relaxes when she speaks. Best of all, her eyes. When she looked at him, he got nervous. The kind of nervous during a first French Kiss.

Brian is in obvious trouble. The quest for overrated pleasures is knocking at his door. Maybe it's the booze, the power of responsibility, the smoggy air. The new $350,000 salary, or maybe, it's the unknown. Change is sexy to Brian. All Brian cares about is sexy and freedom. At least for now. After all, isn't this why Brian moved to Los Angeles in the first place?

Lisa's from Virginia. Her family raises quarter and thoroughbred horses. They have won the Kentucky Derby and are respected politically. The amount of money they make from racing is astronomical. She owns two horses herself. She races one of them at Santa Anita. She drives a Mercedes S-CLASS and for fun; a 1994 Alfa Romeo Spyder. Black with tobacco brown interior. Lisa wanted Brian since the first time she saw him. She is the one that transferred the call, getting Brian off the phone. She already knows who Jenna is. Lisa claims her father is political and they share the same traditions. Their children will be gorgeous, she thinks. She knows all about Jenna and she doesn't like her. Lisa knows what she must do to get rid of Jenna. Her future will be with Brian. No-one will get out of her way, no one will stop Lisa, ever…

"Hi, you are, Brian, right? We meet at orientation."

Everyman that's dated this woman, begs her like a dog. Opens every door for her. Gives her money, buys her jewelry, spends $1,0000 at shitty restaurants, places a love letter and a single rose on her car window. Begs for her love. Then, she dumped them all. Not this time, she's seen his success, and knows he'll make over 5 million a year soon. She's wants to trap him. Her mother and grandmother taught her how.

"Mind if I sit down?" asks Lisa.

"No, not at all, come in. this is great, god knows, I could use the boost."

Brian feels blood rush through his face. What a stupid thing to say, thinks Brian. Lisa went downstairs to Starbucks. She bought him an Irish Cold Brew. She bought your typical girlie sweet coffee drink with a lot of sugar and whipped cream.

She is Jaclyn Smith hot. I mean, 1972 Jaclyn Smith hot. Lisa is incredible. I wonder what my father would think of her. Screw my arranged marriage. Shit, I'd sell my soul to make love to her. Not only is Brian's face flushed; he feels wet under his armpits, and his hands are clammy. A fuckin' disaster. She caught me off guard. Now I must take her out. Show her my good side.

Lisa sits down in front of Brian. She sits at a 40-degree angle, displaying her perfect silhouette. Her perfectly formed, inviting hips, her hands, French manicure. On the left side of her breast is barely showing. Brian sees the outline of her nipple. It is extremely exciting.

"Thank you, Lisa, this is nice."

Lisa is bright and cheerful. She exuberates success. Brian likes this. He will eventually know *everything* about her.

"So, tell me, Brian. How do you like LA so far?"

"Haven't had time to enjoy it yet. Still putting together furniture; boxes are everywhere."

"I know, moving is the pits. I hate it," says Lisa.

"And what is up with cable and internet connections in this city. The wait is six to eight weeks?"

Lisa laughs aloud.

"And saying hello to someone in the elevator. Forget about it. They treat you like you're a disease."

"Brain, welcome to Los Angeles. I mean the people here, the ones visiting, with dreams of stardom. They are the biggest a-holes. I have the same kind of people in my building. It makes me ill." Says Brian.

"Yeah, and the cable, good luck with that one. I waited almost three months. Then when connected, nothing works. Wait until your hacked and get trojan a few times," says Lisa.

Brian laughs. He's feeling more comfortable now.

"Brian. You're from Washington, right?"

"Yes, and you're from Virginia? Nice place. The American tradition is still there. It's also very, beautiful; historic."

Lisa smiles. She adjusts herself in the chair and checks her posture.

"So, you live alone?" asks Lisa.

"Sure do."

"Girlfriend?"

"No, not yet?"

Brian blushes as she looks at her. She knows he's lying. She doesn't care. She likes Brian. She's been eavesdropping on his phone calls. Lisa is more than impressed. She has informed *them* that Brian will be a good business partner.

"That's good to know," says Lisa. "Because I've been meaning to ask." Lisa pauses for a moment, blushes, and bats her eye lids. "A few girlfriends of mine are having a night out. Have you heard of the Golden Gopher, this Friday, what you say?"

"Golden Gopher?" Brian is stunned. It is his favorite place. He pretends he's never been there.

"It's such a cool bar. You will love it. Many attractive women go there. They're not pretentious either."

Brian readjusts his seating and posture. Not there, thinks Brian. Just Horney…

"They have this cool jukebox. Also, Halloween is almost here. The place throws an awesome party. Think about this Brian. Women, in Swiss Nurse costumes, French Maids, Bat woman."

Brian looks her over with a blank expression. How in the hell does she know my taste. He already knows how awesome that bar is.

"Last year they showed '*Dawn of the Dead*.' It was awesome. Lisa left out the sexy costume contest,"

"Excuse me, Dawn of the What?" Brian is not really a fan of horror movies.

"Excuse me, am I rattling on about nothing? I'm sorry. I know your new in LA and—"

"No, it's OK. I had a tough sale a few minutes ago. I'm still shaken," says Brian.

Lisa goes on about the Golden Gopher for a few minutes. Brian tries keeping pace and understanding what she is saying. *A lot of LA lingo going on here,* he thinks.

Brian smiles, nods, then drinks his coffee. It's delicious. Lisa talks about how *hot* her girlfriends are. She talks about all the excellent trance and house clubs.

Lisa losses Brian's attention. His mind is fixated on Sondra now. Sondra and her lips. Sondra and her lush lips. Sondra how beautiful she is. Best of all, Sondra doesn't talk too much. I mean Lisa, for heaven sakes. She sounds like a Czechoslovakian vacuum cleaner.

Lisa finally finishes speaking about herself and her friends. Brian wonders if he has lost a few phone calls. He probably has. Brian wonders if she is testing his threshold.

"I'm hyperactive, I know I am, I can't help it," says Lisa.

"No, it's OK. You're not hyper. I'm just a bit busy today. I've been assigned a new team."

"I know, congratulations, that's what I was talking about. Let's hang out."

Brian's phone rings.

He thinks, *Thank goodness*. He has had enough of Lisa for now. He didn't think like this with Sondra. He never lost interest in Sondra for a second. Brian tells the front desk to send the call through.

"I am sorry, Lisa. This is important call. I need privacy."

"Oh, yeah, of course."

Lisa stands up slowly, then walks over to the side of Brian's chair. She leans over and takes his business card. As she leans over Brian smells perfume. Not ordinary perfume, but French. French custom made, and expensive.

Lisa walks away speaking softly,

"I'll call you later. Don't forget, let's celebrate."

Lisa exits the office door, stinks her long sexy fingers through then waves. Brian is beet red. He feels kind of sick for some reason.

Brian's phone rings. It is Sondra. Brian is confounded. He has not stop thinking about her since their spaghetti dinner. Wow, what a dinner that was. She is smart too. Brian thinks smarter than him. This is main reason he wants her. He won't tell her he's been thinking of her non-stop. He will wait for later. Timing is everything says his father. Sondra tells him, she felt him thinking of her. Brian is floored. She then asked him out for a date.

"Let me get a pen and paper," says Brian.

"OK, ready. No, I've been there once before. No, don't worry."

Brian waits while he impatiently listens to the call.

"At eight it is. Perfect. See you then, Bye."

Brian hangs up the phone and takes another drink of his coffee. It doesn't taste good to him. Not anymore. In fact, he almost vomits. He hates cold coffee. Brian throws the Styrofoam cup in the trash.

He moves his chair to the window and stares out over the city. Brian cell phone rings again. This time, he will not answer...

It's 8:00 pm. Brian picked up Sondra from her apartment. As soon as Sondra opened the door, Brian was shocked by her beauty. She wears a Dolce Gabbana, pull over cocktail dress, with black Prada flats, rose colored lip stick, deep eyeliner and teardrop diamond necklace. To accent the dress, she wears a black knit sweater over the shoulders. Sophisticated and sexy. She looks like the beautiful actress' Violante Placido.' Absolutely stunning. Only difference between Sondra and Violante is the hair style…

Sondra thought its best they walk. This way, she can introduce Brian to the city, Discuss its history, trend spots, and architecture. They walk down ninth street. Sondra wants to show him the Golden Gopher.

Brian laughs as she talks about the time she threw up in the bathroom. She wasn't feeling well that night. She ate a stale burrito at lunch. Her friends dragged her out, to meet someone from Mexico. He was visiting from Baja California. His name is Hector. Her Mother has been trying to arrange their marriage for years. Sondra is an independent woman. She wants no relation with this man called Hector. Brian also laughed at the pictures sent her cellphone. It is cool though. A 1976 Ford Pinto Wagon. 427, custom exhaust and suspension. Custom wheels, black paint. 4 speed manual transmission. Original Ford Mustang Pony Interior. Pretty sweet, thinks Brian.

Later that evening, after four shots of tequila, and three margaritas, she vomited all over the bouncer shoes, he was trying to pick-up on her. Then later, Hectors face, and chest. It was a disaster. Sondra told him, they went out on one date. Dinner, dancing and bar. She just doesn't want him. Her mother drives her fuckin crazy everyday about Hector. Brian now, is completely floored by this incredible woman.

She tells Brian she likes to drink. It's fun with the right people and good food. Food is the most important part. She just doesn't like how booze makes her feel in the morning. Brian feels the same way. It was last Halloween. Hector still calls her every week. She hints to Brian that maybe he can defer his interest. They walk arm and arm. Brian makes sure she doesn't walk street side. Brian is already comfortable. He hopes she is too.

Homeless people continuously ask Brian for money. Brian keeps handing it out. Sondra tells Brian if he keeps handing over money. He will be marked for life. The homeless people in this city, set up networks. They usually live in a one-bedroom apartment with six people. They all have daily duties. One will stay home and cook. Two will be on the corners. One will get pharmaceutical drugs from a doctor. The others will buy illegal drugs off the street. Not locally, but far away. They usually take the metro.

Sondra asks for his wallet, telling him enough. Brian responds by saying, "You never know if the homeless are angels in disguise."

Sondra smiles, then clenches him by his arm. Brian walks on the street side of the sidewalk. This way she is safe from traffic.

Sondra discusses the architecture and historic relevance. She discusses the Westin Bonaventure, and Kennedys acceptance speech for the Democratic Nominee. She also claims the room number he and his mistress slept in. Brian is fascinated by Sondra. Every word she speaks, every step she takes excites him. Sondra refers to some of the building as being sexy, and how the light is romantic, erotic and well placed. She also likes Mexico City and their architecture tour also.

After dinner, Sondra will suggest having dessert at Louie Bottega. Then go to Seven Grand for a nightcap. As for dinner, Sondra chooses Roy's Restaurant on Figueroa Street. She feels it's a comfortable atmosphere. Not overbearing. and not to pretentious, or "stuck-up." The drinks are good, and the staff wears Hawaii Shirts. Sondra thinks it's ironic. Due to the fact. One Hawaiian shirt started the LA riots.

If the date goes well, Next time, they will visit Fleming's. They will enjoy life, and have drinks, steaks. then the Metro, then Martinis, then dancing at Olympic and Grand. 'Timo Mass' and 'John Digweed' are appearing in a few weeks. Sondra likes dancing. She believes men who aren't afraid to dance are more passionate about life.

They wait at the bar before they are seated. Brian tells a funny joke, and Sondra carries on about her overwhelming family. Also, how they have tried to throw her in an arranged marriage. Brian cannot wait until dinner. He has not eaten all day, anticipating the meeting. He's in the same situation she is. Brian and Sondra told jokes over the phone about food and sex. How she's a pig at times. She enjoys staying home sometimes. Ordering Chinese take-out. Watching movies until sunrise. Then "hitting the drive through at Farmer Boys." Now, finally, they break bread together. Best of all, they are both Catholic.

Sondra nervously unfolds her napkin, then shuffles her silverware throughout the setting. Brian is impressed. He's portraying his best James Dean, pulled out her chair, and escorted her to the washroom. Trying to play it cool. He likes Sondra. He wants her badly. However, he doesn't want to make it obvious. Appear anxious or desperate.

Brian looks over the menu. He's never tried Hawaiian Fusion. His taste, a bit more conventional. Dishes like Corned Beef, with red potatoes, glazed carrots, cabbage and rye bread. Plum Jam, and butter of course. He likes the names of the drinks and dinners. He laughs, then references some of his favorite restaurants in Washington. Sondra tells him about the restaurants in Mexico City and Guadalajara. She also tells him about her favorite boutique stores in Mexico City, and how her father owns a shopping center.

"So, Brian, tell me about yourself. Your mom, dad, brother's sister, your life. I want to know everything."

Brian's facial expression changes. Sondra found his weakness. Everyone is Los Angeles is running from something.

"You don't wanna know everything. Trust me. It's not all roses, boosters, dedications, and bake sales." Sondra giggles.

"You're from Chicago, right? Oops, I mean DC, Washington." Sondra burps then apologizes. She begins to feel the effects of the tequila from the bar.

"Cheers," says Brian. "A server, 24 years of age. Blond hair, 5'7", Hawaiian shirt, hair up, black apron, delivers a tray of two dinks. Here you go, two double shots of tequila. Anything else?" she asks.

"Keep 'em coming," says Brian.

"Pardon me," asks the waitress.

"Immediately."

The server leaves the table smirking.

"Check it out," says Brian. "I mean, what's with the attitude in this city? In DC, it's sin not to drink. Politicians get loaded. It's, cool. In this city, people stare at you. Seriously, Sondra. Look at the guy over there, with his tight jeans, oversized running shoes, hoodie and sharp features. See him? He stares at us, flashing his camera, which appears, towards our direction."

Sondra laughs aloud. So loud, other patrons look at her.

"You're ambitious tonight?" says Sondra. "I like it."

"If he doesn't stop, I'll break his arm later."

Strangely enough, the man looking at him, stands up then exits his table. He never returns.

"We're on a mission from God," says Brian. "Seriously, just having a good time. I like having a good time with you, Sondra. You are a good woman, and fun. And that's important. Fun."

"Do tell Brian, do tell. So, what do we toast to?" asks Sondra.

"How about Rome?" says Brian.

"I was there once." Sondra continues laughing.

"I invented the phrase, 'When in Rome.' I am serious, Sondra, I like you. Let us drink."

"Salud."

"Salad, or salad? Did you say salad?"

"Brian, stop it. People are looking. Shit, I can't stop laughing,"

"You sound like a drunk Hungarian. Salud. I want eat Salud."

"Back to Rome. When in Rome, Sondra cheers."

"Salud."

"This woman is nuts. She cheers for salad. I just don't understand. Hey everyone, we're cheering for salad."

Restaurant patrons look at Brian, smirking.

"Brian, stop it. I can't handle this." Sondra does her best to regain her composure. She changes the subject.

"So, tell me about Washington. Your family."

"To answer your question. I moved here from Washington." Sondra laughs aloud. A patron looks at her. She knows this. Brian's being a smart-ass.

"Screwed up the place," says Brian.

"For this new job of yours?" asks Sondra.

Brian regains his composure. The thought of home sobers him up for the moment.

"It's a bit more complicated than that?" says Brian.

"Please, tell me."

"I really don't feel comfortable telling you, at this stage, of our relationship." Brian shifts his eyes throughout the room.

"Relationship?" Replies Sondra.

"Well, I'm working on it." Brian imitates his bet Bogart. Brian notices a few good-looking woman in the Restaurant.

"Brian, look at me."

"Yes?"

"I like you. I would not be here if I didn't. after our last meeting, I think we can get past the bullshit. I don't judge people. I want to know you better. This is why we ask questions. Right?"

Brian relaxes a bit, sighs, then nervously moves his glass around the table. Sondra reaches over and takes Brian's hand. He looks at Sondra in her eyes. She has a light and tenderness her that he has never experienced.

"I have a ghost that follows me around also Brian." The server brings two more double shots of Tequila.

"First we both need to drink this," says Brian.

"Cheers."

"Salud," says Sondra.

Brian grins.

"And don't start with the salad stuff again," says Sondra.

Brian and Sondra surprisingly finish in one drink.

"Whoa. That is the good stuff," Sondra says.

"Yes, it is."

"Ready to order?" Ask the waitress.

"Another ten minutes. We're about to have a private chat here, and you interrupted." Says Brian.

Music is turned up louder in the restaurant. The song is 'Mamouna' by Bryan Ferry.' As the track starts, Sondra takes a deep breath. She blushes and smiles. It reminds her of the first time she made love. It was back seat of a Volkswagen Cabrio, facing the ocean in Mazatlán.

"Ohhhh, I really love this song," says Sondra. Brian likes it too. He won't say anything though. He has it on vinyl. He'll wait until he makes love to her.

"OK, I'm listening," says Sondra.

"To what?" Sondra gives him the eye. She has had it with the games for now.

"Don't be silly, Brian. Your story. Please be serious now."

Brian sighs, then adjust himself in the seat.

"OK, well you see, I come from a powerful family, with money. A very, powerful, family. We date back to the founders of this country. Anything involved with the economic infrastructure, we created. My father works in the state department—"

Sondra quickly adjusts her seating position.

"When I graduated from Georgetown, I wanted to be a teacher, of political science and sociology. My father had other plans. He insisted I work for him. He wanted me to be his assistant in the State Department."

"Doing what?"

"Who knows, who cares."

Sondra is a bit concerned about Brian's statement. She wonders if he is a spoiled brat with too much money.

"He would tell me. Shake some hands, Son. Meet some people. Make a name for yourself. After all, you are the gifted one. You have a calling, you will succeed."

Sondra curiously looks over Brian. Her life has been much more complicated than Brian. Her family has money also, but they killed themselves acquiring it. Sondra was raised to listens to her elders and parents. Especially her father. Now he is gone. The only one left, is her mother. However, her mother, unlike her father, thought for her best interest, not her daughters.

Sondra takes a sip of tequila. Decides to slow the pace of drinking. If they continue, they will crawl out of the restaurant.

"I don't understand, what's so bad about working with your father?"

"The problem is, everything I say, everything I do reflects on him. It's not what goals I want to accomplish. It's the goal he wants for me."

Brian takes another drink of tequila.

"I was always followed," says Brian.

"Maybe you were just paranoid. Aren't there many spooks in Washington?"

"With his power and influence. I mean, shit; the man is head of covert operation for the CIA."

Sondra almost spits up her drink.

"No, firkin way?"

"Ye." Says Brian. I wouldn't lie about this.

"If I went to lunch at the Café Courtyard at work, someone would watch me. On a date, some asshole would follow me. Top that, they wanted me to be in an arranged marriage."

Sondra perks up. She takes a sip of tequila and leans over the table closer to Brian.

"My father would tell me, Son, power marries power, money marries money. Brains marry brains. Presence marries presence. Very, simple, Son. This is all I and your mother ask of you."

"No way. That's kind of scary," says Sondra.

"What a load of crap. Cheers." Brian holds up his glass.

"Salud. And don't start with the salad stuff," says Sondra.

They both drink a sip of tequila. Brian and Sondra are a bit high now.

Just the way it should be, thinks Brian.

Sondra finally drops the big question again.

"So, you have a girlfriend, or engaged?"

"Hell, No! Oops, did I say that loud?"

"Brian, tell me the truth. I once was in love. Once only. It's OK."

"I'd be disappointed if you weren't," replies Brian,

Sondra holds his left-hand showing assurance. Brian sits up changing his bravado.

"There was this girl, her name was Amber. Jenna is the one my parents want me to marry. Amber was hired by my father. He hired her as he used to say, 'protégé.' She was from DC. It was one of his, hey, look at me, she's my not totally white project,' or some bullshit like that. Anyway, she was beautiful, smart, sexy, and totally cool. Her name was Amber."

"You already told me her name."

"Oh, yeah. I did. Sorry." Brian takes another sip of his tequila.

"It was summer. I was broke. My dad convinced me working with him. I really liked the girl; we had a connection. During work, we would text, talk, meet at Starbucks, get a sandwich at the Deli together. It was almost too good."

"Go on," says Sondra.

Brian looks at Sondra and smiles. Sondra looks a tad jealous. He takes her hand.

"Sondra, she's not pretty, as you are. Serious."

"Yeah right, go on."

"I finally summoned enough courage asking her out. One night we, well I, set things up. I even picked a restaurant I thought my father would never know about. So, we're sitting at this hipster, Italian bistro and jazz place. We're having a good time. I look at the other end of the restaurant and see my dad sitting there. Looking at a newspaper. Next to him, sits one of his goons."

"No fuckin' way. What did you say?"

"Holy crap-shoot Sondra. What can you say? Hey, there is my over-bearing dad. Hey, Father, get over here, get high with us. Have a few drinks. It's all good. I mean, holy crap."

Sondra laughs. Brian likes her laughter. It loosens him up.

"I played it off of course. Acted as if they weren't. there. Even though. I was shitting my pants. Sweating from forehead, armpits. It wasn't fun."

Sondra laughs aloud.

"All I remember, was freaking out. My father placed down the paper and began staring at me. Not just looking, concerned. I mean starring, like some psychotic demon from outer space. He was holding the paper, hands shaking. He had a look on his face like he wanted to murder me. I didn't say a word."

"Amber was going on about herself, family, her dreams. All I could do is sweat it out. I never said a word to her. Played it off. Acted if he wasn't there. I will never forgive him for that. It was that threatening, hateful look that creeped me out the most. A look will never leave me."

Sondra gazes off for a moment. She tries imagining what that must be like. She also tries imagining what powerful and wealthy families are like from Washington. All she knows is she is from money also. Rich, wealthy, Mexican money from Guadalajara. She and Brian are both wanted for an arranged marriage. She likes this. Two rebels with a cause. Sondra feels it's romantic.

Sondra returns from her gaze. The sounds of the music in the restaurant bring her back to reality.

"I have an idea," says Sondra. "Let us try the margaritas."

Sondra gestures to the waitress. Brian thought she would run, and she didn't. He's not done with the story yet. Maybe the booze will comfort her more. She may feel a bit more involved with my cause.

Brian wants Sondra. He wants her bad. Brian takes a steak knife and presses it against his index finger. He checks if he is alive. He wants to make sure he doesn't end up a lost lover, in George Orwell's novel.

Sondra sees that Brian's not done with his story. She also sees he loved her. He really loved her. Much more than he will tell.

Sondra digs into Brian deeper. She flirts, smiles, compliments him. Does everything she was taught by her mother. Keeping him interested. She tries the obvious approach.

"Brian, you said you weren't done with your story. I want to hear it. All. Even the wet, juicy parts."

"Darn you woman. You say all the right things. Oh, yeah, well, anyway, by the time the check arrived, I looked down, signed it, looked up again, he was gone."

Brian takes a deep breath, then sighs, "It was way fucked up."

"What happened next?"

"First margaritas for us." Brian waves down the waitress. Brian re-adjusts his bravado again. This time he tries his best Steve McQueen.

Brian signals the waiter for two drinks. He orders Sondra a Blue Curacao Margarita and Markers Mark for him.

Sondra looks at him. She nudges his foot under the table.

"Don't drink too much Brian. I'll have to carry you home."

Not a bad idea, thinks Brian. Woe is me. Woe is me.

"Are you sure you wanna hear this? It's brutal, at least on my account."

"Brian, we are here now, tonight. Everything is about us. I want to know all there is to know about you. Like is said earlier. I do not judge."

"I'm sure you will when I'm done," says Brian.

"Tell, me, tell me, tell me."

"I don't know. You might freak on me," says Brian.

"Brian, it's OK. Trust and respect are most important, right?"

Sondra is tapping her foot under the table.

"OK, first another shot," says Brian.

"I think we are done with the drinks," says Sondra.

Brian remembers what his father taught him.

"OK, yes, you are right. I respect that."

"Good says Sondra."

"Totally cool. I must tell you this, awesome. And you are totally beautiful. Oh my god. I said totally. Next, I'll be calling you dude or bro. Los Angeles is already rubbing off on me."

Brian wants her in the bathroom now. He thinks about banging her atop of toilet. He wonders if she would go for it. He regains consciousness then sighs with relief. This is not 'Carlito's Way' he thinks.

"OK, next. What happened?" Sondra perks up. She looks like she's about to share a deadly secret with her best girlfriend.

"OK, here it goes. At work, I tried to mellow things down. We texted back and forth. She asked me out in all. Anyway, I replied saying I wasn't feeling well. I wasn't lying. I started feeling sick every day. Due to stress. I couldn't hold down food. I noticed people in the office kept staring at me, watching what I was doing. Friday comes around, she's not at work. I ask her friend if she was sick. No one knew anything. I couldn't get an answer from anyone. For about a week, this went on, nothing, not a text. Then about midnight, 4 days later. I figured I will text her one last time. I thought, if this doesn't work, nothing will."

"What did you say?"

"I said, 'I love and miss you.'" There is silence for about five seconds. Sondra's eyes begin tearing. So are Brian's.

"I finally get a response back about four hours later. She texted, 'I KNOW.' In capital letters."

"I know. Those are two words that will fuck up a young man's life, Sondra." Brian takes a deep breath, then sips his whisky.

"Anyway, rumors circulated later, she moved out of state, met someone else, got married. All crap in the end. Well, at least for me."

"So, what do you think happened to your love, Amber. In the end?"

"I know what happened. It haunts and never leaves. My father knows. I think about it often. I can tell by this eyes. You see—"

The waitress walks quickly to their table. She asks them to order. She also says the table is on reservation for 9:30 PM.

They order Hawaiian onion rings, and two pineapple burgers. So far, Brian can say it is a perfect date. And she is the perfect woman. I have yet to see…

Sondra returns from her date with Brian. She leans back against her front door smiling. Her date with Brian went well. She decided to turn in early though. She must work tomorrow. She has new shipments arriving from India and its inventory weekend. Brian stood outside her door, kissing her lips, no tongue; gently. He tried to get inside her loft. He tried every trick in the book. Even coffee. Nope. Nothing. Sondra thought he acted cute. Sondra said it was tempting, but no. She wasn't raised that way. They stood outside of Sondra's apartment until one more kiss. As she moved in, she gave him the kiss, holding his face and pressing harder. Hard enough for him to taste her wetness. It was sexy. Lips parted just enough. Like a Vagina ready for entry. A kiss, so sexy, his legs went weak. His head went dizzy. She said goodnight, and that was it.

Sondra turns on the kitchen light and looks over her loft. She thinks with their combined good taste; they can make the perfect home. She slips off her heels then turns on her stereo. She is a bit tipsy. She thinks of Brian, and what song he would like. Most of her she's moist with desire and inspiration. Being inspired is the sexiest thing of all. She shuffles through her CD collection finding 'Just My Imagine, from the Rolling Stones.'

Sondra likes the Four Tops version also. However, too her; the Rolling Stones version is sexier, dirtier, makes her think of love. Best of all, lovemaking.

The track begins, as she trots along the cold concrete floor. Sondra opens the refrigerator, then takes a Budweiser long neck. She drops it on the floor, but this doesn't care. *Fuck it,* she thinks. *I am in love.* I'll clean up later. Kind of like sex. Do it now, clean up later. She thinks, then giggles to herself. She is hot, frantic, almost in heat as she thinks about Brian.

She holds the bottle up to her neck, cheek, then rolls it over her cleavage area. No man has ever excited her the way he does. She lashes her tongue around the cold bottle, then giggles.

'Finally, I have found my man,' she says to herself.

Sondra lays down on her couch, she places her legs up in the air, admiring her legs, calf and feet. They are almost perfect she thinks. She wonders if Brian would approve. She rubs her hands over her hips and looks at the poster of Jimi Hendrix on her wall. The one at the Monterey Pop Festival. The one where he burns his Stratocaster. Making love to his unknown mistress. The one that would worship him for all eternity. The one woman that would never say no.

She will be that woman for Brian. She wants Brian to man handle her. Sondra takes the television controller. *What the heck,* she thinks. *Here he is.* It is the man with the white hat and white beards. The one that will save her soul with nonsense.

She says to herself, *'If Jesus never needed money, why do you?'*
Sondra effortlessly opens another beer. She takes a good long drink. Beer drips from her chin and rolls down her breast. She thinks of the movie, 'Leaving Las Vegas.' Beer won't hurt, but Bourbon may sting. Sting just a bit much.

Sondra rubs the excess lager over her thighs and between her legs. Beer is good for the skin. Especially on the Mexican Gulf. Sun-bathing.

She places her right index finger and rubs the crevice between her legs gently. Her ex-boyfriend did this to her, while kissing.

She used to tell him, "Think of a kitten licking cream."

Sondra is hot and moist. She moves her hips to the rhythmic music.

Sondra looks up to her ceiling, avoiding climax. She wants to save it for her new profound lover, Brian.

"Dear God, is he the one?" she says aloud. Sondra sits up on the couch Indian style.

Memories of the night swim through her head. Her thighs tingle and tremble with wonder and delight. She wonders if she should kiss him and rub his crotch on the next date. She just may rub his run crotch under the table with her toes. Dark Italian restaurant is perfect.

Just maybe, she thinks. *I don't want to give a bad impression.*

Sondra wakes from her dream of Brian. She could stay up all night. Listen to 'Exile on Mainstreet, 'Stooges, Generation X' Kiss Me Deadly' is her favorite song.

Sondra now has, and finally, access to the cable porn channels. She knows she can pleasure herself to softcore channel. Soon, she will watch the sex movies with Brian, and practice her techniques. She will always please him. He will never look for another lover. Soon, she will call Brian and talk about sex. Get him excited, then invite him over. Call him and say, "Come over, Brian. Come over and fuck me." The words all young men long to hear. But she will not, not just yet. There so much that needs done. And she is madly in love. She will wait. Wait for the proper moment. In her heart, she has found her prophet. In her heart, a man of God, best of all, a man of the people. Her love will be a great leader among men one day. Something in her heart tells her this. She cannot wait to bring him home to Guadalajara. Best of all he is Catholic. Just as she is…

Sondra lies in bed. It is 12:00 AM. Her telephone rings. Sondra picks up the phone. It's her mother from Mexico.

"Hola, Mama."

"Siempre se' cu'ando eres t'u." Sondra rubs her fingers through her hair.

"Mam'a, porque tu' llamas a la hora."

Sondra knows where the conversation is going. Arranged marriage with a wealthy man in Baja California. His name is Hector. It's always about Hector.

Sondra looks at her cigarette pack. She knows Brian doesn't smoke. If he does, they will both stop.

"Nada, trabajo, cene' con un amigo nuevo." Sondra's mother rambles on the other line about how great Hector is. She tries talking about Brian.

"Se acaba de mudra de Washington, es muy agradable," her mother yells at her through the phone.

"Mother, please speak English. I'm in America now."

There is a pause over the phone.

"Because, I don't want him, Mother."

Sondra paces around her loft, she pulls up her silk nightgown, admiring her thighs and buttock, in the standing mirror. She knows she looks good. Much better than the white girls in Washington. She takes the unfinished Budweiser, drunks.

"Yes, I want children. I am not old. Mother, please, enough. I am not in the mood tonight. Yes. Yes, I do mama. I am very tired. Yes, I must conduct business tomorrow."

Sondra turns around and walks to the loft window. She watches the couples in the courtyard below.

"Mother, I must go. I promise we will converse tomorrow. OK, bye. I love you also, Mother."

Sondra hangs up the phone and walks toward the bathroom. She slips out her silk nightgown then turns on the shower. She will no doubt think of Brian all night. She will dream of a new life together.

She fears she may sleep restless. She knows there's another woman in her presence. She knows Brian is on the outside, alone looking in. He has no one to protect him. However, she will. Tonight, she will carve his name in a white candle. Place it inside an oil tray. A special one. Her great-grandmother gave it to her. This is how she'll enslaved her husband, Brian. Tonight, Sondra will light her candles all around her loft. No evil will touch him. Not anymore.

Sondra wakes to the sound of a woman screaming bloody murder. Her loft is dark blue, and rays of light shine through the window. She lays on her stomach, head turned left.

Immediately she thinks of the woman next door. The one that killed Troy. How many times this has happened before. Screams of both pleasure and pain. She remembers she's gone back home. This is at least what the police said. Or did she? She had to of left. I saw her wrapped in a blanket, crying, stepping into the ambulance, saying "thank you," too me.

Sondra wipes her right eye and looks at the clock on her nightstand. It is a Felix the Cat Clock.

Sondra thinks of her childhood. She always liked Felix the cat. When she was punished as a child, Felix with his sense of humor cheered her up.

How can I hear her scream next door? That girl Angie. It must be in my head. Months and months of trauma. In some way, I'm a victim too. The scratching on the wall at night. Playing music that's on my IPOD. Hearing voices saying they want to fuck me. How beautiful I am. They want me to join them. Then in deep sleep, the dreams. The full color dreams. Like a video made in hell. Distorted people, partaking in pornography and hate crimes. Some of the worst is when I dream an Earthquake in downtown. The building cracked in half, below me fire, then I begin to fall. Then my heart. I could never fall back asleep after those dreams. My body burned when I saw a bomb go off downtown in my dreams. Hotter, than hotter, still hotter, skin pealing, than I wake in terrible pain. No more, God please no more. The thought of Troy dead gives me peace. I go back to my life, working hard, sending money to my loved ones in Mexico. Damn it, 3:00 AM. That assholes girlfriend better now mess with me.

Don't people have jobs? Don't people have boyfriends, girlfriends, families? I have a son in Mexico to support. Thinks Sondra.

She thinks about her clothing store, meetings with suppliers, inventory, call returns, employees, customers, pay-roll, customers trying to steal from her. She thinks about the one fat lady, who claimed she tripped in her store and filed frivolous lawsuits. Sondra wondered if she is from New Jersey. Only people from the New Jersey, sue anyone for anything. Sondra thinks about these things when she can't sleep.

She hears giggling next door, then a knock on the wall. She quickly exits her bed and yells through her wall "Chinga Tu Madre Pendejo!"

Sondra can still taste the tequila in her mouth. She wishes it were Brian. She wonders if he's home alone. Maybe she should knock. An overpowering urge to call him overcomes. No, I must wait. Mother taught me; she thinks.

Mi Madre siempre tiene raz' on.

Sondra grabs a bottle of orange juice. She takes a healthy drink from the carton, she gulps at least ten times, then wipes mouth with her wrist. She takes another drink, burps, then slams the refrigerator.

Loud Russian Opera Music hails from the loft next door. Then goes quiet.

Sondra knows she can have them killed. This would be too easy. Maybe, this is what they want. Maybe these assholes are terrorist. Maybe they are

Marauders, searching for death. They instigate, then make monies for their families.

Sondra's loft is completely quiet. An ambulance drives down the seventh street, after that, blessed silence. She chooses a track on her iPod. The song is 'Substance -New Order 1987.'

When listening to the song, she believes she hears whispering through the wall. It is a woman and a man.

The man tells Sondra he wants her. He wants her creamy thighs. The woman giggles and says, "I told you, see. Look at her, she's perfect and easy."

Sondra listens. She is angered, disgusted, yet worried. She thinks of all the young women, that arrived from the train station. The wicked things that happened to them.

Sondra thinks of how he dominated her. She now worries about her. She fears she may be back in the loft. Or maybe, she left a few personal belongings. One's so precious, one's so pure, one's of innocence and romance. One's that remind her of childhood. One's she cannot live without. Sondra wonders this, because she has a good heart. She feels sorry for the woman.

Sondra stands up from the toilet, she flushes, and checks her stool. She always does. She turns on the sink water, washes hand, then faces. As she dries, she hears a female voice next door again.

"Sondra, come. Come here now." Sondra turns off the sink and walks toward the wall. as she walks, she hears tapping on the wall, then a scraping noise. Like a cup or fork scraping the wall.

After the scraping noise she hears a hardball, like a cue ball, bounce on the floor. She hears a man's voice giggling.

The man speaks through the wall again. This time a bit louder than before.

"Sondra, come over. Suck my dick, baby girl." The man's voice giggles again. "Sondra baby girl, come next door. I want to take off your panties."

"Vete a la mierda la traduccion, assholes. Fuckin' white trash, speed freaks. You've been waking me for months!" yells Sondra.

Sondra puts on her black jeans, black vans shoes, a black t-shirt top. She can fight better with this attire. She speaks aloud to herself, *she talks about her job, her family, she is so tired, up for months with this crap. It now ends.*

She grabs a Anolon-German steak knife, holds the blade downward, hidden behind her forearm. *This is good,* she thinks, as she looks herself over. The knife is placed properly for defense and attack. *They will never see it coming,* she thinks. Best of all the gift was purchased in Canada by her cousin. The investigation can take years.

Sondra walks out her front door and heads south down the hallway.

She walks next door and notices the front is partially open. On the door, displays a skeleton Halloween prop, and yellow police tape.

Sondra looks through the opening. There is no light. She hears nobody. She listens for the sounds of footsteps. Nothing. She walks to the right. She places her ear against the wall. she knows where the walk-in closet is. She listens and hears nothing. She is furious.

She runs back to the door throwing it open with her right shoulder. The force of the door shakes the entrance, however; does not faze Sondra. She remembers her training back home in Mexico. Sondra is now inside the loft. She quickly turns on the light.

"All right, assholes, come out." She doesn't hear a sound. She quickly walks to the bathroom, then looks in. There is no one. She turns on the walk-in closet light, Knives ready. She sees no one. Sondra looks throughout the loft. What she sees is shocking. A messy bed with bloodstains. She sees bloodstains on the wall and headboard. The concrete floor is interlaced with cut drinking straws. There are spray-painted messages on the walls.

One says, "We are the children of Manson. The Forgotten Ones." She sees another message. "Warning, Lahmia has been summoned here. The fuck beast from hell. Incubus sucked my cock, and I loved it. There is also a big red swastika on the floor. There are also other messages. Most of them wanna-bee Jim Morrison hippy shit." Makes Sondra sick. She doesn't like hippies, liberals or communist.

Looks like an apartment she saw on the news in Mexico. Mexican Nazis. Work will set you free, right? The home was inhabited by a terror-cult. They ran illegal military equipment, trying to hack humans. Stealing bank account numbers from innocent people, hacking smartphones and computers. Stealing people's art, their creativity, their gifts. Anything *they* create is stolen. As of recent, same for the designers in the Garment District. Hundreds of Central Asian women have filed police reports. She watched a television report about these Satanic assholes. After they made money on the women, they killed some, enslaved. Others, by making black market sex films. Selling them worldwide. This did happen in Mexico. The Police also killed everyone involved. Fuck it, is all these devil worshipers say. That and 'fuck the mother fucker.'

It was good riddance for a while. Now, they must be in Los Angeles. She remembers *them* as a young girl. Following her home from school. Taunting her, yelling rude sexual favors. Now, she feels sick.

The smell of the room makes her almost vomit. Now, she understands why her ex-boyfriend is a surfer, and his gang beats up these asshole. He is a Mexican, and from Santa Ana.

The room smells like dead hippies. The bathroom was never cleaned. The toilet is stained with bits of intestines from LA's dying youth. It smells like dry, filthy, drug-laced blood with ammonia, brake fluid, and 99 cent dish soap. The soap from Little Tokyo.

Sondra smells old bologna, meat and mold. Most of all, death. Sondra opens the refrigerator. The only thig missing is a human head, with candle placed inside. That would be an awesome picture though, she thinks. I would make good money on that one. Sondra chuckles to herself.

She looks at the closet door. There is a picture of Charles Mason with a pentagram drawn on his forehead.

Sondra cannot help noticing a stripper pole in the center of the room. She walks toward the pole looking it over.

She thinks about the young woman. What possessed her to stay with this man?

Sondra touches the pole with her fingers, then wraps her hand around it. She feels a shock of energy jolt through her body, as she gasps for breath. It felt kind of good. Kind of like the feeling when Magic Wand vibrator gently touches your clitoris.

Sondra closes her eyes and sees Angie and Troy on the couch. She sits atop him and bounces fiercely. Sondra's eyes roll back as she feels energy tingle between her legs. Sondra releases her grip and opens her eyes. The feelings pass for the moment.

Sondra places her left hand on the pole. The same energy bolt enters her again. This time, from the top, of her head. She closes her eyes, then prays for their forgiveness.

She sees *him* atop her, kissing her, eyes dilated, sweating profusely. Hips pounding her.

Sondra keeps her eyes closed and continues praying. She tells him to stop. He will not. Troy keeps penetrating her, curing her, slapping her face.

Sondra can feel him inside. His shaft punishing her. Sondra releases the pole and opens her eyes. A blast of energy runs through her body, as she falls to the ground.

Sondra quickly stands up, placing both hands on the pole again. She closes her eyes, as an orgasmic wave of energy strikes her.

She falls to the ground, finding herself atop Troy, riding him backward. The feelings are so intense, she cannot and will not let go. Sondra has never felt this feeling before. She knows the soul of the woman, the one that used to live here. Inside the loft she now stands. She feels if she is now indeed Angie, getting screwed by a demon.

Sondra begins crying out. She feels an explosive, throbbing feeling upside her uterus. It is so intense heat covers her whole body.

A white flash is seen by Sondra. She falls to the ground eyes still closed. Sondra begins to cry. She feels regret, despair, fear and abandonment. Worst part is, she cannot move. She has thoughts of shame and suicide. All Sondra can do is cry out for Brian. She tells Brian how much she loves him, and how sorry she is. Sondra has had a severe nervous breakdown.

Sondra hears the voice of another man. It is familiar to her. It is the voice of Troy. She opens her eyes; her worst fears are confirmed. It is Troy. The devil himself. Her nightmare. The one Sondra fears most. The evil one from Hegang.

"Take my hand," says Troy.

He looks different than before. His body is healthier, hair groomed, no facial hair, eyes gleaming of an angel. He looks attractive; beautiful. His skin perfect and glowing. She notices a warm glowing light around him.

"Sondra, Take my hand. It is OK. Everything will be better now. There will no more pain. No suffering. How, we have waited for you, all these years, my love."

Sondra cannot speak. Her body is limp. She has no control of her muscles or nervous system. Sondra feels dismay, anguish, despair. She cannot speak. Her eyes begin watering.

Troy lays over her and kisses her cheek, then forehead. He sticks his tongue out and lashes it at her. It is the tongue of that of a demon snake. He speaks a language she's never heard before. He chants in tongues.

His tongue is oversized and unnatural. As he stands over her, large wings flow his body. He forces himself, inside her again.

Sondra tries to fight him off, it is useless. Troy has consumed all her energy. All hope is lost for Sondra. She knows this man, Troy. She has always feared him since a child. He was the reason she slept with a light on, the closet locked, flashlight on, toy guns under the bed. Why she ran home from school every day,

Troy represents something inhuman. A deity of hunger, lust, anguish, revenge, hate. Sondra begins to absorb these feelings, as she cries for God's help.

As Troy kisses her, she begins burning. Sondra feels as if needles are poking her skin.

She feels a claw grab her vagina. It hurts horribly. Huge nails cover the outer section.

Sondra tries screaming again but cannot. Troy stands up looking her over. He smiles mischievously. He looks like a lion ready to devour its prey. Like a servant who is sacrificing for his master…

"Take my hand," says Troy. Sondra shakes her head. Eyes filled with tears.

"Take my hand, the pain will stop." Sondra's body now begins to burn. The pain is insatiable. She feels as if her skin is beginning to rip apart. Her teeth, clenching so tight, they make a cracking sound. Muscles tearing between her, ribcage.

Sondra suddenly finds her tongue. She speaks a language she never knew before. His language. The language of damnation. Troy reaches out his hand then begins laughing. Sondra hand trembles as she reaches upwards.

"OK," Sondra says. She unwillingly accepts the demon. She will no doubt, unwillingly regret this decision, rest of her life or worse, all eternity.

Troy grabs on to Sondra's virgin flesh laughing as he laughs, the loft windows shatter. The concrete. Walls crack, the kitchen cabinets are thrown to the ground. The refrigerator falls over.

These symbol of conquest. The symbols of control in the human world. A symbol of all which is evil. A symbol of what Troy wanted from the beginning.

Troy takes her hand and pulls her upward. "Don't be scared, my child." Troy lifts her like a bride. A groom carrying his new virgin wife through the threshold.

A blue dim, greyish light shines out from the walk-in closet.

Troy carries Sondra into the closet. The door slams, while Sondra screams. This time, no one will save her. Not like her mother used to when she was a child. Not like the times, the German Sheppard guarded her, during a stormy night. Or when Uncle Salty visited from Spain.

Sondra is now a victim. A victim of a presence unknown too man. Only God knows this man. The enemy now owns her. Sondra is forever lost. In eternal despair…

Chapter 13

Brian exits the elevator, then exits right. It's the first route he and Sondra took, walking her home.

Brian's returned home from a date. A pre-planned affair with his coworker in advertising. It was a weekend event. He left Sunday night, then called in sick Monday and Tuesday. Brian stinks of booze, stale perfume and is unshaven. Even his armpits smell that of a woman.

Sondra is not committed to their relationship. Not yet. This is what Brian thinks. He's used to having things his way. Women fall in love with Brian, drop of a hat. Why should he sit and home and wait for her? Woman are throwing themselves' at him all over the city.

His only concern is, she usually texts him at least once per day. The past two days, nothing. Especially he not being home. He thought for sure, she could call. They went out Saturday night, he now returns Tuesday evening.

Brian carries two bottles of Beaujolais, Belgium chocolates, and a Tiffany bracelet. Maybe, he feels a touch of guilt? He hopes Sondra didn't knock on his door over the weekend. He didn't call her thanking her for the date. He knows this was low class. Sondra may be suspicious or worse; never see him again. She did say she has the *gift* of clairvoyance.

A couple walking abreast notices Brian, nods then smile. The woman mentions, how beautiful the flowers are. He greets them, by saying hello, then tells the woman what apartment he lives in. The couple tells Brian They moved from Texas. He is involved in city politics; she is in advertising. The couple vanishes down the hall, the woman whispers in her boyfriends' ear, then giggles. Brian knocks on Sondra's door four times. There's no answer. He only hears the voices of people talking, downstairs, in the courtyard.

The late afternoon ice-cream vendor yells in the distance. People buying booze at the market. Brian looks in both directions and knocks. There is still no answer.

A security guard, a large Black American, around 6 feet, 5 inches tall, walks up to Brian. He curiously looks Brian over. He noticed Brian walking with Sondra a few times in the building. So have the *others*. People who are jealous of Brian and Sondra. They sit downstairs, listening to Brian and Sondra talk. Right below Brian's loft. They tell obscene jokes, then make up stories that are hurtful and untrue.

The security guard is a bit concerned for Brian. He knows things about the building and the people who inhibit it. Things have changed Downtown, and not for the better. Santee Court is a haven for lost souls. Evil people with satanic desires. The security officer sees Brian as another naïve, quiet, white man, just passing through. This is what young adults dot. Pass through this part of the county. It's unfortunate, some may *never leave.*

Brian is quiet. He does meet many people. Not many, and so far, only involved with Sondra. Everything else, exterior chaos and Distinctive Behavior. Brian doesn't know Sondra's mother has been calling the front office, and her employees. The police will be asking questions soon. There are only a few hours left, until a missing person report is filed. The police will no doubt be snooping around. They always do, this time of year. The high season. The festival of the witch. The festival of Samhain, the Southern Hemisphere or Capricorn.

You see, the security guard has worked Santee Court since the day it was converted. He warned the residence during those small intimate rooftop parties. Sometimes, dogs and cats are thrown of the building. One Halloween, a human jumped. The police called it suicide. The security says otherwise. This old hat factory on Los Angeles Street. The drugs, the slavery, the lost souls that were sacrificed; murdered during the festival.

"She's not home," says the security guard. He sports a Jamaican accent.

"What?" replies Brian.

"The girl, Sondra. She's not home."

"Oh, OK. I'll come back later."

"Son." The security places his hand on Brian's shoulder. "You don't understand. She is gone."

"Gone son. To another plane. Another world of sweet pain, and unbearable pleasures."

What the fuck, this guy's problem? Thinks Brian.

Brian looks over the security guard. He's always been a bit unusual to Brian. Especially since he heard, a dog was thrown off the roof, on the 4th of July. Brian wonders if this nut sack may have done it. Sondra told Brian that this security guard was seen shooting Heroin under the stairs.

late night.

Brian wonders if this rumor is true. Brian heard from Sondra that the units above Rite-Aid are so demonic. Some, tenants, ended up clinically insane.

The security guard has wild eyes. The kind of eyes that barely sleep. Entertain demons. They kind of eyes that are wishful of things in the spirit world. The kind of eyes that looked *through* Sondra's apartment when she wasn't home. He smelt her under ware, right from the wicker basket. He licked her vibrator and dildo. How does Brian know this? He just does, he's still high from the two-day sex and alcohol binge.

Brian's grandmother told him, "You're just like your father. You must find God or die."

"You're right, I don't understand. Where is she? if you don't mind?" asks Brian.

"She's been gone since Sunday morning, 3:30 AM."

The security guard's eyes glare through Brian.

"How do you know?" asks Brian.

"Nobody knows Brian—" Brian interrupts.

"How do you know me?"

"I know everyone and everything about this building, young man."

The security guard gazes off, his eyes roll and twitch.

"Life is like a voodoo trance. Brian. I have been here since the very beginning, young man. I'm not leaving this place, ever. After a while, you become acquainted with the spirits that roam these hallways. You get to know them. Become friend with them. Soon, it will happen to you; young man."

The security guard moves in closer to Brian. He stands almost face front. Touching his shoes. He is trying to read Brian. Brian sees this man. He knows his lust, and his thirst. He prefers the night shift. This way, he can smoke speed, while drinking gin from his flasks. He knows which lofts have sex with blinds open. The ones, where the tenants do not mind. She bends over the couch, looking out the window lashing her tongue. Talking dirty. He sits with his hands down his pants, smoking a blunt with another tenant as he films the act by smartphone.

Brian glares back at him wondering, why he still has a job. The other security officer, Andy; is a real live wire. He runs around in an NSA style uniform. Black helmet, black face cover, with antenna atop the helmet. He also wears black gloves and carries an oversized radio. He looks like one of fuckers from 'Star Wars.'

He told Brian, "I can melt your face with this, buddy. You better watch it here."

"How do you know her?" asks the security guard.

"She was the first person I met in this building."

Brian pauses, then starts mumbling to himself, *"Don't worry, Son, they know you didn't kill her. They know everything."*

The security guard moves in closer to Brian. His face almost touches his. He places his right hand under his chin.

"They always know what you do."

The security guard looks up at the water pipes on the ceiling. The lights start to flicker, and voices of a few children are heard in the distance. Brian cannot believe what he has just heard. A wave of guilt consumes him.

"What if she went out of town? She does have a mother in Mexico. Maybe there was a family emergency. Maybe—"

The security guard interrupts Brian.

"So, you do know her. She's one of the good ones. A real gem. If I had a chance, mummy, I would go at it, boy. Go at it, really good."

Brian stands in shock and dismay. Brian wants to knock the guy out.

"Thanks for the info. I'm a bit confused. I don't know what to say." The security guard looks upward at the ceiling, then cracks his neck. The noise of the crack sounds like a twig breaking in half.

"Excuse me, boy, I got the ankylosing spondylitis."

"Thanks for the info. I just don't know what to say. What to do?" says Brian.

"We are all confused, Son. I'm sure she's OK, little man. Just let it hang for a while. You know, lay back, smoke some weed, keep things, nice and slow. Slow and real."

"Alright then. Ummm, well, I must get going." Brian says.

Brian looks over the man. He sees a burglary. Brian knows he is involved. He supports his vice one way, or another…

"I best be going, good night, Sir," says Brian.

"Good night, 'big man.' Swing low, baby, swing low." says the security guard. He scratches his testes, then walks away slowly. He turns around one more time.

The security guard laughs out loud, then walks away.

The security guard gave Brian the creeps. I mean, what the hell? In Washington, you would be put in jail for showing up work that loaded. I mean, that guy smells like a Colombian windpipe, thinks Brian.

As Brian walks, he turns around, looking back at the security officer. The man stands center of the hallway starring at Brian. Brian opens his loft door and enters. He re-opens the door and peeks his head out. The security guard stands there, just staring. He smiles, then salutes. Brian quickly closes the door. he wants for a second and re-opens again. Surprisingly, he is gone, without a trace.

Brian leans against his door and sighs relief. He gives the main room a look over, then speaks aloud, "What the heck? I didn't leave my apartment like this."

His dining table is turned over. His nightstand is placed atop the coffee table. Shoes lay in perfect order under the window. His record albums are spread across the floor. His picture of Bob Marley is gone. His painting of Pierre Mass is gone. *They* stole his German blender and German knives. All other utensils are in his sink. All cleaning supplies are in his bathtub. His neckties and watches are tied together. *They* made some sort of pagan sign on the floor with change from his sparklets bottle. *They* stole all his cashmere socks designer under ware. Not the sweaters, though. Brian guesses this was for the inconvenience. Who would wear used underwear? There is a message in white correction fluid. It is written on the floor. It reads, "Come to us, Brian."

Brian's television was left on. It shows the evangelist with a white hat with a black band, He sports a white beard. He's wearing John Lennon style glasses, with red lenses. He holds an Italian silver and black cane.

"It's Satan, who wants to destroy you. It is Satan and all his children, that represents the moral decay of the United States, and its people. We all must turn away from sin or die. You must pray, you must turn from sin now. Not tomorrow, or next week. If you don't do it now. It may be too late. There is no negotiation with God. As none, with the devil. God will throw you into hell, before you enter his kingdom. This is for being Lukewarm in faith. Have you all read Revelations?"

Brian is confounded. Every time Brian returns home, he turns on the television and finds the same evangelist on television.

I must be living in the Twilight Zone. Thinks Brian.

Brian picks up the remote turning off the television. Brian looks upward toward the ceiling. He hears footsteps running back and forth across the floor. Then he hears the voice of a young girl giggling. The television evangelist show turns on by itself again. Brian gasps as he looks at the television.

"You must pray, young man. You must pray, turn from your sin before it's too late." Brian turns off the television.

He is a bit freaked out now. He walks quickly to the cabinet above the refrigerator. He finds a bottle of Makers Mark. Thank god he thinks. Finally, someone who makes sense. And his name is Mark. Brian grabs a glass from the cabinet, then pours the famous Kentucky Three Finger Chaos.

He looks around and sighs deeply. *So, this is fuckin' great. Now I must deal with this shit. I wish I caught these asshole. I'd go A-Bomb on you, assholes. Bring out Hercules.*

Brian takes a drink, then notices that his answering machine is blinking red. He walks over to the kitchen, then listens. There are four messages from Jenna, two from Jenna's mother. Brian listens while he tentatively walks through his loft.

As Brian begins shuffling through his records, he hears footsteps running upstairs loft again. Brian pays no attention. At this moment, he wants to use his training, He is furious. He for the first time, wants to break someone's neck. He wants to beat a man until his head falls apart, then throws him out the window. This kind of crap would never happen in Washington. Brian hears a door slamming upstairs loudly.

"Shut up!" Brian exclaims. Brian looks at his front door for a moment, he sees large footsteps walking by, underneath the door. They stop for a moment, then move onward.

The messages on Brian's answering machine are general by natural. The first ones are Jenna. She asks, why haven't you called me. She calls him a cheater. She refers to Brian as an asshole.

He starts setting the dining room area in perfect order again. Brian takes a drink of whisky. He slams down the glass, then pours another to the rim. He works in the kitchen, getting everything back together.

Brian will stay up extra hours re-organizing his loft again.

He listening to Fog Hat. He starts with 'Sarah Lee' That is a good kick ass tune. Thinks Brian.

Brian starts bopping around the loft. Why not right? If you must clean. Might as well do it too great rock-n-roll.

Next, he will play 'T-Rex' the*n 'Who' young man blues*. 'Live at Leeds.' Best Who album ever recorded.

Brian powers down his drink then pour another. His nerves are a bit on edge tonight. He feels tingling on his arms, and little needle pins of pain poking at his head. The sensations are not pleasing. They irritate offering fantasies of violence.

The feeling of the alcohol runs beautifully through his veins. He thinks of Jack Nicholson at the bar, in 'The Shinning.' Brian slams the glass down on the table.

Brian's phone rings. He hesitates for a moment, then picks up. Brian is in a trance-like mode. Expressionless and emotionless.

"Hello?" the voice on the answering machine is Jenna. Brian's not in the mood. If I don't talk, she will never stop calling, or worse. He is starting to wonder if she did this. Maybe she's here. Maybe she is visiting Psycho Hotel on Los Angeles Street. Brian decides to answer the phone.

"Oh, hi. What's up?" Brian's voice is cold and distant.

"I've been busy, told you this before. Things haven't been going smooth. It's been rough lately."

Jenna's voice escalates on the other end.

"Look, I've been busy, what do want from me? I know things were smooth last week. Now they've changed."

Jenna's now yelling at Brian over the phone. Brian moves the phone away from his ear. Brian takes another drink, then slams it down on the table. Jenna asks what he's doing.

"I am drinking, baby. And it feels good. NO, I am not driving home. Duh. get that out of your head now woman." Jenna starts yelling again.

"Hold on a second." Brian pours another drink. He passes gas loud.

"Wait, speaker time, baby, Say what?"

"Brian, you're an asshole. This is not like you. I know you're seeing someone else."

"What's with the, I know your seeing, crap. That's all you ever accuse of me of now. I ain't seeing shit. My house is a fucking wreck, work is a fuckin' wreck. What do you want from me?"

"I've called you a hundred times, Brian. I want to know, why aren't you answering? Why is that sweetie?"

"Look, I've been busy. I still love you. Don't worry. Everything feels a bit artificial now. I think the security guard walked into my apartment. Turned things upside down. My fuckin underwear and socks are gone. T-shirts too. How bout that Jenna. Underwear and fuckin socks. Oh, and you know that oil painting you gave me. Fuckin gone also. Either way, I'm having a great time, how are your fuckin parents, Jenna?" There is a long pause of the other line.

"I don't feel like you love me, Brian. Love is respect, you don't respect me. I can feel it."

"Look, things will get better. It's been hard adjusting."

"OK then, I am coming out. I want to help with the apartment."

"No, you're not coming out."

"Yes, Brian, I'm flying out tomorrow."

"No, don't fly out yet."

Brian's hand starts shaking. He wonders nervously around the kitchen. He pours another Makers Mark. Brian burps, then scratches his crotch area.

"Brian, my mind is made up. I'm flying out tomorrow. I think your cheating. I want to see the loft."

"The loft is sweet. It's our perfect love nest. We can have a child here, then buy a bigger home in Larchmont. This is my plan. The plan is Los Angeles, baby. I mean, this place is off the hook. You should see the women here. Just kidding kitten. I'm never going back there. The money is here in Los Angeles, not fuckin' incredible. Get that through your head. We'll buy a loft Downtown. Then buy a cool home in Larchmont. Our children will be god's baby doll. And don't start talking about DC. Honey, with my future goals, we will never go back. Things are a bit ruff now. I am getting acclimated. Just wait, well get married, have kids. It will be awesome."

"What the hell is Larchmont?"

"Never mind, girl. I'm a fuckin Dodger fan now."

"So, you still love me?" asks Jenna.

"Fuck, yeah. I still love you. You're the best, baby. Yeah, baby, first things first, when you are here, I will worship you. Lay you on the bed, then worship the juices between your legs. Finally, no parents, we can be real adults now. Our lovemaking will be outrageous."

"You sound like your drunk." Says Jenna.

"I am drunk. Get used to it. Jenna calm things down. My loft's been rolled, I'm drunk. How bout that? Things will normal tomorrow. I'll call, then you'll fly out."

"So, you still love me?" asks Jenna.

Brian changes the music to 'The Church, Reptile.'

"What did I f'n' tell you. I'm going Gene Simmons on you. Then going to feed you. After that, a 69 position. One for hours." Brian is obviously out of his mind.

Jenna interrupts, laughing aloud. She likes it when Brian is sometimes a bit off-color. Brian had a dark side. Jenna likes it, because the sex is incredible.

"I do miss you also. I was driving the Benz today with no panties. I was so horny, thinking about you. Anyway, I shot on the dashboard. Brian, it was sexy. See how comfortable we are together?"

"Sure is. I'm hot for you also pumpkin."

"Brian, do you want phone sex with me?"

Jenna is in complete control now. Just the way she likes things.

"Honey, I love that with you. You are so beautiful, amazing, I do want to feed on you between your legs hungrily. I like it when you explode. That is the best. You are delicious."

"I do miss seeing your manhood stuffed in those jeans. The best part, baby, is when I get on my knees and unbutton those lucky jeans, you wear. I like watching it unleashed. It's always so smooth, clean. And it's so damn hot."

Brian laughs aloud.

"Serious, Brian, it makes my mouth gush."

"Good. That's what I want to hear baby doll."

"Yes, it is. It gets hotter and hotter. Baby, it is even better inside me. I do miss you so much, my love."

"I do also, baby. Man, now it's all big and barney. I can hit baseballs with it. Or spank your butt, making that slapping noise you like."

"Give it to me now," says Jenna while laughing. "Brian, you're crazy. This is what I love about you. I am flying out. I need you now."

"Soon Jenna. But first, let me fix the loft. Seriously. I'll make you a deal. Let me get things finished. Then I will call back tonight. We will have a date."

"Promise?" asks Jenna.

"I promise," says Brian.

"OK, then deal. You better call me back, or else. Brian, I love you."

"OK, OK. Got to go, we will get it on later, promise. I'll tell you a really sexy story."

"OK, bye. And Jenna, answer the phone later."

Jenna talks about her future goals with him, and the children they'll will have. At this point, anything to get her off the phone for now. Brian thinks.

"Brian, can I tell you something else?"

"Sure."

"I cannot wait until we are married. We are going to have a perfect life, Brian. Don't you agree?"

Brian pauses for a moment, he walks toward the television, turns on a football game.

"Brian, are you there?"

"Yes, honey, I am. I heard, you; you're right. In the end, everything will be perfect."

"Bye love."

"Call me later."

Whew, Brian got rid of her. Worst part is. He did it by lying through his eye-teeth. *May God strike me down forever*, thinks Brian.

Thunder strikes outside Downtown Los Angeles. The forecaster said it will rain most of the week. This is good. It will wash away the urine and crap left behind from the homeless.

Brian walks to the refrigerator and takes a six-pack of beer. He sees that the Chicago Bears are playing the Seattle Seahawks. This is good. Brian is a Chicago Bear fan. He always has been. When he was 10 years old, he watched Neil Anderson a run against the Cleveland Browns, on a Monday night. After that, it was all over.

The telephone rings again. Brian looks at the television, opens a beer, then lays back on his couch. For many years he waited for this one moment. He, his couch, beer, and Chicago Bears. Brian just about begins to relax. Curtis Enis runs up the middle 40 yards.

"Alright, here we go!" Brian exclaims aloud.

Brian's phone ring again. He was just getting comfortable. Football, downtown fast food on the corner, and beer is all he wants tonight.

It is Jenna again, he thinks.

He grunts out loud, then answers, "What do you want now, Jenna? Oh, shoot, Mom, I'm so sorry. How are you?" He places his mother on speakerphone.

"Brian, how are you, honey?"

"Mom, I am great. My new job is great. Los Angeles is great; my new job is great." Brian turns the volume down on the television.

"Hi, Mom. How's everything, with you and dad?"

"Brian, we are very, disappointed with you? Did we raise you this way? Where have you been? Why didn't you call when you landed? Your father is very, upset. So is your sister, and Jenna's been crying every day."

"Mother, I spoke with Jenna already. Today, tonight, and a few other times."

"Don't lie to me, Brian. I know when you're lying." Brian feels a rush of blood flow through his face. He tries the logical approach.

"Mother, have you ever moved to a new city?" There is silence on the other end. "I have been busy at work. Did you know, I am the first, the first new intern that now has my own finance team. My new salary is $350,000 plus commission. I destroyed everyone first 30 days, how about that? I produced more income that most do in 6 months."

There is still silence on the other end of the phone.

"I did this in only 30. Mom, I am good at what I do. I'm doing what Father wanted me to do."

"What is this, Son? What is it your father wanted you to do?"

Brian takes a drink of beer. His throat is dry from his lies already.

"I'm developing wealth for the family, Mother. And, for Jenna and me—"

"Brian, I called because your father won't. If you knew what he told me, you would fly home and visit this weekend. When Jack says he is disappointed. Well, I think you know what that means. Right?"

Brian's heart begins racing. His arms and back start tingling. He feels nauseous. As he frantically paces his loft, his knees buckle a few times.

"You understand me, Brian? Son?"

"I understand, Mother."

"Good, now, call your father tomorrow. Lay off what you are doing. Lay off what you are doing now. And do not do what you plan on doing. Do you understand me, Son?"

"Yes, I do," says Brian.

"OK, then, it's late, you're watching the bear game, and you have work. We *all* love you very much. Get some rest, go to work, continue doing well, call us tomorrow."

"OK, Mother, I'm sorry. I do love you all."

"We love you too. Goodnight, Brian."

"Good night, Mom." The phone hangs up. Brian missed a touchdown by the Seattle Seahawks. The touchdown is an unwanted omen. Mom calls, Seahawks score. What a bummer.

The telephone rings again. After the 4th ring, he hears Jenna. She's crying about how she misses him. She reminds him not to cheat. She also says that she'll be watching, and he better have decorated appropriately. If not, everything will be done her way. The phone hangs up.

Brian yells out loud, "Leave me the fuck alone. Shit!"

After Brian yells, he hears a tapping noise atop his ceiling. Then the sound of a bouncing cue ball roll across the floor. Brian will try, paying to attention. He will finish the six back and enjoy the rest of his evening. Hopefully, the Bears will win. If not, I may end up at the Golden Gopher, for a night cap. Brian thinks.

Brian's passed out on his couch. The six-pack turned into a 12-pack, seven tacos, and a cheeseburger. The burger place is on the corner of San Pedro and seventh street was amusing to Brian. It is a raunchy looking place, laced with drug pushers, street walkers, grease and rats. Like Brian said to Sondra, "When in Rome."

The Bears beat the Seahawks. Well, he wishes the meal were as satisfying as the game. Both ended in Omen. It's disappointing not to discuss the idiosyncrasies of the Bears and their Omen's at work. At least for now, Brian's a bit happier than before. The disappearance of Sondra and loss to the Seahawks would have done him in. at least for a few weeks. Sondra probably had to fly home for emergency. He still hopes.

Brian strolls through the cable channels. He watched 'Blade,' then appropriately followed it up, with 'Two Days in the Valley.' then some softcore porn. Brian's not a porn fan. He just likes sex, and wonders what the channels are like in LA, opposed to Washington. He wonders why woman and men would expose their weaknesses to the public. Especially in the form of soft-core porn. It's always a detective story. The acting is absolutely, putrid in soft core porn. Except of one scene. One of the women in the film looked like Sondra. This kind of turned him on. He tried calling earlier, with no success. He wanted to leave a message; her message box was full. She must be around somewhere. This gives reason enough for walking downstairs and buying another six-pack.

He also bought some of those hungry-man, extra man-size meals. Fried chicken, mac, and cheese and pot roast are his favorites. Brian also bought some Hawaiian punch, stale bread, lunch meat, hot dogs, chili, and cigarettes. He never smoked before. Maybe a few times, casually; walking home with his friends, after the pub and its food. Food for the renaissance man. Food for the man on his own. "Food of the gods," Brian tells the merchant. The merchant thinks Brian is making fun. He tells Brian. "Don't forget about my excellent import beer selection." The merchant is from Lebanon. Brian bought Miller.

Brian sees a tenant with a Walter Payton jersey. They sat in the courtyard until 10:00 PM. They both ended up drinking tequila in the courtyard, playing checkers and discussing current events.

A few other tenants joined with their dogs. Nobody knew Sondra or discussed her disappearance. What they did discuss was Troy and Angie. Oh my, how the tenant's gossip about other people. The massage houses, the drug dealers, the rich kids from the "Red States." This place is a nightmare thinks Brian.

All Brian wanted to do, was meet a few new people, discuss football. For god-sake, it is near the end of October. The weather in Downtown is perfect, the booze is good, the women, and the food; excellent. These assholes around him want to gossip all night. What a bunch of intellectual losers, thinks Brian.

The girls did not say much. It was the men; that is the problem. All the gossiping made him depressed. He thought of Sondra, then whimpered away in self-destruction.

Sondra is a Bear fan. This is probably the reason why she is so cool. He really wanted to watch football with her. Get drunk, look at her in his Walter Payton jersey. No under ware or makeup. Trotting around the house, showing off her hips, scratching herself; making burritos at half time. Brian must find this woman. He will, or he'll never be the same.

Brian's finally passed out on the couch by 10:40 PM. In the back of his mind, he hears the ever-famed ambulance drive east on seventh street. The ambulance drives the route all night. Sondra told Brian, "That ambulance is part of the garment districts, mind control program. The fuckin' siren has a hidden message. That is why it runs all night. It warns junkies to leave Downtown, or the rainbow people will get them." Brian absolutely adores Sondra's sadistic personality.

A beer bottle falls aside from the coffee table. In half slumber, Brian hears a woman upstairs loft.

It sounds like Sondra. If fact, it sounds too much like Sondra.

Brian sits up, stretches, then coughs. A bang on the upstairs floor is heard. Sounds if a large boot stomped on the floor. Brian yells at the ceiling. Telling them shut up. Then he hears giggling. Then a man and women talking. He cannot understand what they say, however he did hear a man with an accent, mutter the words, "motherfucker."

Brian looks at the television. He sees the Evangelist again. It's the same old guy, with a white hat, with a black band. He talks about modern-day, new world luciferin ideology. How it is being taught at grade school level. How school children are being taught to mediate, rather than solve animosity amongst each other. He also speaks about Jacob and Isaac, and the paradox between the American Government.

Brian wonders how the channel turned on. He lays on his side watching the show. He likes this teacher. He's smart and makes sense. He also likes his style, and skull-head cane. This is important to Brian. Too Brian style is everything. It goes a long way.

A louder bang is heard upstairs. The strength of the sound startles Brian. Sounds like a large oak dresser being tipped over. Greyish, blue light shines through the blinds as an eerie feeling overcomes Brian.

Brian looks at the foot of the couch. He sees a small, cloaked figure. It his hooded, four-feet-tall. No face is seen. Brian's heart begins to race, and his body tingles in pain. He tries to move with no success. He feels heat over his body. Then he feels the sensation of lightning bolt slamming atop his head.

"Who are you," Painfully asks Brian.

His voice trembles with fear. The small, cloaked figure doesn't answer. The sound of Jax is heard upstairs. Then a ball bounces on the floor. The sound of a woman's voice is heard upstairs, then light laughter, as a cue ball rolls across the floor.

"Who the hell are you?" Brian yells.

"Lamia." Says the figure.

The voice of the demon is deep and snarled. It sounds precise, confident, and defiant. Another voice is heard upstairs.

The voice proudly says, "kill him."

"Shhhhh. Be quiet, he may hear us." The woman upstairs says.

"I thought I told you to shut up." Brian's heart is almost ready to fade out. His head is so dizzy he can barely see.

"What do you want?" asks Brian.

"Your soul." The cloaked demon responds.

The cloaked demon points his long finger upwards toward the ceiling. Quickly, his hands, with long rotten nails jab into Brian's skull. Brian screams as loud as he can. With each effort his voice becomes weaker. The sensations of needles poke through his neck, setting his nervous system ablaze.

The demon is extremely strong for its size. Without effort, he drags Brian from his couch like a rag doll. Brian begins kicking and struggling. The demon drags Brian toward the dark walk-in closet. Blood from the force of its grip squirts blood from Brian's face and eyes. Brian tries screaming for help. Nobody will hear him.

"What are you doing to me!" screams Brian.

"I'm dragging you to hell."

The demon laughs, mocking Brian. He makes fun at him. Calling him "gods forgotten bitch of a son."

The demons other hand covers Brian's mouth. His middle finger jabs his tonsils, pokes at his larynx. Blood continues to cover Brian's face. The demon takes another nail, pushing it through his ribcage, piercing his lung.

Brian can no longer scream. His body in total shock.

The demon laughs, as it continues to mock Brian and his maker.

Brian sees a bright fiery wall in the closet. As the demon drags Brian toward the fiery wall, his skin begins to burn, then peel. Brian's hair begins to burn from his skull.

"NO, NO, NO, GOD, PLEASE HELP ME!!" Brian finds the strength, letting out one last cry.

Brian wakes up yelling. He is dripping in sweat from his head to his feet. The back of his neck and back is drenched with sweat.

Brian looks at the television. The Evangelist with white hat, black band, and John Lennon-style glasses, talks about the book of Romans, Corinthians, the Apostle John, the Antichrist.

Brian looks at the clock over his entry door. It is 3:00 AM. Brian rocks back and forth holding his waste. He feels his stomach in knots, and he needs to defecate. He feels older now. He feels that someone or something drained his energy. As Brian stands, his knees buckle. He looks around the room and it starts spinning. He notices little white dots dance midair.

The left side of his brain feels like hot water dripping.

Brian stumbles to the bathroom, falling on the way. He barely makes it to the toilet throwing up blood. As he throws up, he feels his ribcage shutter, making a cracking noise. The movements are so strong, his spinal column makes cracking noises. He looks in the toilet and quickly sits down. The pains he feels are almost unbearable. As Brian defecates, blood squirts in the toilet. He feels if safety pins are existing in bowels. As he pushes, more vomit squirts from his mouth. Must be Rat Poising thinks Brian. That darn grease pit on the corner of 7th and San Pedro. I'm going to blow up the place.

"Good Lord above, I received your messages last night. Help me get over this hangover. I won't do this again…"

Brian turns on the shower, wetting a towel. He wipes up the vomit off the floor. Slashes of heat burn through his body. They are hot, then cold. Then ice-cold energy pierces his face.

Brian takes a quick shower. As he washes, he brushes his teeth. He vomits again in the shower, as he brushes his tongue, he vomits again. He says a quick prayer. He promises he will get his life back on track. He promises he will not drink like this. He wonders why he started smoking and promise to stop. He prays that he will do better at work. Be number one. That is all that's important in this town. Being number one. He tells God if he makes a lot of money, He'll donate 20 percent to the church. He will rejoin bible studies. He will now be a better Christian. He will be a better man.

Brian steps out of the shower, wipes himself dry, then looks in the mirror. He sees the apparition of an older man dressed in white pajama style clothes. He holds a black and silver cane, sporting a black hat. The apparition grins at Brian, then quickly vanishes.

At this moment, Brian decides to clean up his lifestyle. Do the right thing, try harder. Later he will call his father. Confess what he has been doing. All he needs now is equal. His perfect woman, Sondra. Together, they will walk through this world together.

The last three days have been total chaos for Brian. He looks around the loft seeing too many empty beer bottles, too many whisky bottles, too many pizza boxes, too much root beer, Hawaiian punch, and chocolate fudge cake in the refrigerator. Kentucky fried chicken, too…

He finishes cleaning the loft. He opens the refrigerator, then takes a Corona Extra. Might as well push the alcohol through. He sits on his bed, thinking about Monday morning. He worries his boss will scold him in front of everyone.

"Where were you? Young man. You left a lot of unfinished business with the Norwegians. Lisa took over the file. I need you here Brian. We all do."

Brian takes a drink of his Corona, then a bite of fried chicken. He lays back on his bed, turns on the television. 'I Love Lucy' is on Channel 11. He likes this show. Especially on a rainy day with the perfect woman. He also checks the television guide seeing 'Invasion of the Body Snatchers' is on. Then 'Bladerunner.'

Brian will leave the television on all night. He will change his bedsheets and add an extra pillow. He will crack the loft window open, letting the night breeze flow gently over the remains of his lost weekend. Most of all, Brian will invite all the noises outside. All the noises he hated before. Especially the ambulance. The loud talking downstairs, the taunting of the upstairs loft. After tonight, nothing will bother Brian ever again. He feels that he conquered a malicious demon. Not only a demon from another world, but one that lives inside of him…

Brian wakes to the sound of a siren wailing in the distance. A door slams down the hallway, and a woman calls her boyfriend an asshole. It is 3:00 AM.

Wow, 3:00 AM on a Monday morning.' Again? Says Brian too himself.

The couples walking up the stairs, no doubt, was at that club on Melrose. The electronic trance. If they're on pills, screams of moans and pleasure will echo throughout the building until 7:00 AM.

Brian looks under his door. He notices four pairs of shoes standing below the shadow of the door. They whisper, giggle, then quickly walk. He hears one of the voices tell a woman, "Take off your shoes." Brian indistinctly hears another woman's voice.

She whispers, "Go for it, go. We need more money, shit."

They walk away quickly as their voices fade in the distance. A male curses in the distance. Another woman curse's him back, followed by the sound of a hand slapping a face.

Brian is too tired for this to bother. The fact is, he hasn't slept much since he moved to Los Angeles. He's met a few good women at the Golden Gopher and Seven Grand. He met two and brought them home from Olympic and Grand. Overall, the first month has been chaotic bliss. This is what he wanted and needed. He likes the Art Walk and frequents Cole's sandwiches on the sixth street. Underneath the alcohol-laced evenings, he feels alone, isolated, and discontent. He wants Sondra. And he wants her badly. He wants to break off Jenna. Introduced Sondra to his parents. If his parents don't accept, he'll give up his inheritance, have kids with her, and move to Mexico. This is what he has decided. Brian wants to start a new life with Sondra. Best of all, He tried calling her many times with no success. He called the Police. They said, there was no reason for alarm yet. "This happens in LA all the time. Call us in a few days."

Brian opens his nightstand, then looks over the envelope, he found on the plane. The Chinese symbol and the words, 'Do Not Open' stare at him. They taunt him. He thinks about opening the envelope in the presence of Sondra, on their wedding night. Brian rubs the envelope over his face. The smell inside reminds him of an old short rib, left behind from a barbeque. The fatty one with flies all over it.

Brian places the envelope back on the nightstand. He tries calling Sondra. If she answers he will tell her he is drunk; and he really wanted to hear her beautiful voice. He will tell her he has not slept without hearing her voice, he'll tell her he loves her smell, her skin, her lips, her eyes. He will tell her many things. He will tell her all she needs to know.

Brian picks up his phone and dials. Four strong knocks are at Brian's front door. Brian stands up quickly and stumbles to the front door. It is Sondra.

Sondra looks more exotic, seductive, sexy, and beautiful than before. She wears a white dress, with silver four-inch stiletto heels. Her hands and nails are French manicured. Her hair is worn up, with silver loop earrings, lace diamond necklace, bracelets, and pink rose lipstick. Her face is whiter than before; almost that of a vampire. Her eyes makeup is very seductive looking.

Brian thinks, she is perfect.

He's immediately turned on. Sondra kind of looks like one of the patrons at Club 'Helter-Skelter.' She wears no bra and panties. This catches Brian's attention immediately. Her beautiful double C-cup breast are tucked perfectly in the dress, showing the perfect amount of cleavage.

Sondra runs into Brian's arms. She kisses him, tongue tearing into his mouth. The force, and movements of her tongue, stimulate Brian's nervous system. He's finally alive again.

Awesome, thinks Brian. Each kiss causes Brian's legs to tremble. She kind of tastes like sliced peaches in heavy syrup.

Sondra reaches down and grabs Brian between his legs. She rubs his manhood over his denim, she looks, eye contact, smiles. She looks down and sees the head peeking out over the waist band. This pleases Sondra. She never saw Brian in under-ware. She tears them down from her waste, makes him lift his feet, then kisses him more deeply. It thickens in her palm with each lapping kiss. She pulls smiling.

Brian is excited. The inside of her palms feels that of a vagina.

"How I wanted you, Brian."

Brian looks at her for a moment. He's in shock. Brian's thoughts are moving in all directions from her kisses. He looks her over from the feet up. Should he spoil the moment by asking where she's been? No, he will not. He has waited enough. No time for small talk. Thinks Brian.

"Your everything I ever dreamed of. I mean, I…fantasize about you, every night." Says Brian.

"I know, Brian. That's why I am here."

"I mean, Brian, wait, not yet." Sondra intercepts him. She turns away. Brian picks her up by the buttock and carries her to the bed. They begin kissing, this time Brian is in control. She whimpers. Then moans then whimpers again. Brian feels her body go limp and he carries her.

Finally, she is mine, he thinks. Brian drops her down on the bed, pulls up her dress, then kneels.

Brian ever so gently rubs her clitoris with his index finger. He studies her face, then smiles at her. Sondra's eyes are closed as she breathes heavy, whimpering. Brian grabs her hips then arches her up under a small pillow. He begins searching her with his tongue, as Sondra yells out. He continues as he feels heat fill his mouth.

Brian crawls up on the bed, then places his hand behind her neck. He pulls her upward as he thrust his tongue in her mouth. She reaches downward again and is pleased. She pulls him upward, licks her nipples then works his way up to her mouth again. Sondra is almost frantic with pleasure. Brian moans with anticipation, as Sondra grabs his manhood with the left hand and with the right, skillfully slides it inside her. Sondra's eyes widen as he enters her for the first time…

"I felt you, Brian. I felt you calling me. Now I am here. Take me."

She takes Brian's hands, telling him, touch my breast. Brian stops his hip movement, then lowers her dress down her legs, then through her feet. What he observes is godly. He lashes his tongue over her erect brown nipples, then leans over her head for a few moments. Hand wrapped around his presence, slowly stroking.

"Wait, my lover," she says. Stop.

Sondra quickly gets out of bed. She walks around the loft nervously. She looks around, head moving in all directions. She looks at the ceiling then grins. She feels someone or something is watching them. She avoids the subject. She avoids the thought of a hidden camera and slavery. For now, all she wants is Brian is to Fuck her. Fuck her like no man has ever fucked her before. Brian curiously looks her over.

He thinks, she may have been in a club. Dropped pills or something for more dangerous. Forget. Brian will not destroy this venture.

Sondra runs back to the bed and pushes Brian back.

"Shhhhhh." Sondra places her long finger over his mouth.

"Make love to me, Brian, I haven't much time." Sondra looks at the clock.

"What's wrong?" asks Brian. He tries sitting up again. She forcefully throws him backward on the mattress again. For the force of the throw shocks Brian. She is like no-other he's experienced.

"What are you waiting for?" asks Brian.

"An eternity with you?" says Sondra.

Sondra crawls over Brian. She sits atop him, then squirms, whimpers sounding like a kitten.

"Why do you love me?" asks Sondra.

Brian can only mumble. He is completely consumed by this god. If he speaks, he may this union of perfection. speak much.

"Make love to me, Brian. I don't have much time." Sondra leans over and kisses Brian.

"What are you waiting for?" asks Sondra.

"Where have you been?" This is all the courage he can muster now. Sondra leans into and Brian and kisses him deeply.

"Wait a moment. I tried calling." Sondra smiles, then kisses Brian again. Brian pulls her upward.

"I tried calling your store?" Sondra has a look of disappointment about her. She doesn't want to talk.

Brian carries on about her whereabouts, how she just vanished, almost disappeared. Her responsibilities. Sondra does not say a word. She leans over and looks Brian into his eyes.

"Are we going to make love, or shall I leave?" Brian shuts his mouth. She is serious. Brian sees something in her eyes he has never seen before. Before she was a shy, conservative, and discerning.

Now, he sees a woman who is older. No, not older, but more experienced. One with fire in her eyes, sinful desire, lust, anarchy. She is Brian's perfect woman. Brian can only say one sentence.

"Fuck now. We make love later."

"So, what are you waiting for?" says Sondra. Sondra looks at Brian's nightstand. She sees a wine goblet half full. She takes it, then drinks it down fast. Brian looks on in amazement.

"Now, I'm ready," says Sondra.

Brian tries speaking again. Sondra will not allow it. She places her hand over Brian's mouth. She looks at the clock. Then looks at Brian nervously.

"Hurry up, we don't have much time. Kiss me, Brian. Fast, but be quiet. They might hear us."

Sondra notions her head upstairs. A teardrop runs from her eye dripping on Brian's chest.

"Why are you crying?" asks Brian.

He leans up, wiping the tears from her eyes. Sondra pushes Brian back on the bed, then kisses Brian forcefully.

Brian grows in the palm of her hand. Sondra's head turns and swivels her tongue searching his mouth.

"Touch me," says Sondra.

Sondra directs Brian's hands over her breast, as she moans with pleasure. Sondra looks at the clock again.

"We must hurry my love." Her voice trembles, with a mixture of fear and pleasure.

Sondra forcefully directs Brian to mount. She wants him to devour her. Man-handle her.

Brian slowly enters her as Sondra gasp with pleasure. Sondra violently grinds her hips, while moaning atop of Brian. She moves her hips vertical, then back and forth, again in a circular motion. Back and forth again, then in a fast, circular motion. Her hips moving faster, then faster. Sondra is so excited; the sound of the bedpost was heard bashing the wall.

"Let me get on top." Sondra says.

Sondra begins riding Brian up and down. The bed shakes so violently, the bedpost sounds as if it's going to break.

Sondra and Brian climax together. Breathing fast and heavy, Sondra sits atop Brian backward, with her smell feet on his thighs. She rides atop Brian for a few minutes then climax again.

"Oh, shit!" says Sondra.

Sondra now lays her head on Brian's chest, as she catches her breath.

Her face feels like it's on fire. She kisses Brian's neck and quickly sits up. Sondra looks at the clock quickly, then Brian.

"Kiss me," she says. "Take my last breath away."

Sondra and Brian kiss, as a loud knock is heard on Brian's door. The four knocks are loud enough to startle then both.

Sondra pulls away from Brian. She starts to panic, breathing heavy, shaking.

Sondra gives Brian a sad, devasting look. Her eyes are tearing, nose sniffling.

"What? Where are you going?" Brian looks at her with a dazed look of satisfaction.

Sondra does not answer. She slips on her heels and runs to the exit door.

"What the fuck, wait," says Brian.

Brian stands up quickly but a bit sloppy from his bed. He is feeling the effects. Two days of drinking.

As Sondra runs for the exit, Brian tries putting his jeans on. He loses his balance falling to the floor.

Sondra exits the front door, quickly slamming it hard.

A dog is heard barking down the hallway. Another door slams shut, as heels make a clanking noise down the stairs, to the bottom exit.

Brian gathers himself and stands up. He hobbles to the front door opens and yells down the hall.

"Sondra, Sondra!" yells Brian.

The only thing in Brian's sight, is the flickering lights in the hallway. The ambient electric buzzing that makes him sick. The buzzing noise is eerie and irritating.

Brian walks down the hallway and opens the stairway exit. Nothing in sight. He desperately searches the elevator and other hallways. She is nowhere to be found. Brian limps back to his loft door, opens, and stares out. His eyes begin to tear. He fears he may never see her again. He tries calling her phone. It's off…

Brian walks to his cupboard and takes down a bottle of Makers Mark. It is going to be another long night for Brian.

Chapter 14
The Two French Men
Told by Brian

Clement and Mathis were from Paris. Like me, they had their own dreams and aspirations of Los Angeles California. Strip clubs, and many of them. They lived on the 4th floor, same as mine. And yes, this did happen. Their dream in Los Angeles came true, which turned a nightmare, or was it a lesson about American Culture?

For a city where over 80% of the residence are "passers-through," this story will be their anthem. It will be a story told by the Clement, Mathis, and their offspring for many generations. A true story of *real* renaissance men. Real French men. The kind that shuffles through the dark alleys and mean-streets of downtown; looking for weed or that last kick of opportunity. Sometimes that opportunity came in the form of; 'ladies of the night.' A story *forever* told by French firesides, laced with red wine, cheese, and Marlboro Red Packs. Especially during Halloween. Which is Ironic because the French like Halloween. And this happened around Halloween, Late-October. During one of those dark, sexy Los Angeles nights.

I met Clement and Mathis in the elevator. I was intrigued by the two French men immediately. Not because they looked odd. Not because of the color of their skin. Their height, hair, and clothing. It was because they are French. And being French means something in this town. When Clement and Mathis were introduced to the leasing agent, she said "Welcome to Los Angeles." Like that means something, anyway; they went nuts…

All their lives they waited to hear those words. "Welcome to Los Angeles." The words so long to hear, became words of desire, lust, nightclubs, electronic clubs, and women. Many women. Again, these men are French. And, they had deep wallets. They told me so. That was one of their many mistakes.

When I think of Paris, I think of *cool* movies like *European Vacation,* the *Great Race, the Pink Panther,* and *Killing Zoe.* These movies are a good thing. They are rich in culture and non-demeaning to women. I'm getting sidetracked. Anyway, our two French friends entered a world of strip club culture. Black Strip Club Culture. Americas' only strip club. This is according to Clement and Mathis. I guess they found out about the club at an underground nightclub in the La Weekly.

So, there they are. It's Saturday night. I was in the elevator with some woman I met from the Golden Gopher. Clement was wearing white knickers, white slip-on shoes, and a pink polo shirt. The color was up. He was sporting a black marker beard. Mathis, his life friend; was wearing drawstring pants, flared bottom, with blue slip-on sneakers, blue and white sailor-style shirt. They had way too much gel in their hair, smelt of Gin, Red pack cigarettes, Paco Rabanne, and Old Spice.

The woman I was with noticed the cologne. I noticed their ambitious everlasting style. The women noticed the way they "eye screwed" them. One of the girls thought they were cute. Puppy dog cute. They wanted to take them with us. She was seriously being polite.

"They asked where we were going. I told them 'Golden Gopher.' Of course, I asked them to join."

They politely declined stating they were going to a Black Strip Club in South Central. It is 'invitation only.' A Hip-Hope Strip club owned by Rappers. I don't think our French friends understood what invite only meant. I told them; they should call first.

Clement and Mathis obviously did not comprehend what I was saying. They just looked at me, looked at my lady friends, smiled, and said, "Black American Women have great, big tits, and big assess. Not like Black French Woman. And we want sex." I shook my head and unwilfully smiled.

"How much money do you guys have." They both spoke in French. Mathis translated what I was saying. They told me; they have 4000 US dollars each. I told them. "Not only will you get, but you'll be also surrounded by woman. You'll both do just fine." Like any red, white, and blue American, I shook their hands and wished them a happy holiday. My dates and I walked off into the cool fall night.

The Next Day

I was escorting my dates downstairs the next afternoon. I was a bit tired and decided to take the elevator. This is when I passed Clément's and Mathis's apartment. They were standing outside their door wearing beach style clothing. A bit odd for October.

"So, guys, how was your night?" They both looked at me like two lost puppies. They nervously shoveled their feet, as they looked at the concrete floor. Their door was open. I looked inside their loft.

"Where the hell is everything?" I ask.

Mathis rubbed his hands over his face, Clement scratched his eyes. I noticed they each had one overnight bag packed. That was it.

Apparently, their night went well. Too well.

They had a ball. They dropped money, bought drinks, requested music, they paid for lap dances. Best of all, they had a woman on each of them.

The women stayed with them, until their shift was over. They also mentioned a VISA-cash machine and bottles of champagne. Also, a VIP room.

At the end of the night, two beautiful, busty women. Ones they dreamed about, drive home with them.

Mathis tried to explain how he was almost seeing double. It was very, difficult to drive with this beautiful woman on my neck. Rubbing on me, etc. Smoking marijuana. They arrived home and anticipated the night of their life.

In the end, Mathis and Clement were found by the LAPD in an empty loft. Everything was stolen. Their television, stereo, furniture. Their silly clothes, cologne, shoes. Your name it, it was gone.

All they had left was an overnight bag each. The question remains, what happened in that club. Were they audacious assholes with money? Did they tell jokes that were distasteful? Did they pretend to be black? That's a no, no. Did they buy enough drinks? Did they not tip the bartender? Did they insult the bartender or someone of influence? Did they start a fight? Nobody will ever know.

The lesson here, travelers to Los Angeles, is never assume anything.

Like most of beautiful women in Los Angeles. Just because they're American, does not mean they are easy.

Remember this, they have boyfriends or husbands. I tried to warn Clement and Mathis. They would not listen…

What happened, LAPD told me, their boyfriends followed our favorite French men home. Trousers down, money exchanged, boyfriends, inside the loft, everything gone.

Their passports, cellular phones, credit cards, everything. Most Americans probably wonder today, where Clement and Mathis are. I wonder what they are doing. What we do know is this folks. Wherever they are, they will tell all cultures and everyone abroad.

Do not fuck with the Americans, and "Oink, oink, my good man, oink, oink."

Chapter 15
Back to Reality

Brian walks through Santee Alley, in the Garment District. Vendors are yelling out from their garages, selling various products. Most of them knock-offs. Mexican pop music blares throughout the alley. It's fucking disgusting thinks Brian.

Most of all, thoughts of Sondra fill his head. Both bad and good. Her being from Mexico and having a dress and jean shop can invite the wrong types of people. Especially in Downtown Los Angeles. Sondra is gorgeous, smart, intuitive, and comes from money. She sends money every month for her family to invest. Mostly in the rebuild of Monterey and Guadalajara.

Brian hasn't slept well. He wakes up six to eight times a night. He likes his job, he likes Lisa. However, He doesn't want Lisa. He's obsessed with Sondra. After the other night, he wants to marry her. He dreams of joining her flesh. No guilt, beautiful monogamous love making. Ordained from God.

Brian's smart. He's much smarter than any criminal. He also knows if anyone hurts Sondra. He'll have them killed. His friends as West Point are connected. They never leave you. Brian thinks of how smart Sondra is. There is no way, she would get involved with an asshole. Brian feels Sondra is smarter than he. Just like Hilary is smarter than Bill. And that's a good thing. With her, he can and will build a financial empire. He so worried, he feels deathly ill. He's read about women who've been kidnapped, forced into slavery, and murdered for their gifts. This downright pisses Brian off. These people who kidnap also anger his father. When Jack says angered, or something is a "Problem." Run for your life. Better yet, leave this planet.

Brian walks to a hotdog stand. He was planning on carrying up six hotdogs and four bottles of champagne for him and Sondra. He likes the word Perrito

Calientes. It is a fact; Downtown Los Angeles has the best Perrito Calientes on Earth. Brian's traveled almost everywhere.

He thinks, *Mazatlán is a close second.*

Brian knows enough to keep his wallet in his front pocket. Especially during the holiday. All cities are the same during the holiday.

Buses in Washington, Subway's in New York, or flea markets, rugs in Seattle, it's all the same. Brian can't wait to see Sondra. His hands shake, and he feels nervous thinking about her.

A male Mexican vendor tries capturing his attention with a fake leather jacket.

Brian refuses in Spanish and politely walks on. An attractive Mexican woman walks by Brian. Usually Brian would say hello, or smile. Not today. She kind of looks like Sondra, he thinks.

Brian buys two hotdogs and two long neck Mexican Coca Cola's. He thanks the vendor then walks onward.

He's never seen anything like Santee Alley before. He walks past the cooking store and the guy with the fake automatic watches. He looks at a few fake automatic Rolex. Brian thinks the Submariner looks pretty good. He buys one for LA bragging rights. Hey, MACH 3 Razors. Can' t live without those. Brian wonders if the cooking ware is any good.

Brian stands in front of Sondra's store. Unfortunately, the gate is down, and metal doors locked.

Brian asks a vendor across her store where she is. Nobody knows anything. He starts to worry, and his stomach knots. He's so tense he squeezes the hotdogs until they fall apart. The Coke bottle in his right-hand cracks from his hand clenching the bottle.

If Sondra's gone forever, Brian will walk the Earth in her revenge. This is what Henry's organization wants. A wrath child. Son of Sam. Sam meaning Satan and Master. He thinks about destroying everyone in his path, then takes a deep breathe.

Brian walks to a trash can and dumps the food and drinks.

A female vendor walks out into the alley, four stores South of Sondra. She looks Eastern European, black hair, early, to mid-sixties. She wears a long black dress, gold sandals, and an abundance of jewelry. Brian notices her as he quickly walks by.

"Hey, you," says the vendor woman.

"Hey what?" Brian replies, in an agitated tone.

"Yes you, come here, young man."

"What do you want?" asks Brian.

"You," says the vendor woman.

Brian laughs aloud, "I'm sure you do." Condescending tone. The vendor looks at him smiling, as she places out her hand. She trees *reading* him. She closes her eyes and lowers her head.

What kind of pagan bullshit is this? thinks Brian.

Brian looks her over, her eyes closed, chanting to herself.

"Lady, I have no time for your shit right now. Play your games with someone else. Good day."

Brian walks away. The vendor woman yells out loud.

"She's all around you," says the vendor woman.

The statement immediately grabs Brian's attention. Brian stops, turns around, and walks toward the woman. She grinningly looks at him.

"Why do you question me?" asks the woman.

"Lady, I haven't asked you anything."

"I can read you. Brian is your name. She loves you with all her soul."

"How do you know my name?"

"Follow me, and I will show you," says the woman.

Brian, without hesitation, follows the woman through the entrance of her store. The store looks like something you would see in a vampire movie. Or Venice Beach, Los Angeles. People who are into the essence of garlic, holistic cures, potions for sex, love, marriage. Talisman. It's all here. There are many old and new books. Brian looks at a cover that read, "Spells and Tranquility."

Odd-looking patrons are in view. The kinds of his father told him about. The kinds of people that stand out wherever they go. The kinds that want to be different, and not in a good way. People who don't appreciate arts. They just want to steal it. People who spy on you when your loft window is open. They call the police, and report lies. They pay off the maintenance man, get your apartment key, then illegally record you and your girlfriend, or even wife, when you make love. The type of people that hate Christians, Jews, and Catholics. The types that hate you for any reason. The types that smoke what they want, drink what they, want, snort what they want, shoot what they want, screw whoever they wish, then blame it on the government.

They are "thieves, liars, and hypocrites." These are the peoples' Brian's father warned him about. Candles, oils, incense, masks, paintings, water pipes, and other drug paraphernalia.

Brian follows the odd-looking woman into her private office. Brian can't help to think if she is a prostitute, or just wants sex. She isn't bad looking. The more he looks, the more he thinks about sex. It is bewitching.

"No need praying in here, young man. He's of no hope for you," says a man looking at witchcraft books.

Brian's stunned, yet curious. He's taken on this type before. One on a pier in Washington. The muscles on his back begin to tighten. The hairs on his back begin tingling. With every step, the room feels much colder. Hairs on his arms stand.

He hears a voice in his head, *Leave, Brian, evil dwells here. Leave now.*

Brian walks through door beads, as he enters her private room. The store owner sits down, first showing her cleavage. It looks warm and inviting. Brian shakes off his thoughts, then sits down in front of her. He sighs, while looking around the room. Behind her, stands an old wooden crucifix, with Christ affixed to it. What kind of message is this? Thinks Brian. Brian looks at the crucifix and comments.

"What kind of demonic irony is that crap?"

The woman doesn't say a word. She looks him over like a long-lost lover. Or a dead relative from Tasmania, comes to life.

Brian nervously readjusts his posture in the uncomfortable chair.

"What are you bothered about?" asks the woman.

"Nothing," says Brian. "Nice place you have here. It is warm, inviting, and eclectic. Reminds me of home."

"You are home, Brian." The woman tries being spooky. She looks over Brian like he is a ten-pound T-bone steak. She lashes a long-pointed tongue over her upper lip. It's sexy to Brian. Thoughts of sex fill Brian's head again. Brian cannot figure out why he keeps thinking about sex. She is kind of attractive. However, not that attractive.

"Why are you fighting me?" asks the woman.

"Excuse me?" asks Brian. "Sorry, I really don't understand, or comprehend where you are going with this."

The woman laughs aloud.

"You can't fool me, Brian. I know you."

Brian thinks, *Blah, Blah, Blah, Blah, Blah. She must be desperate for sex or something.*

She continues with her rubbish, "You're easy to read. You are very depressed, in love, you feel lost. Let me see your hand."

They all start with this crap, thinks Brian.

"You're not going to borrow it, dirty it up, then mail it back to me," asks Brian.

The vendor woman laughs so loud, one of the workers check to see if everything is OK.

"Let me see your hand," says the woman.

"I'd rather not."

"Don't be shy, I won't bite."

The woman raises her eyebrows and grins seductively. Brian surrenders his left hand.

"What's this about?" asks Brian.

"It's quite simple for me. I saw you; she called me. Now you are here?"

"How do you know my name? Who called who?"

"Relax, Brian. You're safe here."

The woman looks over Brian as she observes his hand.

Brian looks uncomfortable. He takes a deep breath, then nervously looks around the room.

She looks at this palm, then looks at Brian. She looks at his palm grins, then smiles at Brian.

"What?" asks Brian.

She chuckles, then shuffles her body in the seat.

"Like I said, you're easy to read."

"Thanks, that's comforting," says Brian.

The woman's facial expression changes. Her eyes are now beading. Face narrows.

"Be careful during this two-week period."

"Why?" asks Brian.

"I'll explain in simpler terms. In Eastern cultures, have you heard the 15-day reign from Hell?"

"What's that, and what's it got to do with me?"

"It has everything to do with you, Brian. You and everyone. It happens every lunar year. During this 15-day period, the darkest and most powerful spirits from hell, are allowed free reign upon the earth. It is an act of God. The chances of war, rebellion, anarchy, hate crimes, murder, and other evil deeds, are more influenced upon a man, than any other time. There are ancient scripts that say some of the demons take shape in human form." The woman looks over Brian's left hand again.

"There is a warning here. Brian is very, uncomfortable. He is squeamish and begins to sweat from his forehead."

"Well, I don't believe in this. You do this to everyone. A game you play." Brian tries taking his hand back. He is unsuccessful.

"Let me see your other hand," she says. Brian reluctantly gives her his right hand.

"You know who she is, Brian." Brian quickly takes away both of his hands, he tries to stand, but he cannot. He feels as if some large creature is standing him, holding him to the chair.

"She has a message for you. She says she is waiting and wants you, is looking for you. Her name starts with the letter 'Sssss.'"

The woman pauses for a moment. She grabs both of Brian's hands and squeezes tight.

"It's clear now. She says something about an envelope, she saw in your apartment."

The woman's voice trembles. Her eyes roll back in her head, showing all white. She grabs Brian's hands and starts convulsing. The vendor woman places back her head. She lets out a horrifying scream. One so loud, all the candles burn out. A few pictures fall off the wall, as the woman reaches over the table and begins choking Brian.

Brian places his hands over her arms. He cannot move them. Brian begins to gasp for air as the robust woman scream and yells. In an effort, to pull his hands away, he stands up, falling hard to the ground. The woman continues to scream, as the lights turn off. Her screaming is so loud, Brian sits on his knees covering his ears. The screaming brings another woman into the room.

"What are you doing to my mother. Who are you?" The vendor woman now begins sobbing. She mumbles of hell and pain.

"The horrible pain, the suffering. The children there." She looks at Brian's fearful expression. She starts sobbing again.

"I don't know what happened. She was reading my hand, then she started yelling. I didn't do anything. She attacked me."

"My mother would not attack anyone."

Brian tries offering help, he kneels trying to help calm the woman.

"Go now." Brian offers a hand helping her up.

"I said go! Go now!!" Brian reaches in his pocket and takes out four 50-dollars bills. He offers to the younger woman.

"We don't need your money here. Bastard!"

Brian drops the money on the ground, turns away, then stands at the door. He looks back one last time. He watches the young woman rock the older one, comforting her. Then he looks at the crucifix. The crucifix somehow, mysteriously, stands upside down on the wall.

A cool breeze blows over Brian, and he hears laughing in the store. Brian will exit this domain and never enter again. When he finds Sondra, he will tell her to move. She will. He will help her. They will open a normal storefront in the Arcadia Mall. Tonight, he will drive to Figueroa Street. There he will pray and re-gather his thoughts. Most of all, he will pray for his love Sondra.

Chapter 16

Brian sits at his dining table. He stares expressionless at his whisky glass. He fills another four-finger glass, then looks at the clock on the wall. Brian drinks his whisky, observing the envelope with the Chinese symbol.

The evil satanic bitch earlier didn't bother Brian. He has dealt with people like *them* before. Matter of fact, it was fun. Just another parlor trick to suck money from tourist.

He rubs his thumb and index finger over the round object inside. He thinks of the woman, and the fucked-up things she told him. Brian thinks about her knowing his name; and the woman looking for you starts with S. Sondra's probably been there before, he hopes. She does a portrait of them on her phone. He now thinks the worst. However, he's not scared anymore. He's not scared of anything. He now knows what to do. Who they are?

Brian did go to the church. He prayed and met with one of the priests. He was reminded of demons, and trickery. That demons want good people like Brian. They already have the bad ones. Demons will lie, entice, offer you worldly desires, and use other humans to destroy you. These comforting words made Brian feel a heck of a lot better.

Brian ran to the USC liquor store and bought enough booze to last him for 4 months. His Omen. Or shall we all call it fate?

There are four knocks on Brian's door. He knows who it is, and he really doesn't want to answer. It is Rob and Robert. The man has a dual bi-polar, personality, with Distinctive Tendencies. Guess it depends on his douche bag mood.

Brian promised he would go out with Robert tonight. Brian is a man of his word. It's the way he was raised. He would rather sulk at home, have a few drinks in a hot bath. Watch '*Wizard of Oz*' or '*Raiders of the Lost Ark*.' Then a depressing love movie like 'Leaving Las Vegas'. In fact, Brian believes

'Leaving Las Vegas' may be the best movie ever made. Except for the violence on the women. Why does Hollywood have to fuck up a good movie?

Brian would rather sit watch and fantasize about he and Sondra. Having too much time and too much money. Drinking and fucking their way through paradise. Ending up at Farmer Boys at 4:00 AM.

This is the way love should be, thinks Brian, as he admired his whisky glass.

Brian hears the door knock again. Brian looks at the clock then sighs, clears his throat, takes a drag of a cigarette, then takes a sip. It reads 10:00 PM. He Whisky is Brian's comfort. It's his poison. Reminds him of a depressed Irish Mobster planning revenge on enemies of the church. For him, there is no other spirit.

Brian slowly makes his way to the front door opening. He sees Rob-Robert in the doorway. Smiling mischievously, a bottle of vodka, eyes gleaming.

"Wait until you see what I have planned tonight," says Robert.

"It's Sunday, don't forget we have to work tomorrow," Brian says.

"Don't get all pussy on me now, big boy. If we get too fucked up, we'll call in sick. You're the number one producer, home slice."

"Come inside, for a drink before we go," says Brian.

"Drink, fuck that, man. We have all night for that. Get your shit together. Let's get out of here. Ever since you've been here, all you do is sit on your ass."

"You don't know shit about me." Brian says,

"Well after tonight, you'll never sit home alone again." Robert laughs aloud.

Brian looks at Rob, shakes his head, rolling his eyes.

"Well, come on, let's get a drink, buddy." Rob says.

Buddy, buddy? What kind of reference is "buddy" to a true friend? Brian doesn't like that word. In Washington, it means the enemy. Just like "my friend" in Armenian means enemy.

Brian takes his black leather jacket, leaving with Rob. Rob will not shut his mouth. All the way down, to the courtyard. All he talks about are women he's never been with. It is kinds of amusing how men, those who never have sex, or make love, always talk about it.

Tonight, Brian may see a side of a human male, he despises. It may be quite comical. It might be depressing. It may be tragic. Either way, Brian's not interested in Robert's friendship. He feels the night may end of disaster. He's using this demonic night; to get rid of him; for good. Brian can't wonder enough about how many women will slap his face or punch him in the balls. Robert and Brian look at the other tenants in the courtyard. It's a healthy atmosphere. Many single women. Sitting talking with each other, walking their dogs, drinking beer.

"Dude, the women in your building are hot," Rob says loudly.

Brian covers his ears for a moment, as they walk by the security officer. It is the same weirdo Brian meets in front of Sondra's loft.

"You boys heading out tonight," he asks. *Stupid question* thinks Brian.

"Hell, yes, bro, we're getting our drink and woman on us," says Robert.

Rob tries high fiving the security guard. He refuses. The security guard looks over Brian, giving him the eerie "I know who you are" look.

"Brian. Be careful out there. Bad things are going on tonight," says the security guard. "It's that time of year. Hell walks our earth."

Brian and Rob continue to walk on. Only Brian turns around as they walk. He sees the security guards standing in the middle of the lot, looking at him. The security guards look at each other, then start to laugh.

Brian and Rob drive through the Downtown streets. Rob drives a BMW M5. He's inconsistent with the acceleration; the ride is jerky and unrefined. The exhaust is aftermarket. *What kind of moron places an aftermarket exhaust on an M5?* thinks Brian. Rob likes revving the engine at the red lights. He looks at the other drivers at all the stops. Especially the woman. The woman never looks at Robert. They just laugh. Of course, he turns up the music. It only makes Brian more embarrassed.

"What's the big deal tonight?" asks Brian.

"Dude, there's this place called '*Fugitive Theater*.' Tonight, it's a fetish club. Pretty fuckin sweet buddy. Pussy will be crawling the walls."

"Sex club? Rob, forget about it. I'm not into that sort of thing."

"After tonight, you'll never forget this place The women there are smoking hot. The drinks are lethal, and the music kicks ass. What else you want from a club?"

Rob looks out his window, yelling at a woman in a Porsche.

"Hey honey, you wanna drag?" The woman pays no attention.

"Aww, sugar, no need being stuck up." Says Rob.

Brian interrupts.

"I don't need to hang out at a fetish club to find women," Brian says.

"Dude, they pass out pills there like chewing gum. I mean rock hard baby. Rock hard…"

Rob notices the sour look upon Brian's face.

"Hey, well looks at you. Mr. fuckin' sexy. Casanova, Don Juan Del Douche. I've seen you at the office bro. Chicks are all over you. And you, you fucker, do nothing about it."

Brian sees already that Rob is a complete fuckin' moron. Yet, Brian is intrigued. Again. *How can a man like him exist amongst the female races?*

Rob continues a million miles a second about nothing.

"Dude, why you so gloom. It is a Fetish club. It's different than a sex club."

Like this asshole has been to one, thinks Brian.

"Let's go too that Grand and ninth place. Timo Maas is there tonight. Lisa was telling me about it. I think she's going tonight."

"Ha, Ha. Holy shit. Lisa, oh, man, Lisa? You will see. Fuck Grand man, we're going to the fetish club."

Rob starts laughing aloud. He stamps his right hand on the steering wheel, and pounds on the roof with his other. Then, he starts howling like a Wolfman. Like the fuckin' awesome movie Wolfen. The one in 1981. This act of male indecency doesn't bother Brian. He finally laughs. How can he not laugh at this fool. We all would. Robert gives Brian a flask.

"Drink this dude."

"What is it."

"Dude, it's 151. Used to be my grandfather's. I found it after he died. It is fuckin' awesome." Brian takes a sip and almost coughs up his lungs.

"What the hell?"

"Dude, it's like over 50 years old. I told you, fuck, yeah, buddy; fetish club it is. I have a surprise for you, my good man. Brian, serious of you can't get action tonight, you got a serious mental problem."

Robert takes another sip of the 151. He passes to Brian. He takes a small inhalant sip. Brian feels his lungs get warm. Then a warm wave of ecstasy flows through his body. He feels good now. He wonders how heroin addicts feel…

Why should I sit home by myself? Brian thinks. *I love Sondra, if she doesn't love me, fuck it. There is nothing I can do.*

"Sorry, that I've been putting you off lately, Robert."

"Rob. Call me Rob."

"Yeah, whatever. Anyway, you don't understand. I met the perfect woman, and she vanished. I mean this one was it. I can't get her out of my head. It's almost like when I'm alone she's there, watching me."

"Is she banging you, man?"

"What?"

"Dude is she one of those hot, 'nasty witches that come to you in dreams.' You know, like a succubus."

"Suck a what, Robert."

"Call me Rob, dude."

"You have serious mental problems," says Brian.

"I know, man, that's why we're out. Your new fucked up friends going to show you an ass-kicking time. Fuck it, man. Let it go. Let it all go."

"Alright, alright. Keep your panties on. The fugitive whatever, it is." Robert offers a high-five to Brian. Brian accepts for the first time.

Robert yells out his window, howling at the moon again. "Brian, check this out. Listen to this song. It will get you in the mood." Robert turns the CD player on in his BMW. He plays, 'I Can Tell, By Bo Diddley.'

Robert is now at Grand Avenue. He turns left at the light and floors the Gargantuan V8. It growls like a hungry demon through the thick, sexy Los Angeles night.

Brian and Robert walk through the entry doors of the infamous sixth street, Parkview Plaza Hotel. The interior has not changed much since the Golden Age of Hollywood. It was a very, popular spot in the 1980s. They welcomed Punk Rock and Gothic club goers. It was the first hotel in Los Angeles to do so.

Brian and Robert are in the main lobby. They slowly walk up the red stairs that lead to the main party hall. Brian notices a wide array of women walking by. Some are dressed as French Maids, another a sexy Swiss Nurse. Two women dressed in lingerie, with high heels and garters. One woman walks other women, with dog collars. Some carry whips, chains. Some wear SS hats with aviator frames. Brian's eyes are bulging. He's never seen anything like this. Not in DC.

"See, man, what did I tell you?" Says Robert.

Brian doesn't say anything. A seductive looking Italian woman walks by Brian and winks. As Robert leads Brian up the main stairway, three large bouncers over six feet tall, over 225 pounds, look him over. Robert gives each bouncer a 20-dollar bill. He wants to keep his flask, and the pills hidden in the bottom compartment.

In the background, the music plays from the main ballroom. The track is 'Layo & Bushwacka. Let the Good Times Roll.'

Bouncer finishes patting down Robert, then gives him the stare. The stare only a door bouncer can give.

The stare saying, "We'll be watching you."

Robert responds by giving each bouncer a $50,00 dollar bill.

Brian and Robert enter the main ballroom. Laser lights and flashing colors are seen everywhere. There is also a mist in the air from the fogger, cigarette, and marijuana smoke. The dance floor is full of many *interesting* people. The DJ is known as DJ Dan. The DJ sways his body slowly to the music, while his entourage feeds him booze.

"Welcome to Babylon.!!" Yells Robert.

Brian looks on and smiles. The first thing he notices is a female cocktail waitress, mid-20s white lingerie, pink wig, very sexy and seductive.

"Well, buddy," says Robert. "Let's get a drink."

As Rob leads Brian to the bar. There are laser lights and flashing colored lights are hypnotic, euphoric, blinding. The dance floor is full of many different characters. The VIP sections are full, and couches are occupied. There are many women in this club. More than men.

This is good, thinks Brian. He sees quite a few that are extremely seductive. As the biorhythm of the music vibrates through his intestines, he feels tingling in his legs. It feels erotic and exciting. Something he has never felt before.

What Brian needs now, is a drink. His mouth starts to water as he sees the beautiful woman at the bar. He hopes he hasn't overdone it. The 151 is starting to kick. Brian soon may have to vomit. That would suck. Could you imagine, talking to a hot woman in the VIP section then, of shit sorry, can I have your number?

Brian and Robert are at the bar. Brian grabs the first seat he sees. He's not going anywhere until, he is lured away by a beautiful woman, or the VIP has an opening. An opening close to the bathroom. They'll probably need it later.

An attractive female bartender woman with short black hair, white skin, a black baby T-shirt, and dark eyeliner approaches Brian.

"What do you guys want?"

"You," says Robert. She gives him the *look*. "Just kidding honey; two double shots of Jack Daniels, no ice." The bartender smiles at Brian and walks away.

"Dude, check out at all these tunas. Hope you brought your fishing rod buddy." Brian looks at Robert, then shakes his head. "I said a joke, get it?"

"Hey, Robert," says Brian.

"Call me Rob, dude."

"Anyway, how do you attract woman, or even date a woman with your attitude?" asks Brian.

"Because I don't give a damn. I'm like Damone."

"How the hell is he?" asks Brian.

"Doesn't matter, man. Just sit back and watch the *master* at work."

The bartender returns with the drinks. Robert throws her two twenties and yells keep the change.

"The doubles are 50." Rob reluctantly throws another 20 on the table. The bartender takes the money, walks away, turns, and smiles at Brian. Robert offers a toast to Brian. Laylo & Bushwacka, is now ending. The next track the DJ plays is 'Christian Death,' The Drowning.

"Dude, I'm going into circulation, just like the mix," says Robert.

Brian raises his glass as he watches Robert vanish in the haze. Brian leans into the bar, then looks over the large shot she gave him. It is overwhelming. Everything about the club is overwhelming. A few more of these, I will be finished, thinks Brian.

Brian notices a mirror behind the top-shelf bottles. He looks in the mirror and watches people pass him by. Some stare, others smile while looking. He can feel each person that walks behind him. Some good, some bad, some do it as a release; some are pure evil. It is the evil ones you must look out for Brian always says.

Brian doesn't say anything or tell anyone about the supernatural world. What he knows is his own business. It is all learned. Only Sondra would appreciate his knowledge. The rest all want to feed on him. Extract, steal and make him a slave to their world. Brian's world is more powerful, he thinks.

He'll destroy all of *them* first. What a way to be looked at in life. Slave of a father who is one of the most powerful men in American history.

A woman walks behind Brian. She is tall and curvy. Her hair is dark, she wears a cat-eyed mask, white guarders, white leggings, and clear-silver heels.

Brian sees her standing behind him.

"Hey, there, handsome." Brian turns around.

"Hey, how are you tonight?"

"You don't recognize me?"

"I'm sorry, it may be the—" The woman uncovers her face.

"No, way, it's you."

"Yes, it is. I changed my hair back to brown."

"You look amazing. Seriously. Your hair would look great any color though. Even blue."

"I'll have to remember that, when I wear a wig for you," Lisa says while chuckling. She leans into Brian.

Lisa smells good. Too good. How can she wear it? How can she know? Oscar De La Renta, the pink box stuff. Shit, now I'm doomed.

"You smell really, really good,"

"I know what you like, Brian."

Holy crap, she's doing her research, thinks Brian. *Not bad...*

"What are you doing here," asks Brian.

"This is unusual for me, the first time. Robert—"

"Rob," says Brian.

"Yeah, whatever. Well, Robert said he was taking you here. Remember I said, we must celebrate your promotion."

"Yes, I remember."

"Well, here I am."

"And., I like it," says Brian.

"You do?"

"Oh, yes."

Lisa smiles at Brian. She moves in closer and wraps her right arm over his shoulder. She's very seductive. Every move. Every word, every touch to his hands and neck is felt all through his body. He has always liked Lisa. She calls the bartender.

"Two double shots of Jack Daniels," says Lisa.

Just like Brian was thinking. Every word she says turns him on. Lisa doesn't waste any time. She's wanted to fuck Brian, since the first time she sat with him. Lisa moves in again. This time she places his hands on his face. turning it toward him, then slowly places her mouth on his. Her kiss makes Brian dizzy. He feels like he is losing his legs. He pulls back. The smell of her perfume makes his penis dance.

"I'm a bit high," Brian says. "Been drinking 151."

"So am I," says Lisa.

"High? Really."

"Absolutely."

One of the bar patrons stand up and leave. He immediately offers the seat to Lisa. He takes his leather jacket and places it over the seat. The bartender brings the drinks over. He sets them down in front of them. Brian takes out a 50-dollar bill and sets it down.

"It's on the house."

Brian looks at Lisa smiling.

"I thought you said, this is unusual?"

"I come to these parties once, in a while. Janet, the receptionist, her boyfriend works in production."

Brian's expression goes emotionless. She sees he's thinking. Not in her favor.

"Don't worry, Brian. Don't think. Relax, like I said. It's not my thing."

"Cool," says Brian. A word he thought he'd never say.

Lisa looks over Brian. She knows he's thinking of Sondra. It makes her furious with envy and jealous. There's an uncomfortable silence between them both. Lisa tries to ease the situation by rubbing Brian's shoulders. The DJ cues the next record. The tract is 'Crystal Method, High Roller, Myagi Remix.'

Brian looks around the club.

"I wonder where Robert is?" asks Brian.

"Rob's a fuckin' asshole Brians. A dick less warrior. Don't pay attention. He is probably trying to pick up on some slut. Brian seriously, the man's pathetic, a real douche. He's tried to screw every woman in the office." Brian laughs aloud.

"Yeah, I must admit, Robert is a modern art masterpiece."

Lisa smiles. He's coming back to her.

"I know, it's funny. He tells the new girls he's the manager of the marketing division. When he finally convinces someone to go out, he has her pay for half the dinner. And drinks. To top that off, he tells her, about all the connections he has in Hollywood." He actually lost a bet at work. He had to wear a pink shirt, saying 'chick magnet.' The idiot enjoyed it. That's how he is Brian. Any attention he receives, any, in his mind, is good.

Brian and Lisa are laughing together. She offers cheers again. Brian is unfavorably comfortable with her at best. For now, she helps him forget Sondra.

"Now, we must finish one drink." They both finish their shots. Lisa immediately orders two more.

"And Roberts's hair. I mean, what does he use? What does he use? Lemon juice and egg whites? Brian, I am serious. Believe me, all the girls laugh at him."

The bartender delivers two double shots of Jack Daniels. The way things are going. Brian may sit at the bar until 2:00 AM. Lisa is going on about Robert. Honestly, it's starting to bother Brian. He looks at Lisa's eyes. She's high. She took a pill. That doesn't bother him. Brian doesn't judge anyone. It is your life. You want to fuck it all up, good riddance.

He thinks about Sondra, then looks at Lisa. He wonders where she is. He already tried calling four times today. Her voicemail is full.

Screw it, he thinks. *Lisa is good looking. She might be fun when she's high.* He hopes *this* isn't a habit for her.

As she references Robert, Brian takes a good long drink. He looks around the nightclub. He's kind of worried about Robert. The way the bouncer looked at him, anyone would worry.

"So, what's the deal, are you and Robert like buddies, or something?"

"I'd say like something. He dragged me here tonight," says Brian.

"Dragged?"

"Yes, dragged. I'm missing those movies, *Two Days in the Valley* and *Welcome to the Dollhouse.*"

"After that, *Adams family and Farmer Boys, Burgers…*"

Lisa looks over Brian. She's gossiped enough about Brian. She knows what she wants, no; must have him. No woman will *ever* get in her way. Brian looks at his Jack Daniels glass and finishes.

"I wonder what creature's dwell in here?" asks Brian.

Brian's a bit high now. Booze only, so far. With each drink, Lisa is looking better and better. This is what Lisa hopes for. This is what she planned with Robert from the beginning. She looks like the hot woman in the movie, the Bond, movie. 'Thunder ball.'

This upsets Brian. He can be home with Sondra; he wishes; watching the first four Bond films. He catches himself ghosting and remembers Lisa is chatting away.

"I can't believe I'm here, you wanna leave?"

Lisa's eyes light up her expression.

"Where?" asks Brian.

"Anywhere but here? I hate this crap."

"Why waste time?" Lisa laughs.

"Brian, I am not the easy woman, you may think."

"First of all, I never thought, or assumed you are easy. Secondly, and most important, you are the one, that wanted to, what was that you said? Go out and celebrate. Well, here we are celebrating. I know we can do better than this, and I don't see what the problem is. I do like you; you are a good woman, Lisa. And totally cool. And—"

Lisa interrupts Brian then kisses him again. He smiles and calls the bartender. He orders two more double shots of Jack Daniels.

"Shit, Brian. We're going to get smashed."

"Nothing wrong with getting smashed. It is wasted. That's what we must be careful of."

"You got that right," says Brian.

The attractive female bartender. She was eavesdropping on the conversation. She looks at Lisa and frowns. Lisa without Brian notices; slips her the middle finger.

Lisa moves into Brian slowly. She kisses him again lightly on the lips. Then gently bites his lower lip. She whispers in Brian's ear.

"I think we should cool it after this."

The bartender brings back the shots. She glares at Lisa, this time asking for money. Lisa lays down 20 dollars for the shots. The bartender walks away giving Lisa the finger. Lisa moves the glass toward Brian.

"Let us toast, Brian. To new friends."

Lisa savors the moment. She secretly toasts to her, future pregnancy with Brian.

"To new friends," says Brian.

This time Brian leans into Lisa and places a quick kiss on her lips.

"It's about time you loosen up. I have a surprise for you," says Lisa.

"What?"

"Stick out your tongue, close your eyes." Lisa gives Brian a deep long kiss. She pulls away and looks at him with straight eye contact.

"From this moment on. You will never be the same, Brian."

"What are doing to me?"

"I'm saving your life." Lisa replies.

Lisa grabs him behind the neck and kisses him deep and much harder now. As they kiss the DJ cues, 'In the Flat Field, By Bauhaus.'

Lisa pulls away from Brian grinning.

"Tonight, your mine." Says Lisa.

Brian has an uneasy feeling. His head feels dizzy, his arms, legs, and hands tremble. He feels if he might vomit.

"Lisa, I must go to use the restroom."

"You, ok? You don't look like you used to."

Brian stands up, then looks over Lisa. Suddenly she doesn't look the same either. Her eyes look uneasy, demonic, self-serving.

"Swell. I'll be back."

"Hurry up." Replies Lisa.

"Wait here. I won't be long." Brian walks away into the crowd, the more he walks the music is louder. The guitar of Daniel Ash slashes through Brian's brain.

He has visions of Sondra, then hell. His body starts to burn, and everything around him is synthetic now, fake, surreal. It is not comforting.

He looks back and Lisa from across the nightclub. He can barely see her. What he does notice is a man in a black suit talking to her. Black suit with red tie.

The strobe lights flash now as Brian vanishes deeper into the crowd. Brian finds his way to the stairs. He sees a sign with a devil pointing.

It reads, "Restrooms."

Chapter 17

Brian stands in front of the bathroom stall. He places his head back, takes a deep breathe, then yawns. He's impressed by the deco architecture. The green and black tile look like mint ice cream, with black chocolate. He also likes the 1940s French sinks and beveled mirrors. Brian places his head back and breathes deeply again. He's now having trouble. His heart feels like it's burning. His back is tight. Brian's bladder is so full, it hurts him to urinate. He knows in his heart, now, he's over done it. All he can think about is home and Sondra.

The music is good though, Brian thinks. The DJ cues another 'Bauhaus Track, Hollow Hills. Brian thinks, the song is dark, but appropriate for his mood. He wonders if Lisa would mind having sex to this music. Sonra too. That would awesome, thinks Brian. A dark loft with candles lit everywhere across the room. How can light exist without darkness? Another theory that he will soon discuss with Sondra. If the conversation goes well, his clarity will reach another plane of conscience. Brian will try taking it easy, rest of the night. Take it easy, Brian thinks it sounds like 'The Eagles' Non-threatening party music. Not his thing. He'll soon be hone with Sondra. Hell, or high water, he will find that woman. It is only Los Angeles. She cannot be that hard to find. I can find anyone. In any country, anytime. Brian's thinks. All I do, is use my connections…

As Brian urinates, he looks at a newspaper clipping on the board. He reads them over. Most of them are from LA X Press, and La Weekly. " Bad girls. We're twins.' Full-sized, amateurs, and small. I'm your one-armed bandit. If you thought Pinocchio had a problem, call me. Freak show Mary wants to bury you. And. I'll whip your heart out."

Brian looks over the adds curiously. They're much different than in Washington. He called a few women in Washington. It was for knowledge and life experience. It was at best interesting. He paid $250.00 dollars for the woman to walk in his apartment. She sat and starred at him. That was it. She said, "no sex, and for every item of clothes I remove, you pay $150.00." What he learned from this woman was her son had cancer, she needed the money. Her family needed money. All the other women said the same. Makes you think. Are *all* these woman victims. Stuck in a world of brainwashing, and compromise. Brian remembers the woman being robotic, emotionless, trance like. A compromise that benefits their owners only. As Brian looks at the ads. He thinks of Troy and the girl that killed him. He snaps out his thought process, noticing two guys talking about the SS twins dancing to the 'Cramps.'

Who gives a damn? The evil son of gun deserved it anyway. Brian mumbles to himself.

Brian shakes his head, chuckles aloud. He flushes the toilet, then heads toward the sink. He washes his face. The cool water feels good over his skin. He is also thirsty, craving bottled water. The music outside, oddly, becomes a bit faint. He hopes the club isn't closing yet. Lisa is not Sondra. However, they might become friends. That would be awesome thinks Brian. I feel so high thinks Brian. What did that evil bitch, Lisa do to me. My heart, my head, my left arm is starting to tingle…

To Brian's left, sits in the corner an older man in his late 60s. He wears a formal tuxedo with Ray-Ban sunglasses. He looks over Brian like he is reading a book.

"May I please have a towel?" asks Brian.

"I'm on break. Get your own damn towel; fool."

The old man stands up, looks at Brian, shakes his head, then lights up a cigarette.

"I'm too old for this shit," says the attendant. "I've been working this hear hotel for over 44 years. I've seen it all young man. Demons, mistresses, The Messiah of Evil. Eternal pleasures to no end. Be careful tonight boy."

Brian looks over the man, not saying a word. His heart feels if a needle quickly jabbed it.

The old man quickly exits the bathroom, then slams the door. Brian looks at the mirror in front of him. He notices every crevice. Every imperfection, every pour on his face. The blackheads on his nose look huge, oversized. Paisley shapes being to move on the deco painted walls.

I am one ugly disgusting human, thinks Brian. *Holy crap, I must be at a looney farm.*

Brian walks back to the sink. He really liked the feeling of the cool water on his face and hands. He thinks he will give it another try.

A man in late 50s, dead pale skin, black suit, black shirt, and purple tie, with white dots, stands directly behind Brian. His hair is almost white and noticeably short. There is no color in his eyes. They look dead grey. Kind of like 'Linda Blair in the Exorcist.' Brian thinks of his training. 'One move by this weirdo and his arm is mine.' Brian mumbles to himself.

Brian continues washing his face. He dries off, then dries his hand. He throws the towel on the attendant's chair. The man stares emotionlessly as Brian looks back in the mirror.

"What are you looking at?" asks Brian. In situations like these, always let the individual know your conscience. The man continues to stare at Brian unemotionlessly.

"There are plenty of other sinks, old man." Brian says.

The man doesn't budge. Brian decides he is in danger. He's going to lay this asshole on the floor. Brian immediately throws a right elbow to his nose, then grabs his right arm, twist, and goes for the break. Problem is, no man is there. Fear overtakes Brian. He looks in the mirror, then man reappears. He knows he's not real, maybe some ghost or even demon. Robert said the Hotel is haunted. The man places his pale white hand over Brian's mouth. His other arm wraps around Brian's head. The force on Brian's head feels like his skull will crack. Brian cannot move. He tries with all his strength. All his training is useless. All muscle control is lost. He feels as if he's in the presence of an entity that wants him. Whatever it is, it's satanic. He now knows. It's the same demon that attacked him, home the other night. Brian can't breathe. This creature, this monster is taking his life. His heart begins beating slower, then slower. Brian hopes someone else will soon show up. His arms and hands begin to swell and tingle. He cannot feel his feet below him.

Brian now hears nothing. Not even the noises from the nightclub. All he hears is his heart weakening. All he sees is pure evil behind him. The man-entity, speaks to Brian,

"Why do you mock us." Son.

Brian places his hands around the man's arms. He tries to pull away. He's overpowering. Brian's body tingles and becomes numb. The pounding of his heart is now transferred in his ears, followed by ringing.

"What the hell are you? Let me go," says Brian.

The man grins at Brian, then whispers in his ear, "Settle down. She is waiting for you. And you betrayed her. You turned your back on her Brian. Did you ever think of Jenna, your mother, your father?"

Brian begins coughing. His face is starting to turn red.

"What are you talking about I love her." Brian Says. The man picks up Brian's sideways and throws him down on the floor like a rag doll. Brian lands on his side. His spine feels if it may explode. He looks up at the standing wall mirror. He doesn't see the man.

"Love, ahhhh, love Brian?" Says the demon,

The man laughs aloud. "What do you know about love Brian? All you are, is a wealthy spoiled brat. Life has been too easy for a pile of shit like you."

Brian prays someone will enter the bathroom. He prays this nightmare will soon end.

"Self-sacrifice, dedication, belief in the family? She loved you; she'd die for you. It is all your fault, Brian. Remember this, Brian. When the body burns, your memories will follow." The demon pauses for a moment, then licks Brian's face. "For all eternity."

Brian begins screaming. He feels heat burn through his blood. His heart continues to grow faint.

"I do love her, it's not my fault. I do love her."

"Yes, it is," says the demon.

"Stop, please. Stop please, it hurts."

"Leave this realm or die Brian. Go now, or the pain will be eternal."

Brian screams turn into cries of pain and anguish. All he wants now is to stop. If death means the end of the pain. Brian would choose death.

"Go to her now. NOW, NOW, NOW!" says the man.

Brian screams are torturous. The pain escalates to a point he can no longer take, then everything goes black.

Brian is now asleep. Brian sees his father, mother, and sister. He sees Jenna. His dog, and the horses. He sees his glory days at West Point and Georgetown, he sees the love his family has for him. He now feels regret, isolation, and despair. Now, all he sees, and feels is darkness. Eternal darkness.

Darkness that people don't believe. Painful and alone. He sees a vortex of energy in the dark, at first like a kaleidoscope, pulling him to a din light. As he travels through the dark, the vortex of energy turns to heat. It begins to consume his body. He tries to open his eyes but cannot. He tries to pray; he can't find his tongue. He feels someone dragging him across the floor, with long nails in his skull. The same feeling, he had during his loft nightmare. He feels being chocked, he feels the heat tearing, consuming his skin, sounds of smacking, slurping, and licking around him. It burns hotter and hotter. The heat is now so intense. All is lost. His screams echo, and nobody can hear. He is now consumed by eternal fire. He cries for God, however; he does not listen. Brian begs for mercy. God will not give it. Brian begs for forgiveness. God will not forgive. Brian fears he is damned for all eternity.

Brian lays in the bathroom fetal position. There are four club patrons, starring him over. Brian wakes and gasps for air. Drool runs from his mouth. He notices his under ware is a little soiled front and back. Brian begins to regain consciousness, extremities, and senses. Brian's complexion is dead white. One of the clubbers looks him over.

"You OK, man?"

"He's probably a Buddhist," says another patron.

Brian now comes his senses. He stands up from the tile floor and looks at everyone. Brian stretches, yawns, then cracks his neck.

Another club-goer looks at him, then comments, "Go to her, she's waiting."

"FUCK OFF!" Brian yells at the small crowd around him, then quickly stumbles out of the restroom.

"Check that guy out. He has a hot woman, waiting outside, and he's sleeping in the john. What an idiot." Says a patron.

The other club goer shakes his head, then chuckles in front of the stall.

"Fool. Stupid Honkey."

Brian stands outside the bathroom. The lighting, a bit delirious, and the music is louder than before; more chaotic. There are also more people. Twice as much as before. The club smells like raw meat and sweat. The song playing in the club is 'Gimmie Danger, By the Stooges.' Strobe flashing everywhere.

Brian stumbles down the stairs. Dizzy, sweating, eyes blurred. Robert intercepts him.

"Dude, where the fuck, were you man?" asks Robert.

"Hey, Robert, what's up?"

"Call me Rob, man. Are you OK? Everything cool?"

"I was in the bathroom?"

"Dude, obviously. you've been gone for over an hour." Robert's voice is condescending and non-sincere.

"No way, impossible," says Brian.

Brian looks at his watch. It shows 1:00 AM. "I was there." Brian points upstairs.

"What did you take?" Brian looks at Robert dazed.

"Well, shake it off buddy boy, the night's still young. You probably came across bad dope. Don't look so glum. Look at all the trim out there. Let's hook up, later, go to Denny's, then we'll hit Santa Monica Beach." Robert offers an opened bottle of water.

"Besides, Lisa's been crawling the joint, looking for you."

Robert leads Brian to a vacant VIP couch. He shoves Brian down, then runs off again.

"Don't forget to drink the water, buddy."

Brian places his head back, ablaze by lights flashing around him. He takes a drink of water almost finishing the bottle. Everything around him, still artificial, chaotic, not real. Not as bad as before, but now a bit more manageable.

Lisa sits atop Brian's lap, then leans over and kisses him very gently. She can taste the toxic runoff on his lips. She has him just where she wants him.

"Look at me, Brian."

She tries kissing him again. Brian tries moving his head. She looks different now. She has a look of evil self-centered, egotistical satisfaction.

"Brian, what's wrong?" She asks.

"I want to leave this place."

"Why?"

Lisa leans over, then licks his neck. "I like the way you taste."

"I'm leaving you now. I'll call a cab," says Brian.

"I'll take you home," says Lisa.

Brian tries standing up. He loses his balance and falls back on the couch.

"Come with me, Brian. Get up."

"I don't want to inconvenience you."

"Don't worry, you won't."

Brian tries standing up. Lisa grabs Brian's arms and grunts as she pulls him forward. Brian's knees buckle.

"Good boy." Says Lisa.

Lisa's statement makes Brian want to puke. He feels it sounds like a dog and owner.

I hope she is not some sick control freak, crazy, whatever; Brian thinks. Brian's too high and tired, to think of anything. All he wants his bed. That and 'I Love Lucy' on the cable network. That is all he wanted tonight. Now's he is fucked up, out with Satan's son and daughter.

Lisa escorts Brian over to Robert. He is in the corner speaking to a woman dress up in full leather. The other looks like Alice in Wonderland, or some weird thing. Brian's eyes are so dilated, each laser light feels like it penetrates his brain.

"Robert, we're leaving," says Brian.

"Call me Rob."

"Whatever, says Brian."

"Wait, get over here," Rob yells at Lisa.

Brian watches as Lisa walks to Robert, leans over, and whispers in his ear. He looks at Brian, then smiles cynically.

Brian wants to walk right up to the human douche bag and flush him down the toilet where he belongs. He'll wait until Tuesday. Tuesday will be perfect. There is no way, Brian will make it to work tomorrow. Take the fucker out to lunch, punch the asshole right below his heart. Then walk away.

Brian is starting to snap out his daze now. He walks quickly up to Robert.

"Hey buddy, you are leaving with us. After all, were buddies, right? After all, you are my transportation," says Brian.

"Are you kidding? Look at these two hotties. I'm not going anywhere. Just chill man."

Brian sees murder now. He remembers all his father taught him to maintain and channel his anger.

"Chill, Chill? Robert, don't fuckin' say it, I'll drop you here."

Brian changes his stance to an attack position. By the look in Brian's eyes, good ole Robbie sees he is serious. He also sees a look in a man eyes, he has *never* seen before. Fear strikes Robert. Brian looks at Lisa and singles her to leave.

"We'll discuss this Tuesday." Robert doesn't say anything. He's in complete shock. The two women with Robert giggle and whisper in each other's ears.

Brian takes Lisa by her arm, quickly escorting her through the dazed club goers, and out of the hotel…

Chapter 18

Brian's feeling better now. A different stage of the drug is affecting him. He won't say anything to Lisa. He works with her. Worse comes to worst. They will remain friends. Brian wants to know what she gave him though. Thereafter, he will decide if she's worth seeing again.

Brian walks eastbound on the sixth street, leaving the hotel. The site of people standing outside makes him sick. Brian walks in front of Lisa. Lisa knows by his mannerisms he's upset, and she must explain her actions. Brian hails for an empty cab driving by. It is green and white. Much to Brian's surprise, the fuckin' cab does not stop. It's empty but doesn't stop. Lisa tries catching up with Brian as he hails down cabs. He waves, he dances, he stomps on the ground, he even swings his hips. Cabs will not stop.

"Lisa why is it, in Los Angeles, cab drivers, they don't stop. What is their story? Hey, look at me, I'm Mexican, I have a job. I'll just sit in my car and drive around. Drive around and sell fuckin' dope all day. Serious girl. Tell me."
"LA is the only city on earth, where cab drivers DON'T FUCKIN' STOP! HEY THERE, LOOK; THERE GOES ANOTHER!!"

Brian walks in the middle of the street waving his arms. A cab maneuvers around him.

"HEY, HEY, HEY! Ahhh, Fuck it." Brian laughs; chuckles to himself.

"Holy crapshoot. I must be losing it."

Lisa cautiously observes but likes what she sees. She folds her arms and grins. Grins as a mother would, watching her son score five touchdowns at Virginia Tech. This is her man now. Pretty soon, he'll meet her parents. Then Back to Virginia. Politics, money, power. Everything she has ever dreamed of. Lisa grabs Brian by the arm.

"Brian, wait. Why don't you let me drive you home?" Brian is breathing heavy and sweating.

"You don't get it. All sorts of weird shit's been happening the past few weeks." Brian looks over at the park across the street. A thick fog is present. It is dark and eerie. He was told about this park. Many people have vanished. Children kidnapped, people missing who walked under the bridge. The drugs, the suicide. A real playground for the wicked. Brian senses a presence at the park. Lisa is also starting to get on his nerves.

"I drank too much tonight. And you gave me something. What was that crap? My head is still spinning. It's better I go home alone. I'll flag down a cab at a McDonald's or something."

Brian begins walking away quickly. Lisa immediately runs after him.

"Brian, please, wait. I'm sorry for what I gave you. It is my fault. It's a light hallucinogenic. A yellow pill. Some people have a bad reaction to it. Maybe your one of them."

"So, you drugged me. You fuckin' drugged me?" Brian turns away and chuckles. Then looks at the park.

"Drugged, yippee, drugged. That's swell, fucking great. Thanks, Lisa."

"I wanted us to have a good time. I like you, Brian." Her voice is robotic, artificial, and unnatural.

Atop the synthetic drugs and abnormal behavior, Brian is having what Rob said, "A kick-ass time."

Brian jumps and down like a child and twirling in a circle. He is still unsuccessful stopping a cab driver.

"Look at me, I'm having a swell time. Oh, boy, I can't wait to tell my father. Hey, Dad, you were right. LA's a fucked-up place, with many fucked up, people. They drug you because well, Dad; they like you. And the best part is, they think it's OK. It's fun, and a good time."

Brian looks over at the park again. He sees a large figure, over seven feet tall walk through the fog. He wears a black jacket, has very, long arms and fingers. Brian thinks he still may be hallucinating. He dares not to tell Lisa. The figure stops walking, then stares at Brian.

"It's my fault, let me make it up to you. Whatever you saw or felt in there isn't real. It's all in your head." Brian stays fixated on the park.

"Brian, look at me."

Lisa takes Brian, then holds him. She grabs both his hands and kisses him. She holds him tighter now.

"Alright, this is enough," says Lisa. "I'm not letting you go, unit you accept my apology." Lisa kisses Brian gently.

"Brian, this is reality. Me and you here, right now." Brian looks over at the park again. He notices another odd-looking mass move through the fog. The figure is small, wearing a hood. It runs through the grass, then vanishing through the fog.

"That's comforting to know," says Brian.

Lisa gives Brian a playful slap on his face. Brian tries another escape. He likes Lisa. However, tonight has been a bit much for the man. It is Sondra he wants. And now, he has thoughts of Jenna in his head. He thinks of the bathroom and what the man said, or devil, or whatever he was. *What if it is Jenna? What if she committed suicide or something? Her family has some deep connections. The kind of that can put a man six feet under. The kinds that can or will blow up your yacht. I loved Jenna before, not now. What if she is the one? I better get home and call her. I will call her tomorrow though. I still want to have sex with Lisa. She drugged me, and I deserve it. I may not get this chance again. I'm just going to play it as if I'm not interested. The drugs are still in my Brian. Thinks Brian. They won't leave.*

"I don't want to ruin the rest of your night," says Brian.

"Are you kidding? You are the reason I'm here. Look, I have had a bad experience before. I am sorry. Yes, it's my fault I gave it to you. Let me help now. I know how to bring you back." Lisa kisses him again, pulling him in close. "After some water, bath, a rub down, you'll feel much better."

Lisa wraps his arms around his neck and kisses him again.

"Later, we'll order Farmer Boys."

How can Brian deny her request? What man would? Seriously. He's in love with another woman, but he's not a fool. I'm not married yet, thinks Brian. *Why should I love a woman, while she doesn't have the manners to call? Why am I always worried about others and not myself? Screw it, Lisa is a fox, and I'm going in.*

"I just can't handle this crap anymore. It's everywhere. I feel like I'm constantly being hit by something," says Brian.

He finds a beer bottle in the gutter. He picks it up and throws it across the street, toward the park.

"GO BACK TO HELL!" yells Brian.

Lisa immediately grabs Brian, pulls him in close.

"This is the only thing you will handle."

She French kisses Brian and grabs his crotch are.

"Very well, let's get out of here," says Brian.

Lisa smiles. She has him now. She thought she may have lost him for a moment there.

Lisa and Brian join arms and walk away. Brian walks the street side. They walk east on the sixth street, and Brian looks over his right shoulder. In the park, at the edge of the sidewalk stands the same demon of his dreams. Brian sees Lamia. The same four-feet-tall asshole, that tortured him a few nights back. Brian looks at him, then thinks of Psalms 23. Brian will not say a word to Lisa. He knows what he must do. He decides at this very moment, he is going home. they both fade into the hazy cold night until the darkness consumes them. Now they are gone forever…

Chapter 19

Brian opens the door, then walks into his loft. Lisa follows him, immediately slips off her heels. She skillfully places them on the shoe rack by the door, then pulls her hair up. Brian notices she's not that tall after all. She's all heel. Her forehead would rest upon Brian's chest.

"That feels better. They look good, but hurt like hell," says Lisa.

Brian takes the envelope he found on the airplane and places it on his nightstand. He looks over Lisa. She looks good. Too good. She looks like Gwyneth Paltrow in that movie 'Great Expectations'. She's already shuffling around the kitchen, moving things around like they're married. She takes a few glasses out of the cupboard and finds microwave chicken wings in the freezer. She helps herself, without asking.

Brian watches her. She reminds of one of his relatives. One of the relatives that knows everything about you, and your kitchen. They never say a word, ever. Just devour, and change everything.

A real natural, he thinks. One of the types that Mother and Father would adore. One of the types of women that if you screw up, her brother takes you for a long drive. A woman that has the dark side and is sexy. She believes in American Tradition, lives it, breeds, then dies by it. Now that's Virginia, thinks Brian.

. Lisa still wears her peacoat because of the lingerie underneath and from this moment on, she will *never* leave Brian's loft. He was doomed from the minute they first meet. Like told Robert. She will destroy anyone that gets in her way. Brian lays on his bed, while looking her over. His thoughts race between her and Jenna. *If Sondra doesn't work out, why not Lisa. Dad will approve. Mom also. Why not? She's obviously a control freak. Why not Brian thinks. My mother controls my father…*

"Did you say something?" asks Brian.

"Nothing," says Lisa.

She feverishly creates a buffet from unwanted man-food.

Lisa picks up a bottle of Makers Mark and sweet and sour mix.

She thinks, *it will go well with the spicy chicken.* And she is right about that.

"Mind if I pour us a few?" asks Lisa.

"Not at all." Brian replies.

Lisa lays out a display of chicken wings, sliced apples, grapes, French bread, and butter. Sausages from Alpine Village adds a nice touch also.

"Come over here, Brian."

Lisa walks to the bed with her hand out. Brian stands up from the bed. She seductively guides him to the dining table. He takes a glass of water then drinks it down. Then pours another. So far, the water is good. It's finally relaxing him. Lisa sips whisky, then takes an apple slice. Brian hears footsteps running upstairs. Then giggling. Forget it. Tonight, Brian will pay no attention. At least for now. Why screw up the remains of good morning when it's been a horrible night? The front door upstairs opens and slams shut. Again, Brian pays no attention. Lisa doesn't notice. She sits legs crossed moving her foot back and forth, as she seductively eats, and rubs the index of her toes on the metal foot of Brian's chair. Lisa planned on his night. She brought extra clothes in tote bag. Condoms too, just in case.

"Can I use your bathroom?" Lisa looks at Brian, smiles, and winks.

"Sure," says Brian.

Lisa leaves the table and heads toward the bathroom. Brian rubs his hand over his face, then hair. truthfully, he really wanted to be alone tonight. How can he say no? A gentleman never says no. He's still uncomfortably high and dehydrated. He continues to drink water quickly and in volume.

Brian quickly shuffles through his kitchen drawers and finds High Absorption B Vitamins. "Highest dose available in American, and all-natural."

"It will also boost your sex drive," says his doctor. Like it isn't high enough already.

Brian quickly drinks another glass of water while chewing on two of the tablets.

He hears a bouncing ball upstairs, followed by giggling again. He wonders if this will go on all night. If it does tomorrow, he will walk upstairs and introduced himself. Tomorrow, he will call his parents. Tomorrow, he will talk to Jenna. Tomorrow, the nonsense ends.

Brian sits back down at his dining table and listens to partygoers walk up the side stairway again. He hears *them* talk about the night. He can hear high heeled shoes, splitting the concrete floor, along with every word they say. He would never repeat what is heard. Some of it sounds almost plotted, and evil. It's the same almost every night; four people, two men, and two women. The crap that flows them their mouths is not only distasteful, but it also proves that there are a handful of assholes in the building.

"It must be fun living here," Lisa speaks from the bathroom.

"What? Oh yeah, it's been charming." Says Brian.

Brian studies his whisky glass. He doesn't take a drink. He wonders what this wretched woman is capable of next. Like all men and others between. He makes another mistake.

"The building, it must be fun," says Lisa again.

Lisa exits the bathroom in a black pullover dress. It is a dress almost identical to Sondra. Now, she caught his attention. Lisa looks awesome. Not only is she attractive, but she's also attractive with no makeup. Lisa hurries to the table and kisses Brian on the cheek. She takes her glass of whisky-sour sour then toast Brian.

"To both of us. So, tell me. How do I look?"

"Beautiful," Brian says.

"Imagine if we're married. You can have me all the time." Brian's stomach turns. He now knows what a mistake she may be. She said the word marriage. He doesn't even really like this woman. Lust only at this point, thinks Brian. Now, all he wants is sex. And she is perfect for now. Remember, he feels she owes him…

Lisa leans into Brian and French kisses him. She takes him by the hand and walks him to the bed. She sets down the drinks and pushes Brian lying on the bed. She sits atop his waist. She leans over and kisses him again. This time Brian responds, as she moves her hips, she feels the bulge in his jeans. They begin kissing again, as laughter is heard upstairs. Brian's phone rings. The ringer is heard four times then the answer machine picks up.

"Brian, it's Dad. Listen, we are tired of your games and disrespect. As of now, your cut off. You hear me, buddy boy, cut off. At least have enough dignity to call Jenna."

The call ends and the answering machine cuts. Lisa looks at Brian and smiles. This is good for her. If he has family trouble, he will be an easier catch. Forget his money. She has plenty of money herself. She is already dreaming of a colonial and horses back in Virginia.

"Yup, that's my dad," Brian says.

"And who is Jenna, if I may ask?"

Lisa sounds like a wife already. It makes Brian want to puke. Brian regains his conscience.

"She's a girlfriend of mine. I was supposed to—" Lisa interrupts.

"Don't worry, my family is completely whacked. Anyway, you're with me now." Lisa reaches over to the nightstand and takes a sizeable drink of whisky.

"I'll deal with them later. He's upset I haven't called."

"Here, sit up." Lisa adjusts the pillow behind Brian's head. Lisa places her drink down on the nightstand and lays down next to Brian. She sees Brian is still a bit tense. She feeds Brian water then cuddles over his chest.

"You know what you need?"

Brian shakes his head.

"A bath. Remember?"

"Not now, why don't we watch '*I Love Lucy*' or something."

The drugs are now at the final, drawn-out, fourth stage. The speedy stage. The final stage can go on for at least another 12 hours. Just enough time for Lisa to convince Brian, she's the perfect woman.

Brian is feeling a bit mellow now. His eyes twitch, and he feels as if his body is cold, needles are prickling his skin. Lisa will try to inspire him.

"Seriously, I don't remember much of anything now?" says Brian.

"You promised you'd let me do anything I want. And I want to make you feel better. So, a bath first."

"And later?" asks Brian.

Lisa leans over and kisses Brian. She bites his lower lip. Then kisses him again, then sucks on his neck.

"OK, sounds good to me," says Brian. He turns off *I love Lucy* and puts on *Chill-House*, then will follow with *Enigma*.

Might as well leave a good impression, thinks Brian.

Water flows from the large tub faucet. Brian checks the water with his hand. It is perfect. He takes a bottle of Mr. Bubble and throws in a few caps.

The water quickly boils over with bubbles, and Brian's anticipation. The high dose B-vitamins have helped calm his nerves for now. He hopes this high isn't sadistic, evil, and time released.

Brian sits in the tub, then takes a sip of water. He looks at Lisa standing in front of the mirror. She admires herself for a moment, smiles, rubs her breast; then looks at Brian.

"Do you think I need a breast job?"

Brian removes the hot rag over his forehead and checks her over.

"Hell on, Earth baby. Your tits are perfect."

"Really?"

"Yeah."

"I bet you say that to all the girls."

"Nope."

Lisa turns sideways, turns around, looks at her legs, then arms.

"Do you like my legs, my stomach, hips and arms?"

"Yeah. Sure."

Brian has a rag over his forehead, covering half his eyes.

"You're not looking," says Lisa.

"I can see you in my mind," says Brian.

"Besides, your body and boobs are perfect. Your cup size is what, a 36 C? For god's sake, woman, look at your body. Designed by God and built for me. That's all that matters."

Lisa slips off her black panties, then sits atop the sink. She wants to show Brian her asset. *It's beautiful* thinks Brian as she shows the crevasse between her thighs. He peeks at her then grins. He's immediately excited. Lisa is driving him mad. His heart pounds, and pulse raises.

Still, he remains cool. Lisa puts her hair up in a bun, then touches the water. Her perfectly manicured black toes and the foot is in view.

"You ready for me?" asks Lisa.

"Oh yeah," says Brian.

Lisa slowly sits down in the oversized bathtub. She settles in while placing both legs around Brian's waist.

"We can have a lot of fun here," Lisa says.

"Girl, you say all the right things," replies Brian.

"The main reason why I signed the lease is this tub." Lisa adjusts her body to a more comfortable position. A position she is familiar with. She lays across Brian's front side and lashes her long tongue around his chest. She removes the rag off Brian's forehead, then throws it in the sink.

"Good shot," Brian says.

"You haven't seen my best shot yet," says Lisa.

Lisa continues kissing Brian's chest, slowly working in her way downward. She follows his hairline, slightly above his belly button, she circles her tongue around it, then follows the hairline, trail. It leads to the top of his pulsing head. As she licks to the side, she sees his manhood, shift, quiver with excitement.

"Who taught you that?" Brian watches her tongue slash over him. "Oh, I get it, never mind. It's a college thing." Says Brian.

Lisa laughs aloud, moves upward, French kissing him.

"Make love to me, Brian."

"Get over here," Brian says. "Ride it."

Lisa moves in on him. She sticks out her tongue and places it in his mouth. Lisa begins to whimper as Brian rubs his hands over her back, breast, thighs, and buttock.

"Give it to me now," says Lisa.

Brian quickly takes control. He thrust his hips deep inside her, as she gasps for air. Lisa responds like a wild animal in heat. She accepts his offering, like a woman starving for satisfaction. She climaxes quickly, then sits back for a moment. Her dilated, almost shocked. Brian quickly stands up. Lisa maneuvers in position, then places her hungry mouth over his member. She moves frantically over him…

Brian almost explodes, telling her to stop. Lisa sits back saying how delicious he tastes.

Lisa turns around, positions her buttock up then sits backwards.

The first thrust throws Lisa into a frenzy. Brian moves rapidly, then slow, then he enters her deep inside, and does not move. The only movement is from her release. He undoes her hair into a ponytail, then pulls her hair back. He slowly moves as Lisa accepts, she quickly sits atop him forward, offering him her tongue. They will both climax together. This bathing session will be like no other. It will take a few hours until they are *both* finished. After, Brian will carry Lisa to his bed. This is when the real action will begin…

It is now 4:44 AM. The only light in the loft are the candles placed and lit by Lisa. Dark, greyish blue light creeps through the drawn blinds, and everything for once is silent.

Brian has never slept so well. Brian's snoring as Lisa lays wide awake. She lays next to Brian as she stares at the door entrance. Under the door, she sees the shadows of shoes. Then hears giggling in the upstairs loft. She notices a very slight noise from the closet, as well as shadow areas of the loft. Her eyes shift nervously, and she wonders if she has made a terrible mistake. She loves Brian now. She will not leave him. Ever.

The voice of a young woman is heard upstairs.

"Open the envelope," the voice says.

Lisa gasp for air as her heart is now pounding. She can feel her skin burn and bones start aching. However, she made herself a promise. She removes her head from Brian's chest, then looks him over. He is dead asleep. She hears the clock above the entry door ticking loud, as candles lights begin dancing throughout the loft.

Lisa hears what sounds like jax being thrown across the upstairs floor. The sound of a cue ball is heard rolling across the floor. Then another ball bouncing. Lisa hears the voice of a younger woman. She giggles and tells someone to remain silent.

"They will join us soon." Another man's voice asks "when?" The voice of a younger woman says "soon."

"Lisa, open the white envelope now," the woman's voice says, upstairs.

Lisa quickly sits up, looking up at the ceiling. She looks back at Brian, seeing he's till sleeping. She sits on the side of the bed and takes a bottle of water from the nightstand, then drinks.

On the nightstand, she sees a white envelope with a Chinese symbol. Lisa finishes the bottle of water in a hurry. She *knows* the drugs may be playing tricks on her mind. Yet still intrigued by the upstairs jesters and offerings. She quickly stands up, then walks over to the kitchen taking another bottle of water. She hears a quick tapping noise on the front door; four quick taps. She runs to door, looks out the keyhole. Nobody there. She walks back to the bed and sits next to Brian. She drinks the water and looks at the white envelope again.

"Lisa, open the envelope, or else." The voice is that of a younger woman again. Lisa takes the envelope and curiously looks it over. She rubs her hands over it and notices a round object inside. She then looks at the Chinese symbol.

Lisa is overwhelmed with curiosity. Brian must have left it here for her to open. After all, he does love me. He wouldn't have made love to me the way he did. Now we will be together forever and ever. Lisa's thoughts now turn solemn. Soon, I will have his child she thinks. Soon the prophecy shall be revealed.

Lisa hears footsteps running up the side staircase exit. Then she thinks she hears a soft demonic voice from the closet. It tells her to open the envelope.

"It's a gift from your new husband. He loves you," says the deep gurgled voice.

She slowly opens the side of the envelope. Then uses her long index nail. Slowly and precisely, she opens the envelope. A round object falls to the concrete floor. That size of a silver dollar. There are two other ancient symbols on the coin. Lisa cannot make out what they are. They look Sand script or Samarian. The object makes a loud clanking noise, that is ear piercing; followed by a loud thump from the walk-in closet. A high-pitched demonic scream is heard.

Brian sits up quickly and yells, "WHAT THE FUCK!" Lisa screams atop her lungs.

The young woman that killed Troy, comes running out of the closet full speed. She carries two sharp steak knives from Brian's kitchen. Her hair is mangled, skin is blue, with track and burn marks all over her body.

She makes horrible growling demon noises. Brian and Lisa try fighting her off with no success. Lisa screams bloody murder. The psychotic woman grabs them both, like two small infants from a crib. Brian and Lisa scream and yell, nobody will hear. Nobody will come to their rescue. The woman drags Brian and Lisa's naked bodies inside the walk-in closet, then the door locks. Behind the door, screams are heard. The blows to their flesh sound as if they are being jabbed with a large sewing needles. The screams now vanish, and the room goes silent…

Realtor Jane walks down the hallway. It is the same apartment on Los Angeles Street. The one Brian moved into. She places the key in apartment 400. Behind her is a Black American couple. They are both in their late 20s, professional and attractive. The perfect couple thinks Jane. She was taken by them both immediately.

"You're going to love this loft," says Realtor Jane.

She opens the door and peeks through first. She wants to make sure it has been cleaned and ready for the show. She lures the couple in the loft with a look of satisfaction about her.

"As you can see, everything is white. You can paint any colors you wish. Just don't spray the kitchen and the darn bathroom area."

"Oh, we're not into that kind of stuff," the man says.

"They never are. Well at least, not at first," says the Realtor.

As she speaks, she admires herself in her Mac.

"Honey, this is perfect. You can walk to work. I can do my clothing design's here. I love it," says the attractive young woman.

Realtor Jane sees a light around this woman. An angelic gleam in her eyes. The look of peace, love and excitement. Feeling the Realtor must feed on.

"Yes, that is true. It would be nice to walk occasionally. Get some coffee, pick up the paper," says her husband.

She jumps into her husband's arms and kisses him. Realtor Jane looks them over and grins.

They are perfect, she thinks. *I sure know how to serve 'em up. Especially when they are black.*

"The price is @1,400.00. You can't beat it for Downtown Los Angeles." The realtor cell phone rings.

"Excuse me, darlings."

"Hello Henry. Oh, it's you, I have been waiting for honey. How it goes big guy?"

The realtor speaks over her phone about a property on Ardmore Blvd. She mentioned how it's a lovely place. A famous local model was murdered there. She mysteriously vanished. She also mentioned how wonderful the home is. Realtor Jane tells the prospective tenant over the phone they will meet at Bob's Big Boy on Wilshire later. The couples finishing looking over the loft.

"I love it, we'll take it. When is it available?" says the young woman.

"Immediately. OK. So, let us go downstairs, do some paperwork, have some coffee. I want to know everything about you both. I'm sure you have a lot of dreams about coming to this city. We are the city of dreams you know."

The realtor escorts the young couple out of the loft. She tells them about the history of the building and all the wonderful deaths in Los Angeles. She also tells them about the missing children from the building, and how a woman killed her boyfriend, named Troy. She tells them it is a marvelous story. How wonderful pain and suffering can be. Especially when they are bad people. The realtor escorts the couple to the elevator. They are excited and whispering in each other's ear.

"Be with ya' in a sec honeys. Wait at the elevator," says Realtor Jane.

The realtor enters the loft again. She walks into the middle and looks up at the ceiling. She turns away and looks at the walk-in closet, then smiles. The look upon her face is pure evil. Evil that's satisfied its hunger. The realtor walks to the front door then exits. She walks down the hallway singing 'Rated X by Loreta Lynn.'

Four different voices upstairs begin a conversation. One of them is Brian. The other Lisa. A young girl and an older man.

"When are they coming here?" asks Lisa.

"Soon, gosh, can't you wait. Be patient," says the young girl.

"But when?" asks Brian. "I need more."

"Soon, very soon, they always do," says the older man.

"Will they join us?" asks Lisa.

"Yes, they will join. Join us forever. For all eternity," says the older man.

"They always do, and I can't wait," says the younger girl.

The four voices in the upstairs loft start giggling and laughing. A cue ball is heard bouncing on the floor. Then jax are thrown on the ground. A young girl runs across the floor and begins singing followed by a muffling noise and then silence.